RETURN TO LOCH STRATHKIN

ELAYNE GRIMES

Storm

This is a work of fiction. Names, characters, businesses, places, events and incidents are either the products of the author's imagination or used in a fictitious manner. Any resemblance to actual persons, living or dead, or actual events is purely coincidental.

Copyright © Elayne Grimes, 2025

The moral right of the author has been asserted.

All rights reserved. No part of this book may be reproduced or used in any manner without the prior written permission of the copyright owner. This prohibition includes, but is not limited to, any reproduction or use for the purpose of training artificial intelligence technologies or systems.

To request permissions, contact the publisher at rights@stormpublishing.co

Ebook ISBN: 978-1-80508-789-2
Paperback ISBN: 978-1-80508-790-8

Cover design: Rose Cooper
Cover images: Shutterstock

Published by Storm Publishing.
For further information, visit:
www.stormpublishing.co

ALSO BY ELAYNE GRIMES

Loch Strathkin

Secrets of Swanfield House
Escape to the Highland Retreat

Le Scrittrici
Where it all began

ONE

The little tousle-haired blond boy stood barefoot atop a pine high-backed chair with one hand around a battered recipe book. The book was held together with elastic bands, with old, yellowed pages spilling out. The boy's other small hand was noisily clattering stones and pebbles in his stuffed trouser pocket. His pale blue shorts were layered with a dusting of snow-white icing sugar, and his striped T-shirt tried hard to disguise many recent stains and smeared fruit cake mixture attached to it. He stared at the words on the page he was studying with mild curiosity.

'My mummy always said oz was short for Australia, but I don't know why this says, "five oz".' He shrugged his shoulders, puzzled.

'Well,' explained Marcie Mosse, standing next to him with a bowl nestled in her arm, a wooden baking spoon in the other hand, 'it's an old-fashioned way of saying grams.'

'Why can't they just say grams?'

'Because grams hadn't been invented in the olden days when this book was written.'

'In the black and white days?'

'Exactly. So how many does it say?'

'Five oz.'

'Ounces.'

'What's that?'

'Well, the proper name for oz is ounces,' she said, then realised this was extremely confusing for a child of tender years.

She emptied the dish of whisky-soaked sultanas into the bowl and began to beat energetically with the spoon.

Once she had finished beating the mixture together, she deftly transferred the dough into a large loaf tin, then handed the spoon to the boy, who shoved it into his small mouth as far as he could. Cake mixture covered his pink lips and clung to the sides of his cheeks as he made a face.

'Yeugh! Whisky!' he exclaimed but it did not stop his tongue from licking the thick, sweet mixture from the spoon. 'My daddy likes whisky, but my mummy called it danger juice.'

The words 'called it' hit Marcie like a punch, and she bit her lip and squeezed her eyes shut for a moment.

'I know, darling.' She smiled and ruffled her sous chef's blond hair.

He jumped off the chair, spoon discarded into the sink as he left, and darted out of the house. The cake tin was swiftly put into the oven, the table wiped down in record quick time and the baker reached for the flour-dusted object in the centre of the table. The timer was in the shape of a cockerel; an old tourist trinket from Portugal, brightly coloured in blues and yellows, with one wing missing and a bright red plume. She turned the timer until it clicked in agreement and walked across to the sofa, where Ruaridh Balfour was gently dozing, flat out, breathing softly. Marcie sat down noisily on the chair opposite, and the man stirred. As he turned, she threw the timer to him, and he caught it quickly with an outstretched hand, still in a half sleep.

'Okay, sleeping beauty – I've set the time for seventy-five minutes so switch the oven off and take the cake out when it rings. The other one is already on the worktop on the rack.' The heady smell of the recently baked offerings sat heavily in the air. A warm aroma of fruit and sugar bathed the room in a pleasant and sensory-filled reminiscence.

'Okay,' was the weary response.

At the side of the sofa a half-empty bottle of a young, blended whisky was sitting idle on the floor. She picked it up and examined the amount of golden liquid left, which shimmered in the light. 'The only thing this is good for is soaking fruit, and it's exactly what I'm going to do with it.' She picked the cork up off the side table, pushing it in hard to the neck of the bottle.

'Yes, miss,' replied the dozy man as he tried to pull himself up, wincing at the constant buzzing in his head. He gave a slight moan. She ignored it.

'I'm not having it, Ruaridh,' she said in a tone he knew well, and he took it as a warning. 'Your mum is going to be back with the kids soon. Snap to it!' She clicked her fingers twice, close to his ear, and slipped the half-empty bottle into her blue tartan ANTA tote, which was resting on a chair by the kitchen table. As she searched inside for her car keys, he was suddenly beside her.

'Thanks, Mars,' he said and outstretched his arms to envelop her in one of his hard-to-beat bear hugs, but she recoiled. This one-time love of her life was more than a little dishevelled with unpressed clothes, hair cropped short, and his carefully trimmed beard now no more than a black and greying stubble.

'And a shower wouldn't go amiss,' she stated and headed towards the kitchen door.

She glanced around as he gently sat down at the table, watching as he lowered his face into the palms of his hands, elbows resting on the long carved wooden table he had lovingly made for his wife on the birth of their first son.

Marcie wanted desperately to rush over to him and take him in her arms so they could weep together, but she just stood in silence, taking in the domestic scene she was leaving behind. She walked out the door to find the little boy who had been helping her was immersed in the water on the shoreline, singing to himself, and paddling in the ice-cold water of Strathkin Loch. She waved at him, unseen, then made her way around to her car, which was parked at the side of Lochside Croft, and quietly slipped into the driver's seat.

When she inserted her key, the radio jumped into life. D:Ream's 'Things Can Only Get Better' blasted out of the speakers, and she slammed her hands onto the steering wheel hard and violently. As she continued to bang them against the wheel in her fury, tears that had been slowly welling up in her eyes flooded out like a bursting dam, and suddenly she could not see. Her body was a ball of tension – her head felt like it was caught in a vice. Her furious hands glanced against the channel change on the steering wheel wands, and it moved to a classical station.

Magically, the beautiful pastoral skylark cadenza of 'The Lark Ascending' filled the car, and her mind drifted to one of her favourite memories of listening to the music on a long-forgotten picnic. Immediately, she snapped into reality. Wiping her eyes, she caught sight of two swans on the loch in front of Douglas Balfour, as he stood ankle deep in chilly water, absorbed in collecting stones and pebbles. The birds drifted high with sweeping, gliding wings, softly dancing in the air before they turned and headed in a circular motion to return to the reed bed in front of her former home. Across the expanse of water, Swanfield, now surrounded by scaffolding, had no roof but still sat powerful and imposing. Marcie took several deep breaths and turned the car out on to the small road that ran alongside the loch, passing the tiny hamlet's hospitality offerings in the form of The Strathkin Inn and Strathkin Trekking Centre. She drove until the road became a single track with only passing places as it stretched up into the vast wilderness of the Swanfield Estate.

When she pulled the car up in front of Tigh-na-Lochan, she sat for a moment outside the cottage. The small white house, with a pond in front, often felt isolated from civilisation, as if no other life existed. Once inside, she locked the door immediately behind her, turning the handle several times to ensure it was firmly shut.

Marcie stood in the living room, and her eyes glanced over the empty kitchen. The old silver Carlton teapot sat in the middle of the table, a glass placed inside it, a spray of flowers in the glass. Her mind cast back to the previous day when her two girlfriends were tucking into cake and gossip, sitting opposite each other, laughing until their eyes fell on her. Now, she looked towards the end of the table. The empty seat. The space that should have been filled with the missing piece in their four-person jigsaw. Heather McLeod and Isabella Forrester had exchanged a look, both knowing what their friend was thinking. A person that cannot be replaced. A seat that would remain empty.

Marcie could still see Dina Balfour in her mind, leaning forward, laughing at some ludicrous thing her children or husband had done, smiling, not a care in the world. She walked over to the small table in the corner, now repurposed as her home workstation. An unopened letter sat centre stage, Dina's beautiful calligraphy on the front of the envelope. Each of the women had a letter. None of the friends knew when to open it, each one thinking if it remained sealed, maybe Dina hadn't really died at all. Opening it would bring it all back, make it too real, cement in their minds that their friend was never coming back.

She made her way into her bedroom at the back of the cottage and lay on the bed and started to breathe slowly and deeply the way her therapist had told her to try. She could hear his voice say softly – *in* and *out*, *in* and *out*. His soporific tone was inside her head, and the rising and falling of her chest made her start to drift off.

Marcella Mosse, she said, in her meditated trance, *you are calm, you are at peace, and you are strong. From that strength you will improve and be grounded. From that strength will come tranquillity and freedom from your nightmares.* She breathed slowly. Deliberately. Inhaling. Exhaling.

You are in a period of serene stillness, said her inner voice.

Except she wasn't. She was still grieving for a life lost, for a relationship in tatters and desperately hoped, as the song had said, that things would only get better.

Ruaridh had to admit, the visit from Marcie had been the wake-up call he needed. When she left, he stood on the small lawn that led down to the shimmering shore of Strathkin Loch, hands in his pockets, eyes settling on the house across the water. It had snuck up on him, this devil. The insidious creep of loneliness and sadness that simply would not leave. He faced it every morning like an unwanted guest; on his shoulder when he looked in the mirror; reflected at him in the window when he stood at the sink in the busy kitchen. Chaos of children and noise all around but all he heard was silence. Silence, apart from that last gasp of breath playing over and over in his mind. *It has to be done*, he thought to himself. Now was the time to leave the past behind. The visit from his first love had been the catalyst. He needed to make that call to the other side of the world and do the thing he thought he would never do – ask for help.

TWO

To some visitors, Inverness felt like the end of the world, considering how long the journey took from other parts of Scotland and beyond. At the main train station, a young woman stepped off the overnight train from London's Kings Cross and carefully examined the long platform thronging with passengers. She nervously began to make her way into the station. Deep down she knew already that she had done the right thing by escaping.

'Can I help you, dear?' The man's voice behind her, so close, made her jump in her uneasiness. When she spun round, it surprised her to see it was an elderly man in a flat cap, who carried a thin local paper under his arm.

'No, no, thank you. I'm just trying to find the bus station,' was her swift response. She leaned down to lift the pulling handle of the old, charity shop-bought suitcase and glanced around for an exit, anxious to get away.

'I'm just heading that way. I'll walk round with you,' he said with a genuine smile.

'No, seriously, it's fine. Just point me...'

'Not at all, lassie. Here, give me that! We'll just go out the back way.' The man took her case, which she reluctantly gave up, and they walked side by side out of the rear entrance of the small railway station which led them into Strothers Lane. When she saw the bus station ahead, she felt a sense of relief.

'Now, do you have your ticket?'

'Oh, no, not yet.' She was wise enough not to buy her ticket online with what little she had in her bank account. And she made sure to use a cash machine far enough away from her home address not to draw attention from nosy neighbours.

The two strangers stood at the entrance to the long, low bus station, and she bit her lip.

'Er, could you just look after this for a minute?' she asked with a smile.

As she stood in the ticket queue she glanced around. Her plan to travel this far north was made days ago, and she intended to stick to it. It was what she had discussed with the woman who had become her guardian.

'Did you get a wee chance to pick up something to eat for your journey?' queried the stranger when she returned.

'Oh, no. I don't really have a lot of money. I'll see if they're selling anything on the bus.'

'Here,' he said and offered her his unopened bottle of Highland Spring water and a bar of four finger KitKat with two fingers already broken off.

'Oh, I couldn't!' she protested as the chocolate bar was thrust into her hand – the bottle pushed into the side flap of her backpack. She broke into a smile, revealing a dimple on her young, fresh face as an announcement was made.

'Off you go!' he said with a nod to her bus about to depart, and she leaned over and unexpectedly kissed the man on the cheek, something she had never done before in all her almost seventeen years. The driver helped her to place her heavy case in the open side section of the vehicle, its gaping wing already jam-packed with bags, rucksacks and boxes. She climbed onto the bus, found the empty bench seats at the very back and lifted her tired legs. Taking three seats to herself, she was asleep before the bus driver signalled to leave.

On the concourse, a woman with a baby in a pram passed the old man as he waved to the departing bus.

'What a lucky man you are.' She smiled. 'Your granddaughter is gorgeous.'

'I know.' The elderly gentleman smiled, his ruddy cheeks letting off another blush as the beep-beep of the reversing bus pulled out of its stand and began its long journey through rugged terrain to the western Highlands.

He wasn't the only one smiling. The tall man beside the water machine, half hidden by a strategically placed newspaper, was watching the scene.

Too young to be a victim, he thought, *but it's always wise to keep ahead of who's coming and going to Strathkin.*

THREE

Early morning rituals at The Strathkin Inn were the same as at hostelries the world over. The chinking of cups and cutlery; the smell of fresh coffee hanging in the air; light chatter murmuring in the busy dining room; the aroma of freshly made toast mingling with the mouthwatering smell of bacon drifting upstairs to quicken the morning pace of the rising guests at the small country inn. Quiet voices eased the patrons smoothly into the day. The sound of newspapers rustling was a welcome return to normality for the owner, Heather McLeod. She glided around the room picking up plates and cups, and she encouraged guests to linger a little longer over their breakfast table. Each table had a printed copy of that day's weather nestled between the condiments, and today, most patrons were delighted to see there was a week ahead of bright sunshine – except for the unsurprising half day of drizzle midway through. A light breeze was also forecast, which suited those who had decided to spend the day fishing either on the loch they could see from the dining room window, or in the river as it meandered its way across the glen before narrowing as it descended the hills to the loch. The kitchen was returning to normality after the usual chaos of a breakfast service, and Heather sighed as she leaned on a tall cabinet and took a gulp of coffee, long gone cold.

'No arrivals, no departures.'

'Dishwasher,' said Ally, her bar manager, server, and stock controller in response.

'I'll get it fixed,' replied Heather and drained the cup with her eyes raised to the ceiling.

'I'm going to hang a sheet on the fridge and put a tick on it every time you say that!' sighed Ally, elbow deep in scalding water, yellow gloves wearing thin. 'If I'm washing dishes, I'm not serving customers.' She thought this might urge her friend on, but Heather had a number in her head of how much she wanted in her bank account before she started paying money out, particularly on what she felt were *unnecessary and expensive repairs*. And fixing a dishwasher when she had a perfectly helpful wash-hand on site was not top of her priority list.

When she made her way out to the dining room, she found it blocked by a guest with an open map.

'You look as if you need a bit of direction in life,' she joked, and the man gazed at her, completely unaware of the intended joke.

'I'm trying to find Assynt,' he said directly. She recognised him as one of her week-long guests who left every morning after breakfast, enjoyed a light supper when he returned in the early evening and was likely to be in bed by no later than nine.

'You're a bit far away, to be fair.'

'A bit far away?' he asked in his heavy accented tone. 'I want today to visit Beinn Alligin and Liathnach. It's possible, yes?' He pronounced the names perfectly, and she smiled.

'Oh yeah, it's possible. About two hours' drive? I mean, it's less than a hundred miles but a bendy, twisty road. It's the A896 the whole way but build in plenty of stops.'

'Why?'

'The scenery. It's spectacular.'

'It's possible to go via Ullapool?'

'Oh, yes, with a stop off at the Ceilidh Place!' she encouraged. 'A bite to eat and a wee-wee stop.' He looked at her quizzically. She shook her head. 'It's a lovely drive and you'll get a beautiful view of Loch Broom. I hope you have a good camera. When I say stop, I mean stop: you'll think someone has pulled down a hand-painted backdrop like in a movie – it's breathtaking.'

The guest thanked her and headed up the stairs before returning with a backpack and an expensive camera minutes later. She watched as he made his way out to a German plated Audi parked directly in front of the Inn.

Back in the kitchen, she glanced at the high stack of dishes on the drying rack and the dismal pile waiting to be washed. She knew Ally was on a morning-only shift so, with a sigh, she made her way into the office at the rear of the building and took out her well-worn household book, flicking through pages until it reached 'repairs'.

While Heather was searching for a repair man, the Trekking Centre was a hive of activity. Horses were being tacked up and saddles heaved onto broad-backed Highland ponies. Once the morning visitors had set off on their hacks, silence settled in the stable yard, and Isabella Forrester, Bella, knew it was time now for the owner to take her own beast out into the early morning mist and lose herself in a fast country gallop. Bella loved the feeling of the wind in her wild auburn hair. She had planned her route carefully to finish her daily ride on the high ridge which overlooked the whole of the tiny village of Strathkin. She had a freshly made omelette roll in her pocket which would be at the right temperature for a snack when she reached the viewing platform. The mare was a light bay called Pebbles, and this morning she was enjoying the opening of her lungs as much as the rider, free from the confines of her stable, with the warming sun beating down on her broad back.

Bella left her charge tucking into an early lunch as she climbed the last few metres to the top of the ridge and took in a deep breath of the clean fresh air, raising her arms wide above her head in an exaggerated stretch. She continued this deep breathing for some moments before throwing herself on to the bench to take in the whole view of her home. On her right were her beloved stables, nestling near the water where she had taken her horse for an early morning dip. Beyond that, the village hall with its new roof glinting a shiny black against the blue sky. In the foreground, Lochside Croft was quiet, Ruaridh's two cars parked up and no hot smoke puffed out of the chimney into the stillness of the day. A few hundred metres in front, The Strathkin Inn had finished disgorging guests for their day trips to the surrounding villages. Guests would be hunting for lost treasures, panning in the rivers and searching for elusive fish in the many sea lochs which nestled in the glens and valleys. It was a truly striking day, and no one could enjoy it more than Bella, who had known the loneliness of the loss of freedom that comes with a prison sentence. She appreciated every day she awoke in her own bed and fell asleep to the sound of an owl hooting its presence in the tree outside her window.

Her eyes drifted across to what used to be the jewel in the crown of the village: Swanfield House. The huge rambling house kept watch over the rest of the village and its people like a protective parent. Now it stood as a memorial to those who perished, not in the fire that destroyed it, but at the hands of others. Next to what had been known as the *big house*, was the white-painted cottage of Sweet Briar, Callum McKenzie's cottage, untouched by flames or fire. Swanfield remained empty; it had been uninhabited for over a year. Her eyes wandered back to Lochside Croft, directly opposite the big house on the other side of Strathkin Loch, and a shiver ran through her. Her beautiful friend, her childhood partner in crime, her bewitching and dazzling Dina, the matriarch of the croft, was now another ghost in the history of Strathkin.

Bella reached into her pocket for her one-person picnic and decided not to eat it. An overwhelming feeling of sadness came over her and she had an urge to cry. Cry for her friend and cry for all those who had lost their lives in this beautiful place. *Maybe Strathkin is cursed*, a thought that had drifted through her mind more than once. Sometimes she thought she should have started a new life elsewhere after leaving prison, away from temptation, away from her past, away from what she had known her whole life. But she found herself back here in the western Highlands, drawn by the inexplicable thread which tied her to her childhood home and back to the warmth of her family and friends.

Bella hauled herself up from the bench, ran her fingers over the plaque that simply said CALLUM, tapped it twice, and then made her way back down to her rested horse. It was normal in the Highlands and elsewhere in the country to have memorial benches to remember loved ones around beauty spots. Callum, however, was very much alive and simply taking time out, but this, his favourite spot, offered family and friends the chance to take a moment to enjoy the vista and maybe prompt a call or text to the Strathkin stalwart to share news, gossip or both.

It was only the quick reaction of an experienced rider and horse that prevented a more serious accident just moments later. Cantering along the low, quiet, car-free road, the last thing Bella expected to see as she turned a sharp corner was a young woman in the middle of the road with a large suitcase and a haunted, fearful look. The horse snickered, whinnied, and then reared, casting Bella to the side and into a deep puddle of soft mud and sand. When Bella sat up, the woman appeared genuinely horrified at what had happened.

'What the...?' began Bella, struggling to her feet, half caked in mud and grateful for the strap on her hat and a soft landing.

'Oh, gosh, I'm so sorry!' pleaded the woman, still standing in the same spot, hand gripping her old-fashioned suitcase. 'I didn't expect to see anyone else.'

'Neither did I!' ranted the clearly annoyed rider, dusting herself down with her crop. 'What the heck are you doing standing in the middle of the road?'

'I think I'm lost.'

'No kidding, Sherlock,' continued Bella, wiping the wet mud off her filthy jodhpurs.

'I got off the bus and I think I've taken the wrong road. I couldn't remember what the driver said, left or right.'

'Right,' qualified Bella. 'If you keep on this road, this will take you to the back of the Drovers' Road and you'd be off the cliff and next stop – Canada.'

'Oh,' replied the young woman in a disappointed tone.

Bella saw her flinch as the horse shook her head and whinnied at her in annoyance at the hard stop of her playtime.

'It's okay, Pebbles is fine, she won't bite – seriously, she's a big softie.'

'I've never really seen one up close,' said the woman, a worried look on her face.

Bella walked the horse over to where she was still standing with her fingers tightly gripping the handle of the suitcase.

'This is Pebbles,' she said, patting the horse. 'And you are?'

'Hannah Hurley,' said the woman, blurting the words out quickly.

'Well, Hannah. It's been lovely to meet you, but here's some advice for Highland walking – stick to the verge.'

Bella began to lead her horse back down the slight incline

then stopped. 'Where exactly *are* you going?' she asked, cocking her head to one side. 'Strathkin?'

'Yes, I think that's where I'm going. I'm not really sure,' Hannah replied, eyes flitting from side to side.

A loud gurgling noise interrupted them both, and Hannah placed her spare hand on her stomach.

'I'm sorry. Haven't eaten.' She gave Bella a look of apology at which the rider reached into her pocket and took out the foil-covered roll.

'Here, didn't manage to eat it myself,' she said with an outstretched hand.

Hannah hesitated for a moment then took the package, unwrapped it, and took a bite, sublime gratification covering her face.

'Oh, man. That's delicious,' she sighed, biting into the offering with gusto.

Bella smiled. 'Yeah, you're hungry all right.'

They stood for a moment in silence as Hannah wolfed down the food, licked every finger with relish and gave out a long sigh.

'Give me your stuff.' Bella pointed to Hannah's backpack and cross-body bag.

She handed them over, with a look that told Bella she was positive that the kindness of this stranger meant she would not make off with her only possessions in such a remote location. Bella heaved the bag on the saddle, hooking it over the pommel and placed the cross-body bag over her own shoulder.

'Crikey, these are heavy! Are these all your worldly goods? Don't tell me the kitchen sink is in there?' she joked as she pointed at the suitcase, standing on its side. Hannah smiled back. Bella clicked her tongue twice against the roof of her mouth, a signal for Pebbles to start walking, led by reins.

The two women began to exchange polite pleasantries as strangers do. Bella quickly noticed Hannah gave closed answers as she carefully navigated the narrow road. She made a point of stopping on several occasions to let her admire the view and rest her tired arm. By the time they reached the small junction, Hannah appeared weary and exhausted. They stopped. Bella began adjusting Pebbles's saddle, but in fact was just wasting time until Hannah regained her composure and cooled off. In the warm sunshine, her bulky clothes only added to her overheating.

'What brings you to Strathkin, Hannah?'

Hannah said she was on holiday, but Bella sensed immediately this wasn't true. There was general chitchat as Bella eyed her suspiciously, and it did not take long for the truth to be revealed.

'I'm running away,' Hannah blurted out as if in confession. Her eyes were open wide with a hope she could trust this worldly-wise woman in front of her.

'I thought so.'

Hannah looked relieved to have stated her case but also appeared on the verge of tears.

'Have you anywhere to stay?'

Hannah shook her head, and Bella took stock for a moment.

'Do you think you could walk as far as that Inn up there?' She pointed to the building in front of them, along the road to The Strathkin Inn. Hannah peered past the junction and her eyes rested on the white building.

'I know that's a heavy case but it's not really that far. I can take it if you want to lead this girl?' suggested Bella.

Hannah seemed immediately terrified as the horse chewed on its bit and frothed at the mouth.

'Okay. Maybe not,' said Bella.

They started the slow walk along the road and as they neared the Inn, Hannah let out a sigh as if a weight had been lifted off her shoulders.

. . .

When Bella had left the stables no more than an hour before, all had been quiet. Her house guest had been sitting nursing a cup of tea, facing the loch, on the small patch of grass before the shingle and sand shore, reading her newspaper,

'One minute you can see as clear as day, next it's as clear as mud.' She took a gulp from her teacup and made a face.

'Tea,' she muttered. 'I don't know why they can't make tea taste any better than, well, tea. I've tried it with milk, with sugar, with honey, with that fancy, what is it, oat milk? Milk? From oats? Well, I've never seen the like. Only drink it to join in.' Maureen continued her morning rant until she looked up. 'Where've you gone, Jim?' As she turned, her large Gucci sunglasses slid down her face until she caught the blurry sight of a small Shetland pony called Jim, who had wandered away. She sighed and returned to her newspaper. The *Press and Journal, Highland Edition* had been handed over that morning by the postman.

'Poor girl,' she read aloud, 'found in Edinburgh. Scammed out of all her money. Tut tut. Met some guy who, what's that, catfished her. I'll ask Bella later, she'll know what that means.' Maureen, disappointed with the lack of interest in her conversational skills from Jim the Shetland pony, had gone back to her favourite pastime, having a one-sided conversation with her deceased husband, Brian Berman. 'It's all this online stuff, Bri, not seeing people face to face, look them in the eye.'

Maureen's one-sided discussion with Brian was interrupted as Bella strode into the yard covered in caked-in mud, leading her horse up to where the woman sat.

'Fell off again, luv?' asked Maureen with a chuckle. 'What a state.'

'Long story,' sighed Bella with a shake of the head.

Rosie, her fourteen-year-old eager, horse-mad stable hand, rushed down, took the reins from Bella and started leading Pebbles back up through the yard to the tack room. Bella walked round to stand in front of Maureen, and her eyes fell upon the house on the opposite shore.

'It's a pity, ain't it?' Maureen said, following Bella's gaze.

'Hmmm,' was the response.

'I was speaking to that Jamie fella, you know, the copper. He says they 'aven't found the owners yet. Not traced them. It was well insured, too. Cost a bloody fortune, if I recall. Poor Ange. Bless her.'

Bella stood in silence, her mind drifting to the night of the fire at Swanfield and all that had led up to it.

'Do you ever wonder where they are?' she asked as she took her seat next to Maureen, being careful not to allow any mud or grass to escape onto her carefully curated outfit.

'Him and 'er?' Maureen knew immediately Bella was referring to Doctor Moran Maguire who had stolen her heart, her fortune and her future. 'Can't say I do, but wherever they are, I hope he's left her with some money of her own. He's a one,' she added, referring to the gambling, womanising doctor whose gentle bedside manner and touching Irish lilt belied the scheming machinations of the twice-married man from Ballycastle.

'I met a young girl on the hill,' began Bella, 'who told me she was running away.'

'We're all running away from something, love.'

'She looked very vulnerable. I've left her with Heather. Asked H to see if she could have staff accommodation for a couple of nights. She might go home after she's sorted herself out. From down your way.'

'Streatham? I shouldn't have thought so, love.'

'Well, Englandshire. I've absolutely no idea where, Mrs B. I got lost leaving Inverness Airport.'

'We should do a girls' trip to Marbs, you and me,' Maureen suggested.

Bella turned to her permanent house guest. She was eighty-three according to her hospital records, early seventies, if you were to guess, late sixties, if you were to ask.

'Marbs?' asked Bella.

'Hmmm, now I think about it, don't think I have a working passport no more. What's the nightlife like in Skye?'

Bella shook her head and decided it was time to get into clean clothes and left Maureen sitting planning on the bench.

FOUR

A long and scenic drive away, Marcie was standing in the car park with the sinister mountain Stac Pollaidh ahead of her, disappearing into thick mist. She had driven twenty-five minutes north of Ullapool and was dressed in well-worn wet weather climbing gear, but as soon as she had arrived, a fear took over her. She stared up at the jagged mountain ahead, hoping to walk, hike and climb the trail anticlockwise, as she had done some years before when she had arrived one damp Monday with Simon. She recalled the stunning scenery, the spectacular views, the unbelievable sound of silence, just like she did today. She even remembered the exact spot where Simon had taken a selfie of them both with the vast landscape stretched out behind them. When she had let her eyes drift over the photograph on her phone later, she realised her smile showed her in a happy place. If only she had known what was ahead of her. The photograph brought back memories of escaping with him from their busy legal life in chambers in London. She had been drawn to the great outdoors of her childhood, taken up mountains and swimming in cold rock pools before it became the latest fashion. She had made a deal with herself that she would do it one last time – this time on her own and with him in her memory – a remembrance of better times. Times before the acrimonious split. Before the arguments and distance. When all they had to do was look to the future. Now, alone, she was looking up at the peaks and a fear came over her. *What if something happened? What if she fell? What if she was never found?* While the other part of her brain was thinking – *What has happened to fearless, adrenaline junkie Marcie?* The first one with her hand in the air, eager to take charge. The first one out of the plane on their charity sky dive. The first one to jump into the water off the small jetty on their picnics. A shiver ran through her, and she made her way back to her car. It was a beautiful still day, the sky cloudless and the car park not as busy as normal. She was still swithering about what to do when she walked straight into the man who had parked his car beside her.

'Oh, I'm so sorry! I wasn't paying attention. Apologies,' she said as the man smiled then headed over to the signpost that announced in Gaelic *Crimean's chromogen*, which explained to climbers the crumbling and tumbling they could expect if they took on the challenge of the Stac. The man read the information board and made his way back to the Audi parked next to Marcie's car.

'I nearly bought one of them.' She smiled as the man climbed into the driver's seat, where he sat motionless staring into space. She watched him unobserved for a few minutes then, curious, knocked on his window, which he slowly opened.

He looked confused as to why this woman would interrupt his moment of peace. He said nothing, waiting for her explanation.

'I'm sorry, but is everything okay?'

'Yes,' he said and waited.

'It's just that I thought you were going to climb or...'

'No,' said the man in response.

'Okay,' she conceded, holding her hand up in apology, and

was about to get back in her own car when the man opened the door of the Audi and stepped out.

'I'm more of an observer than a climber. My son is the climber in the family. Sorry, was. I'm just appreciative of the stunning scenery.' He had an accent, but she couldn't make out from where it originated.

'You've caught it on a good day. We say when you can't see the mountain it's raining, when you can see it, it's about to rain.' She laughed at her Uncle Callum's joke, one that never failed to amuse her, but the man didn't seem to see the funny side, its play on words lost in translation. 'It's just a saying. It's about our lovely Scottish weather and our glorious liquid sunshine.'

'Ah, but I'm told it's the water that makes the whisky so tasteable, no, not tasteable,' he corrected, 'drinkable.'

'I think you've created a new word; I think *tasteable* will catch on. I'm going to use it at every opportunity!'

The man's face broke into a smile, and Marcie was struck by how incredibly handsome he was. His demeanour had relaxed and behind his Oakley sunglasses, she saw the laughter lines around his eyes. His open inviting smile revealed a warmth, and neat hair and well-cared-for stubble showed him to be perfectly groomed. He held out his hand.

'Dieter,' he said.

'Marcie,' she responded, and her smile back to him was genuine and welcoming. 'I'm sorry if I put you off the climb. I was going to go up myself, but I've bottled it.'

He pondered for a moment at her language, looking to Marcie as if he had never heard these words in his English classes.

'I got scared,' she explained.

'Ah, well, it is a big hill – a big mountain if it is a first time.'

'Oh, no, I've climbed it before. It's challenging but doable. I took my husband here for his first climb. He was off like a mountain hare.' Another quizzical look. 'He climbed it as if he knew every rock and ridge. He was a very experienced climber.'

'He doesn't climb anymore, no?'

'He, er...' She stopped. She took a breath in like she was taught to do, one of the very few things she still did as recommended by her therapist. 'No. He's quite ill.'

'I'm so sorry to hear. How sad.'

As he spoke, she gazed up at the majesty of the mountain. 'I'll leave you to it,' she said and turned to her car.

'It was so nice to meet you, Mars...' He extended his hand again, and she turned around to shake it.

'Marcie, Marcella... Mosse,' she said, hesitating over her name.

'Dieter, Dieter Frum.'

She pulled the car out of the car park and decided she would stop at the Ceilidh Place in Ullapool for something not only to nourish herself but to eat up time before she drove back to Tigh-na-Lochan.

Once home, for she now called it *home*, her eyes once again fell on the unopened letter from Dina Balfour. She took a shower and then found herself circling the room before sitting down at her desk with the envelope in front of her. She pulled out her laptop and opened a blank page, her fingers starting to run over the keys.

Dear Dina

I miss you.

I haven't opened your letter yet even though you told us we shouldn't keep it like a museum piece. I just can't bring myself to do it. I thought I would after we said goodbye to you. We all did. Then I thought I'd wait a few days, then weeks, then a month and now it's almost a year later and I just keep putting it off.

*I keep thinking of our last days together, the laughs we had and that you're looking down on us from way up there. I even thought I saw you in the sky the other day; the sun was trying to break through the cloud, and I thought I saw it melt into your face. I've not been drinking, by the way! Talking of which, I suppose you've seen Ruaridh? I think he's coming out of his schlump. You've affected so much of us down here by leaving! Why did you have to go? I miss you so much. I miss someone to talk to. I mean, I know you figured out about me and Simon without me having to drone on about it, I don't think I really **had** to tell you. I don't know why I went through with it – caught up in the magic of wedding planning, I imagine, like a lot of giddy women. I often think of us all piled up on the bed in that hotel in Edinburgh surrounded by magazines and Prosecco and laughing about the future. It makes me smile, D. It makes me smile because we weren't thinking ahead to what would befall us – we were just lost in the excitement of it all. And then everything changed so quickly.*

*Deep down, I knew Simon and I would never last. Yes, I loved him in the beginning but we both know I was never good enough for his mother, and I think of how much Flora Balfour adored you. I never had that. I'm so sorry to pile this on you but I'm just lurching from one thing to another, D. I need direction. I need you back. We **all** need you back. Your family, your children, your husband. Everyone in the village.*

*You probably know that me and the girls talked about going to see a spiritualist! I know – **US**! The most sceptical people on the planet. I can hear you laughing, telling us all it's nonsense.*

Remember we talked about Lisanne reading the tea leaves – do you think I could? D, I miss you so much. Could you send me a message? Could you send me a sign? Could you send me someone just like you? Please?

Marcie looked at the words she had typed, tears drifting down her cheeks. Then her finger moved to the DELETE button, and she wiped the screen until she was left once again with a blank page. It was like a metaphor for her life. Blank. Divorce on the cards, a job that she was drifting away from and indifferent about. She got up and looked around the empty space. She heard her Uncle Callum's voice in her head telling her to snap out of it – *plenty of people would give their right arm to be in your position*. And of course he was right.

She dialled his number, and a blurry face appeared on the screen. His wide smile made her happy, seeing him so content thousands of miles away. She told him it was nearly their time, their moment to chase the sun on the longest day, and he told her he was heading out to watch racehorses on the beach being bathed from the local stables on this small Caribbean paradise island. He seemed blissfully happy.

After she hung up, she wandered out to lean on a chair that overlooked the lochan. She looked around the spectacular mountains that surrounded her. She had everything she could ever need. Except contentment.

FIVE

At The Strathkin Inn, Hannah Hurley's eyes scanned the room she had been offered. It was basic. A single bed and bedside table with a tiny lamp. There was a chest of drawers and a wardrobe, which had both seen better days. The room, thankfully, was en-suite and it, too, had seen better days, but the shower curtain was new and still had the folded lines from the packaging clearly showing. It was a blessing to her when she realised that she did not have to queue for a bathroom or strip off in a communal space. Her body still bore scars of recent events, and she did not want to be faced with questions and interrogations. One thing about The Strathkin Inn which struck her was that it was spotless. The carpet may have seen better days and the décor questionable, but it was one of the cleanest places she had ever been in. She ran her fingers along the windowpane. It squeaked and she could see through it, albeit only to the staff car park and the bins. The girl who brought her up was so friendly and had a lovely calm voice with a soft Highland lilt, but she was going on and on about a new dishwasher, and Hannah had switched off. She had, however, listened to her lovely laugh. It was quite husky, naughty, her grandmother would have said, and she immediately liked her. The owner – *she couldn't remember her name either* – was also very welcoming after speaking with Bella and they took her in like a long-lost friend. This would not have happened in London, she reminded herself, and it cemented in her mind she had done the right thing.

Hannah opened her case, and her life spilled out. Packing her bag in such a hurry, she knew there were clothes which would be entirely inappropriate for this new setting, and she was unsure whether to hang them up in the wardrobe. Her backpack, however, had been carefully packed, and she had kept it in the kitchen larder cupboard, knowing Chester would never look in it. Every piece of her short life was now in these two bags. Money that had been squirrelled away over months and years was carefully stored in an envelope, then placed in a plastic carrier bag, and hidden inside a zipped pocket inside the backpack. She searched around the room for somewhere to hide it. She remembered the owner saying everyone was responsible for cleaning and taking care of their own room and that she occasionally did spot checks with a two strikes and you were out policy. She shoved it under the mattress near the bottom of the bed, otherwise she would always have it with her, arousing suspicion.

'Hannah, you want a bit of lunch?' shouted a disembodied voice from the hallway downstairs. These people were giving her a place to stay and now they were feeding her. Her only regret was not coming here sooner.

SIX

'What's Netflix when it's at home?'

Marcie raised her eyes to the ceiling. 'For the umpteenth time, Maureen.'

The four women sat in the reserved bay window nook of the lounge bar at The Strathkin Inn, in what had once been the go-to table for four schoolfriends who occupied this seat on a regular basis, most often when Marcie made her frequent trips from her life in London, but the make-up of the table had changed. Dina Balfour's space had been taken up by the force of nature that was Maureen Berman, who seemed to both fit in, despite the fifty-year age gap, and drive the other three women to distraction with her strange ways and inability to adapt to life in a modern world with all its mod cons and quirks.

'It's new. It's called streaming,' Marcie tried to explain.

'Streaming meant something different in my day,' muttered Maureen in response, pushing her large glasses up her delicate nose.

'Maureen, can we go back to the conversation in hand, please?' said a weary Heather. 'So, I've taken this girl in. She seems lovely. Could do with a bit of help around the place now that business has taken off with Adam in the kitchen, but I was thinking...' she began and caught Marcie's eye, 'Ruaridh.' All eyes drifted towards Marcie.

'What about him?'

'We think he needs a hand,' Heather continued.

'*We?*'

'Me and Bella. He's looking awful. We think he's struggling.'

'Of course he's struggling, but he's too proud to ask for help. I've offered. Dina's mum is there virtually every day. She looks as exhausted as him. She's not a young woman.'

'What age is she then?' queried Maureen.

'Sixty-eight,' replied Marcie.

'Child,' replied Maureen and took a sip from her cup of what appeared to be water, but Heather knew otherwise.

'I'm thinking maybe she could help at Lochside Croft with the boys – it's nearly the summer holidays. Ruaridh will be busy with the tourists and whatnot. Renting out the pods in the garden at the back.'

'I don't know if he's still planning on doing it this year,' replied Marcie.

'He's a handsome man in a kilt, I'll tell you that,' interjected Maureen, apropos nothing.

Bella picked up the cup, sniffed it and put it back on its saucer.

'Kind of like an au pair or a nanny,' Heather went on, 'mother's help kind of thing. Well, father's help in this case.'

'We'd need references and letter of introduction from her previous employers,' began Marcie, slipping into lawyer mode.

'Marce, it's hardly a job for the Bank of England. She seems like a nice girl.'

''ow many serial killers had *that* on their CV – "seemed like a nice girl"? I was watching this forensics programme on me iPad the other night and—'

'Maureen. This isn't downtown Chicago. It's Strathkin,' interrupted Bella.

'Whatevs,' responded Maureen indignantly. 'I'm off to powder me nose.'

'Give me strength,' said Bella, sighing at her girls.

'You must have the patience of a saint,' said Heather, patting her friend's hand on the table once Maureen had gone.

'Nothing from Jamie about the other two?' asked Marcie, speaking, as Bella had earlier to Maureen, about the recent owners of her family home who had been untraceable after the fire which caused so much devastation to Swanfield House. Marcie's eyes were drawn to the scene from her favourite seat with a view of the property across the loch. Even now, occasionally when the wind swirled up, a vague smell of charred timber was carried in the breeze. The last time she parked her car at the Inn a small piece of black splintered wood had floated onto the roof of her white car as if it was a relic from her previous life.

'Nada,' responded Heather, and Bella nodded in agreement.

Both Angelina San and her husband, Doctor Louis De Groot, had disappeared into thin air. *An accidental fire* was the official conclusion of what had happened, and foul play had been ruled out.

'Talking of which... Plenty of Fish?' she asked, turning to Heather and her dalliance with online dating.

'Same old, same old,' replied Heather with a sigh. 'One of the builders on the new Strathdon Road showed some interest, told me he was a quantity surveyor, so I asked to see his theodolite.' The three girls burst out laughing and ended up in fits of giggles and sniggers. 'No show,' finished Heather, and they were still laughing when Maureen drifted back into view.

'I see *himself* is in,' she announced and nodded through to the saloon bar.

All three girls leaned forwards at the same time, but the bend in the bar was too long and they could not see any patron with a pint. Marcie sighed and pulled herself from the banquette.

'Go easy on him, Marce,' encouraged Heather as her friend made her way to the bar next door.

Ruaridh was indeed propping it up. A pint of stout was placed in front of him, and as his hand reached out to pick it up, Marcie swept it away.

'Oy!' he complained before realising who it was.

'It's twelve thirty in the afternoon!' she scolded.

'It's alcohol free,' he responded with a scowl. 'I'm picking people up from the airport. I'm not *that* stupid!' Marcie took a sip of the dark, strong liquid, and caught Ally's eye behind the bar who pointed to the pump which did indeed say zero per cent. 'Just checking,' she said by way of an apology and slid the glass back along the bar.

'Don't want it now,' replied Ruaridh like a petulant child.

Ally disappeared from the bar into the back storeroom, not wanting to be drawn into any unnecessary confrontation. Ruaridh gave out a great sigh and stretched to his full six foot three, heaving out his chest and drawing his arms round in a circle. He was dressed casually but neatly, as always, for an airport run. His thick socks gathered around his ankles, while his feet were firmly planted into his well-worn Timberland boots. He appeared thinner than his frame allowed, his beard trimmed to barely a stubble and his thick hair cropped. Marcie thought this pale shadow of the ebullient, self-effacing, funny, rugged Ruaridh was now a shell of the man he used to be before his wife's tragic and untimely death. She stood at the bar for a few minutes wondering to herself how it had come to this; her first boyfriend from school, all those years ago, before grown-up life got in the way, now unable to reveal their true feelings and a chasm between them. She caught herself in the mirror behind the bar and realised she had the same haunted look as Ruaridh, who had turned and headed out of the door without so much as a goodbye.

A young woman meandered down into the main bar, catching her eye. 'I can get someone to serve you?' she suggested to Marcie.

'I'm just leaving.' Marcie smiled before realising this must be the person Bella had found on the road. 'Oh, hi, you're the new girl?'

'New girl?'

'Well, I think Bella rescued you from certain death on the main road – well, when I say main road...'

She smiled a genuine smile and laughed a little.

'Marcie,' she said, and offered a hand. 'And you're Hannah?'

Hannah nodded and waited a moment before putting out her own hand in response. As the sleeves of her sweater ran up slightly, Marcie took in the lines on her wrists and the marks on her arms.

'I work in London,' she continued, 'but I'm doing a bit of hybrid working and travelling down once a month. Bella said you were from Kent, I think?'

'Maidstone.'

'I had some clients down your way. We used to go to Sutton Valance every couple of weeks for a bite to eat. Lovely part of the country. I like the fact it's so accessible to Europe from Dover.'

The girl seemed to have no idea what Marcie was talking about.

'Do you go across?'

Hannah shook her head.

'We went across to one of the big hypermarkets for my husband's birthday. Stocked up on champagne – it was so cheap compared to here.'

'Was it a special birthday?'

'His thirtieth,' replied Marcie, remembering the time before it all fell apart.

'I've never understood these birthdays. Why would you want to count down your life?'

'I suppose that's true,' agreed Marcie, 'but it was thought that when you reached eighteen, it opened so many opportunities as you prepared to leave your teens. Then at twenty-one, you got the key to the door.' The girl appeared baffled. 'Metaphorically speaking,' qualified Marcie. 'I suppose nowadays it's just a turn of phrase. So,' she began, changing the subject, 'how long are you planning on staying in Strathkin?'

'I'm not really sure,' Hannah offered in explanation, with a bite of her lip.

'A job here, maybe? Long term?'

'Well, the owner here...' she began, and Marcie noticed her struggling to remember the name of the owner who had offered her bed and board. 'She has some work I could do but I'm willing to turn my hand to anything to make a bit of cash.'

'To enable you to go back to Maidstone?'

'No, I really need to—'

'Listen if you're looking for any extra work, I know Bella is always after a bit of a helping hand up at the Trekking Centre.'

'I'm not exactly mad about horses.' She seemed to almost recoil at the very thought of mucking out.

'Any good with children?'

'No, not really,' replied Hannah before seeming to realise she was talking herself out of staying in this magnificent place.

Marcie smiled at her. The girl looked pallid, and Marcie thought a bit of time spent outdoors might do her the world of good.

Both women turned as a man entered the bar, and Marcie greeted him with a smile.

'Hi.' She beamed, openly. 'We meet again!'

'Indeed, we do.' Dieter smiled and offered a hand to shake. When she turned to introduce Hannah to Dieter Frum, she saw the tail end of a black Doc Marten boot as the girl reached the top of the stairs.

'I think you've just missed the lunch service but I'm sure the owner can make you a sandwich or something?'

'No, no, I ate at a place on the road. Very good seafood. I was just coming in to book a table for dinner.'

The bar was empty and a glance through to the restaurant would tell him there was only one table occupied with an older lady and two women chatting animatedly. Marcie, no stranger to the Inn, picked up Heather's reservations book that was sitting on a nearby table. She advised him that he could have a table at eight in the evening and waited for what she thought was the inevitable invite to join him. It wasn't forthcoming.

'It's a bit late but I'm sure it will be fine,' he agreed with a nod of the head and gave her a smile. 'Thank you very much, have a nice evening.'

She smiled, knowing he was struggling to remember her name. 'Marcie,' she said and held out her hand again. He took it, kissed the back of it and then turned to head up the stairs to the bedrooms on the first floor.

'What was all that about, you and the *silver fox*, old Prince Charming if you ask me?' said Bella with a glance to where Dieter Frum had disappeared upstairs.

'I met him up at Stac Pollaidh.'

'Good God! You didn't climb it, did you?' asked Heather, horrified.

'I'm still here so clearly not!' was the response from Marcie as she took her seat again with the other three women.

'Where's he from?' quizzed Bella to her friend.

'I think he said Frankfurt,' replied Heather. 'Maybe a doctor? Orthopaedic surgeon? Here on some sort of pilgrimage or something, he said when he checked in.'

Marcie, Bella and Heather suddenly looked at each other and the same shiver ran through them.

'You don't think?' asked Bella.

'Surely not,' responded Heather.

'Oy, you three, wos going on?' asked the confused woman from behind large glasses.

'There was an accident up here a couple of years ago,' started Marcie, 'quite a bad accident on the mountain. There were several deaths. German lads. It was horrible.'

'Yes, I remember, Bells told me, but who's he then?'

'I think he may be the father of one of them, but surely he would have said?'

Marcie thought back to the three young German men she had met on the high ridge on a glorious day only a few years ago, before tragedy struck on their mountain climb. Now the only reminder of that time was the occasional relative who visited the small Highland village to pay homage or respects.

Marcie stared out the window, across the water, and for the second time that day she felt tears in her eyes. A single drop ran down her face, and she felt a hand gently rest on hers. She was more than surprised to see it was Maureen who was reassuring her, and she smiled weakly at the woman. When Marcie turned, she saw that Maureen had removed her large glasses and she, too, had tears in her eyes. She gave Marcie a nod of recognition. The recent trauma of the fire had affected them all. Silence fell for a moment, until it was broken by Maureen asking if it was too early for another gin.

SEVEN

After a late night with overdue paperwork at Tigh-na-Lochan, Marcie was only too glad to escape to the loch. Early spring, the sun was high in the cloudless sky, the sun was warm with a gentle breeze, and Marcie let her right foot hang off the low jetty to skim the water. She was still dressed in a wetsuit but had taken off her surf shoes that had protected the soles of her feet against the shingle shore. Bella and Heather were swimming towards her, Bella shouting that the race was on, while Heather struggled to breathe in the frigid still water of Strathkin Loch. Further along the jetty, Maureen Berman sat in a low wicker chair, head to toe in white linen. She wore a large straw hat which Marcie had dug out of a box that had belonged to her late grandmother. The holey hat slid down the elderly woman's small head away from her perfectly coiffured white hair.

'Why is it called wild swimming?' shouted Maureen from beneath a large golfing umbrella strategically placed on a low camping table and held between two large boulders. 'Looks a bit uncomfortable, but I wouldn't say *wild*.'

The scene was unlike any Highland picnic you might imagine; instead, it was like a scene from an expensive movie set.

Brightly coloured blankets and rugs were scattered over the jetty as it reached out into the still loch. A white metal picnic table with a lace tablecloth (Maureen's idea) was set with plastic tumblers, and a large thermal jug was filled with a mix of various fruit juices. Maureen sat near her flask of clear liquid, the tonic water and ice watering down the alcoholic mix. A distant red kite swirled in the thermals above their heads and gave an occasional squawk of warning.

'Tell me that then,' Maureen indignantly went on as Bella gently swam towards the shore, and Marcie rolled her eyes.

An old, battered Land Rover arrived on the small road behind them. Four excited children tumbled out and headed straight to the small shingle shore, all in plastic sandals and long-sleeved neoprene. Bella and Heather splashed them with water and shouted for them to enter the loch.

'Bloody typical,' moaned Maureen just as Ruaridh, carrying a large cool box full of food and treats in one hand, and a five-litre bottle of water in the other, strolled casually past her.

'Oh, ello.' Maureen moved her sunglasses down as he passed her with long, strong legs, his flip-flops slapping against his feet. He was wearing a Hawaiian shirt which appeared incongruous in the setting. He sat the cool box and water down next to Marcie and surveyed the scene before him. His eyes scanned the mountains that reached up as if trying to grasp the sky. A tiny puffy cloud appeared then disappeared as if by magic, and the only thing shattering the peace was the sound of screaming, boisterous children. The women's eyes all trained on the boys as they whooped and splashed and then to Ruaridh as he turned and began to walk back to the car, silently slipping into the driver's seat. Eyes then drifted to Marcie who pulled herself up and gingerly walked across the warm concrete to tap his window.

'Oh, 'ere we go,' said Maureen and moved her seat around so that she could face the couple at the car.

Ruaridh wound the window down.

'You okay?' asked Marcie as she leaned down.

'I've not had anything to drink in a week,' Ruaridh said sharply. 'Nearly ten days.'

A few weeks before, Marcie had gently suggested a slowing down of his alcohol intake and that he take a bereavement counselling class run at the surgery. Though it had taken an unexpected visit by local doctor, Arshia Brahmins, on the pretence of checking the children, to persuade him to go. Marcie knew that it was Ruaridh's pride, his fear of people seeing him in such a vulnerable position, those who saw him as a mainstay of Strathkin, which all conspired to put him off.

Still talking to him through the window of the car, Marcie noticed that Ruaridh was not listening to anything she was saying. Without warning, he suddenly turned and said, 'Can you take care of the boys? I'll be back in an hour.'

Marcie stood back in astonishment as he started the car, turned it sharply on the narrow single-track road and took off, leaving her standing staring at the dry dirt.

'What the...?' she said aloud and watched as the Land Rover disappeared behind the pine trees and passed onto the main road out of the village.

Twenty minutes later, at The Aizle coffee shop, Ruaridh balanced two mismatched cups and saucers on his tray before he took his seat at the rear of the restaurant. The table faced a long window which looked out to the glen and meant he had his back to the busy restaurant. He pulled out his phone when he felt it vibrating. It was only the local garage telling him his old Land Rover needed servicing. He had missed both a message and phone call from Ruthie Gillespie, saying she had an unexpected visitor, and she apologetically could not make their get-together. It had been sent an hour previously and he mentally scolded himself for not checking his phone before he left the village and dropped the boys at the loch.

He had finally attended the bereavement class, where he was greeted by Ruthie, and his mood had eased considerably. Ruthie's husband had been in the same Mountain Rescue Team as Ruaridh when events unfolded on the mountain which had left six dead: two team members and four climbers. She was still grieving the death of her beloved Geordie, and it had been a relief for Ruaridh to see a familiar face at the class. Ruthie had gently held his hand as she guided him to his seat in the small backroom of the surgery. Later, outside the surgery, she had explained to him there was absolutely nothing to be ashamed of. Grief was grief. Some people bounced straight back into their previous life, others never got over the shock of losing their wife, husband, mother, father, child. Ruthie was bereft at her loss and said to Ruaridh she would *never* get over it.

Ruthie had suggested she meet Ruaridh at The Aizle, away from the village and its prying eyes, and far from the surgery. Unexpectedly to both, he had taken her up on her offer more than once. Sometimes he was there to listen, sometimes he was there to talk about the emptiness he felt. Sometimes they laughed at stories of their loved ones and often shared tears in the corner table near the rear of the restaurant. He reminded her of how she'd reprimanded him in the post office when, as a child, he'd stolen the little caramels near the Chupa Chups stand at the end of the counter. Ruthie gently told him that she had put them there to give visiting children a small treat.

Ruaridh realised having someone to speak to outside his friendship circle, someone who had known him since he was a child, was mutually beneficial. Although he had prepared himself as much as he could for Dina's death, it still hit him like a runaway train. He had lost his spark. He had lost the light from his eyes and the love of his life. And the one person he thought he could talk to about his trauma was herself caught up in her own tragic life story.

He moved his seat in as someone bumped into it, clearly searching for a table at this busy time of day, and when he turned around, he realised it was Arshia Brahmins who was scanning the room for a seat. When she caught his eye, panic spread across her face.

'Busted!' she said as her eyes drifted to the huge cream-filled meringue which sat proudly in the centre of a large plate.

'Not practising what you preach, doc,' he joked, and she laughed. 'I've just had a dizzy, so you're welcome to join me,' Ruaridh then offered, leaning over to push the seat out in front of him. 'I've been stood up,' he qualified as he saw her baffled expression.

'Ah, I'm still trying to get used to the Scottish vernacular!' she joked and sat the tray next to his, taking her seat opposite him. She deftly and expertly separated the large treat and, with a fork, split the cream evenly on each side.

'You realise if you weren't here, I would just shove this in my face! When really, I should be like one of those men in, is it France or Spain, where they eat tiny birds and must cover themselves with a sheet out of shame?'

He shrugged and smiled as she shovelled a huge piece of the mixture into her mouth, then let her index finger wipe the excess from each corner. Very naturally, he picked up her paper napkin and leaned over automatically to wipe a piece of cream off her cheek then realised what he had done.

'I'm so sorry! I'm so used to doing it with the kids, and my wife loves a cake like that and was such a messy eater,' he apologised, hand covering his mouth.

'It's okay. It's something my husband would have done, too.' Arshia smiled.

He suddenly became aware of her wedding ring, a very thin

band of gold, so small it could be missed. She caught his glance, and she turned her hand to gaze at it herself.

'I, too, lost the love of my life,' she said wistfully.

'I'm sorry,' he felt himself apologising again. 'I wasn't aware.'

'Well, we don't go about broadcasting it, do we? He was a doctor, too. Médecins Sans Frontiers. Doctors without Borders. He was in the Middle East.'

Ruaridh was suddenly unsure what to say, so he simply listened.

'I couldn't bear to be in the same house, go to my same job when a hole as big as that had been cut out of my heart. It's why I'm here. Then, I find out Strathkin has its own heart cut out. To me, it feels like we belong together.' He noticed her huge brown eyes had tears welling up in them. 'Me and Strathkin, that is.'

Still listening, he closed his eyes slowly and when he opened them, he turned to face the vista beyond, his own tears in danger of flooding out. Arshia continued talking but he was again caught in his own reverie: struggling with concentration; struggling with conversation; struggling with life itself. As she spoke, he watched as her mouth formed words he didn't hear.

After a suitable time, he excused himself with the false promise of something to do. He drove back slowly, knowing the boys would be eager to fill him in on their day of wild swimming and picnicking in the warm sun. He pulled the car up the steep incline on to the high ridge and got out and sat quietly for a moment, watching from a distance as screams and laughter below him danced in the air before being swallowed up into the sky.

For a moment he observed the goings on across the loch below. He watched as his children tomb-stoned off the jetty with squeals of laughter. His eye was caught by the car pulling up to Lochside Croft. Dina's mother bent down to take a young child out of the back seat, his child, *their* child. He sighed.

'Man up,' he said to himself and turned to head back to his car and drive down into the quiet, still village. Listening to Arshia talking about losing the love of her life had made him realise he had to draw a dividing line down what had gone before and what was still to come.

He pulled the car into his drive behind his mother-in-law's car and took a deep breath. Persuading Dina's mum to stay a little while longer was not difficult, but he knew he needed more help.

Ruaridh knew what he had done had taken a lot of courage – making that call to the other side of the world. He hoped it would help him, maybe even help his friends. What he did not realise was how much life in Strathkin was about to be changed forever.

By late afternoon, at Tigh-na-Lochan, Marcie was going round and round in circles with her continuing work project. She had escaped the picnic early, leaving the Balfour boys in the capable hands of Heather and Bella, to catch up on a piece of work that was causing her sleepless nights. She had pushed her paperwork to one side and sat with her head in her hands when she was jolted out of her reverie. The slamming car door outside made her jump a little before she realised it was accompanied by the heavy feet of Ruaridh coming up the path.

She opened the door wide, inviting him in. 'Oh, so you decided to come back?'

Ruaridh did not respond as he made his way purposefully into the cottage: a man on a mission. 'Any chance of a...' he began.

She raised her brows at him, expecting him to finish the sentence with *beer*. Instead, he nodded to the French press that was sitting on the worktop. 'I'm happy with instant.' Comfortable as he was in her house and in her company, Ruaridh began to open cupboard doors, searching for a jar of coffee, looking for cups. She handed him her freshly washed mug and then milk from the fridge and watched while he busied himself.

He asked, 'Did you get the message from Callum? He said he's emailed with possible flights.'

'Oh, flip, I've not been in my personal emails. I've just been on work stuff and I'm woefully behind with them, too. I did FaceTime him, but he was otherwise engaged. Is it just me or does time stop up here? I really couldn't tell you what day it is,' she replied, searching for her phone then absentmindedly finding it in her back pocket. She pulled herself on to the kitchen table, phone in hand, swinging her legs.

'He's obviously coming back for your solstice get-together. As soon as he's firmed things up, I'll arrange to pick him up.'

'You came all the way up to tell me this?'

'Yeah, so it means I'm kind of on standby, I just wanted to let you know...'

Marcie knew immediately this was not the real reason for the visit, what with the summer solstice still some time away, but she waited, unusually silent, for him to open up. He looked anxious.

'Look, do you want to...?' he began.

'Yaas?' she said eagerly.

'Go outside? It looks lovely by your wee lochan.'

'Sure,' she said and slipped off the table, following him out to the front of the cottage. Two weatherbeaten Adirondack chairs stood facing the water, but he indicated to the old stone bench that sat on the path against the wall next to a window and a rambling climber of pale scented roses. They sat together.

'Listen, I just wanted to say...' he began. She waited. 'I've been going to this "grief group",' he said with air quotes, his coffee cup nestled between his knees. 'I mean, you kinda told me to go, so. Anyway, we've been advised to talk a bit more. I had a chat with Lachie Bateman not that long ago. Lachie's good at this sorta stuff – I mean, he's had his fair bit of trauma to deal with in his life.' As the head of the Mountain Rescue Team, it was true, Lachie's own life sometimes had to be shared openly with others and an unexpected loss took so many shapes and forms, but she had no idea where this was going. 'Uh-huh,' she encouraged.

'About the other morning,' he began again, thinking of her scolding as he lay sobering up on the sofa.

'It's okay. You don't have to apologise.'

'I wasn't going to apologise,' he said and turned to face her next to him on the stone bench.

'Oh.'

'I've gone off the rails a wee bit. I mean, you've seen it in action. And now, well, I've been in a period of reflection, from my counselling. So... I came to say, I've got to walk away from my past. I need to close the door on what has gone before to enable me to open the door to my new life.'

That's exactly what my counsellor told me, she thought to herself. She was going to make a joke about not listening to all that mumbo-jumbo therapist nonsense, wanted to make light of the situation and give him a nudge and rest her head on his shoulder. But she simply could not summon up the courage.

'So,' he went on, 'I know I've been taking advantage of your good nature and whatnot and ignoring the fact you have your own stuff you're going through.'

'I'm not sure *taking advantage* is what I would call it. You know me well enough to know I'm not going to do anything that I don't want to do. You needed help, I provided it. Listen, I'm sorry if I've been a bit harsh, but sometimes you need to face a harsh reality.'

As Marcie spoke, he stood up, wandered to stand at the lochan in front of the cottage, water rippling in the evening breeze. A chill settled on her. She had a strange feeling drift over her. It was as if she knew what he was about to say, and she wanted to close her ears to it. When he turned around to face her, there was a dawning reality of what was about to come, and she realised he was only moments away from him closing the door forever. She thought of the letter she had written to Dina before erasing it. Was Ruaridh about to delete her from his life? She opened her mouth to speak, to delay him saying what he had come all the way to Tigh-na-Lochan to say. And here she was, Marcie Mosse – the great debater – struggling for words. She bit her lip to hold back tears.

'You and I, we both have lives that ran in parallel, but I think we've come to the fork in the road, and I need to go one way, and you need to go the other.'

Marcie sat stock still with her palms resting on her thighs.

'I'm still in love with Dina and even though I know there may be someone else in my future, I don't believe that person is you, Mars, I'm sorry. It's not that I don't find you, well, you know... and another place in time I could have but, I just... I'm sorry. So, I guess I *am* apologising.'

She could hear him breathing as if it were laboured, as if saying these few words had used up all his strength.

'I wanted to say thank you for getting me here. It could so easily have gone the other way what with my drinking and stuff, but I need to take the next steps on my own. Put on my *big girl pants* as you kept telling me. And you need to do that, too.' He turned around again, back to the water, tears in his eyes. 'You were Dina's best friend. I'm sorry. I just can't,' he said, wiping the back of his hand across his running nose and then lifting it to stop tears coming out of each eye.

Marcie reached up, her finger drawing a line around her lip. She didn't know what to say despite the fact her mouth was full of words that wanted to spill out. *We can try. I have so much patience for you. We can get through this together. Take my hand and we can navigate this new chapter as a lost pair of old lovers.* That was what she wanted to say. Instead, she stood up and walked over to him, where he took her in his arms and squeezed her so tight she thought for a moment it would fuse them together like the ancient people found in Pompeii, and all the things that he had just said would float away like molten ash in the wind. She pushed her cheek against his chest and simply said, 'Thank you. Thank you for being honest.'

'We're good?' he asked, looking down, wiping a tear away from her cheek.

She nodded, managed a weak smile. It was as if time had suddenly stood still and, like him, a door had fiercely and firmly shut behind her. She wanted the moment to last forever, feeling him like this in her arms, vulnerable and emotionally open, until she felt him let go and release her and knew she would never be in his arms like that again.

She made her way back to the bench and sat heavily on the raw stone. Silence descended like a cold blanket on even colder skin. They took in the scenery, silent and still like them. She waited, not knowing what to say.

'Arshia Brahmins seems nice?' Marcie finally said after coughing to clear her throat.

He sat down next to her and poured the rest of the undrunk coffee dregs on to the gravel.

'She encouraged me to go to the bereavement counselling, too. She's very kind, she's been through her own personal trauma.'

'Oh, I didn't know. I hope she knows what she's letting herself in for with you,' she joked.

'I've never really been on a real date,' he stated out of the blue.

'Oh! Thanks very much for that!'

'Och, you know what I mean. We were always just together. I wouldn't know where to start to woo someone.'

'*Woo someone*? Have you been watching Turner Classic

Movies instead of your usual police documentaries? We *have* moved on from nineteen fifty-four.'

'I'm old-fashioned.'

'When you want to be.' She smiled at him and leaned into him a little.

'The boys like her.'

'Halfway there,' said Marcie and rested back against the wall. He pressed forward on his knees.

'Seriously, though, Mars. *We good?*'

She ran her hand over his back and patted it. 'Yeah, we're good,' she sighed, appreciating his honesty, appreciating his vulnerability, and appreciating all the good times and tough times they had shared that had turned them into the strong people they were today.

In years past they would have sat on the back seat of the school bus, secretly holding hands. Who knows what would have happened if they had married all those years ago? As they grew into the grown-up versions of themselves, would her go-getting attitude have been at odds with his laid-back style? Would they have fought for primacy at home? Would they have been the kind of couple who bickered in public, bringing each other down when the love ran out? Fate and their own destiny had taken them in different directions and taken them to destinations where they had been at their happiest, their most comfortable, their most settled.

'What do you think, Mars? Am I being stupid? Is Arshia out of my league? I mean, she's a doctor.'

'Er,' she said and pointed to herself, 'lawyer!'

'Yeah, well, you know what I mean. You're just you, though.'

She leaned up and touched his temple with her finger. 'It's in there that counts' – and then tapped his chest near to his heart – 'but it's what's in here that's more important.'

'You're one in a million, Mars, thanks.'

He leaned forward, kissed her forehead at her hairline and gave her a friendly nudge. He stood up and stretched slightly before he turned to wander back down the path and slid in behind the wheel of his battered old Land Rover. When his car was out of view, she made her way into the quiet cottage and looked around at the beautiful home she had created. She felt the pain in her heart and pulled her phone back out of her pocket.

Alone again.

Marcie realised in moments like this, the first person she would turn to for help and advice would be Callum. She missed him and his wise counsel. He could always see both sides, gave her a choice and she always, *always*, picked the right one. His guidance from her childhood was what she desperately craved. She did not want to come across as needy and desperate, but she dialled his number, and it went to voicemail. She left a message about seeing him soon and went into in her bedroom. She looked at the perfectly made bed, the designer décor and expensive wall coverings. What was all this material wealth without someone to share it with? Her marriage had failed, her friendships were changing, her job was not satisfying her. Her work was piling up and she knew that putting off her London trip was not going to play well with her boss either. There was a decision she knew had to be made. *Does London continue to be a viable option for me?* With Simon no longer in her life, what was her long-term plan? A plan that now had nobody in it but herself, Ruaridh had suddenly made that quite clear. She appreciated his honesty, his openness about his plans for his own future. If he could plan a way forward, then she, *too*, would have to put on her *big girl pants*, as he had said, and do the same thing.

Marcie dialled Simon's number and got what she expected – a message saying the phone was switched off. She dialled his home number that no longer went to voicemail. It simply rang out. And that made her decision for her right there and then. She called Richard MacInnes, her solicitor, and left a message. Technically, she and Simon were separated but to end their union completely would be straightforward enough. There were no children to consider. Marcie wanted to get it all over and done with quickly to enable her, like Ruaridh, to move on. She took herself back out to the front of the cottage, looked at the scenery that surrounded her house and sighed. She felt something akin to a physical release in her body. Marcie knew immediately she needed something new, even challenging, in her life – right at that moment, though, she simply didn't know what it could be.

EIGHT

'I'm so sorry!' said the man who bumped into Marcie coming out of Strathkin General Stores a day or so later as she clutched several bottles of juice. She had snapped herself back to reality and had decided to get a head start on her next visit with the Balfour boys by raiding the small store. Her work, completed after late nights and early mornings, and a particularly rainy and wet day, had made an indoors working from home day ideal.

'Ah, I knew we would meet again!' said the stranger with a broad smile. Dieter Frum stood before her in sunglasses and a pink polo shirt with the collar stylishly turned up.

Marcie smiled. 'Well, hello, or should I say guten tag! It's the only German I know, to be honest. Oh, that and bier bitte!'

He smiled at her failed attempt at his native language and reached out. 'Can I help you? You look overburdened.'

'My car is just here,' she said and indicated the white car directly in front of the shop, 'and as you can imagine, it's full of shopping bags I always forget to take wherever I go.' She pressed her key remote and the car boot opened automatically, displaying a carton full of jute shopping bags.

'Told ya!' She laughed. 'I hope you're not trying to find something extravagant – it is the village store, after all. They don't do flashy. Roddy will keel over if you ask for anything more exotic than a Milky Way.'

'I was trying to find wine,' he explained.

Marcie made a face and shook her head. 'Better up at the deli at The Aizle unless you're after a California Blush. You'll get a half-decent bottle of whisky here, but he'll have to dust it down,' she said, only half joking.

'Ah, maybe not for me then.'

She thought for a moment. 'Actually, if it's a nice wine you're after, and you don't mind a little drive, it's a lovely evening to sit outside. I'm up at Tigh-na-Lochan.' She saw he was confused. 'It's the name of my house. If you want to follow me? I'd be more than happy to share a glass of decent wine. I could do with some adult company,' she suggested.

'That would be very pleasant,' he agreed and headed to his car directly behind Marcie.

The drive to the little remote white cottage was spectacular on this beautiful afternoon. The undulating road took them from the lush green Glen of Strathpine up past the fork in the road that split for both Strath Aullt and Strathdon, then through a gentle landscape to a small lochan where Marcie's house sat with a commanding view of the mountain range beyond. She parked her car at the side of the house, and Dieter parked neatly next to her. As she opened the door and made her way in to deposit the bottles for her next Balfour boys' picnic, Dieter took in the scenery which lay before him, breathing it in. The lochan in front of the house was still, the image perfect.

When he entered the house, he was met with a stylish room with décor in muted colours. It was not what he was expecting in this remote white cottage. The rear wall had at its heart a heather-coloured Aga in the middle of a row of floor cupboards with open shelves above. A long handmade wooden table stood in front with six chairs, each chair having a tartan blanket strategically placed over the back, all at the same angle. A low tartan ANTA bowl sat in the middle of the long table with a display of thistles and greenery, and the whole room was like it had been staged for a photo shoot. A huge green velvet sofa sat at the other end of the room alongside a fireplace with a wood-burner with sparkling lights inside, glowing softly even on this bright day. Large prints adorned the walls displaying modern seascapes, and a tall charcoal drawing of Marcie's wedding dress hung proudly in an alcove, lit by a single wall light.

'It's beautiful. It could be out of *Architectural Digest* – the small house division,' he joked and slid his hands into his pockets.

Marcie smiled at him in agreement and internally thanked Dina, her interior designer, for the little touches that had turned Tigh-na-Lochan into a home.

'Wine!' she said and pointed to a large wine rack laden with bottles behind the front door.

'My, what a spectacular selection,' said Dieter as he made his way over to the wine rack, pulling bottles out to examine each one intimately. 'You have a lovely collection, some exceedingly good wines. Possibly a bit heavy for a day like today,' he suggested, holding up a deep green bottle and examining it closely.

'Oh, there's more!' she joked and opened the large fridge where bottles of white and rosé were on the shelf. He wandered over and picked out a tall green bottle of German Reisling.

'Nice!' He took the glasses that Marcie handed to him and followed her outside to the Adirondack chairs. He unscrewed the bottle and expertly poured the wine, handing her one before checking the bottle again and placing it on the wide arm of the chair.

'*Prost!*' he said as he gently offered his glass, eyes locking on hers, and then he turned to gaze out again to the vast landscape before him.

'I'm startled by the beauty. I understand now why my son loved your country so much.'

'He died on the hill?' she asked gently, already knowing the answer. She sat down and he remained standing, staring into the wilderness. 'I'm so sorry for your loss.'

'It killed my wife, you know, inside,' he said quietly. 'She was never the same woman. It separated us. She just became like a shadow, a different person. It traumatised her so much. You lost people, too, yes?'

'Mountain rescue people, yes. It devastated the community. Like your wife, some people have never truly recovered.'

'I came to the, I think, Fatal Inquest?'

'Fatal Accident Inquiry,' she gently corrected.

'They spoke about a man. A Russian man suspected to be poisoning the water?'

'Yes, Poytr Medvedev. The man who brought a catalogue of chaos with him,' Marcie agreed. She wondered about what to say next, how far to go with the relative stranger who stood in front of her. She took a sip of wine.

'I am not a violent man, Marcie. I am a surgeon. It is my life's aim to help people, my life's work to cure the sick. But I have also made it my life's work to track down this man – this murderer, the man who took the life of my son, destroyed my wife – and make sure he faces justice.'

'He ruined my marriage, too. My husband died inside, just like your wife,' she blurted out and expelled a long sigh, suddenly glad to share her grief. 'We're no longer together.'

'We were meant to meet, you know? You, too, have unfinished business with this man, this killer,' he explained. 'We should join forces, yes? Is that the expression? Two heads better than one?'

She reached up with her glass and they tapped them together, the light noise they made carried away in the breeze.

'Absolutely,' Marcie agreed, not sure what exactly this man meant. Was he suggesting they make a pact to destroy another man's life? For someone whose own life was set by the rule of law, she felt somehow detached from this suggestion and didn't really believe that he, this gentleman, would go through with such a suggestion. As they continued to talk about families and life and their countries, Marcie felt a smile return to her face.

When it was time for him to leave, she screwed the top back on the bottle. She waved as he drove away and closed the door to Tigh-na-Lochan once more. Inside, she looked at the photo of the four friends that sat on a kitchen shelf.

'Did you send him, D?' she asked aloud but already knew the answer as she shook her head.

NINE

At least a few times a day, at The Strathkin Inn, Hannah patted or looked under her mattress to ensure her backpack was still safe and secretly hidden in case she needed a quick getaway. Like last time. *Always have running away money.* Remembering her grandmother's words, she managed to stash a tiny bit away from the many jobs she kept, then lost. A couple of pence here, a couple of pounds there, and it soon stacked up until she had a hundred pounds, then almost a thousand. It was a fortune to her.

Since she'd arrived in Strathkin, Hannah had been careful to build a relationship with the older woman who worked at the post office whenever she took in a bag of loose change to exchange for notes, which were much easier to hide. The slight nod from the older woman told Heather, *I know what you're going through.*

That night when Hannah showered, a stolen scented candle perched on the sink, she pretended to be in a luxurious spa. She tried not to glance at the marks on her arm. Once she had dried herself with the most luxurious towels she had ever used, she sat on the bed and pulled open the drawer to the bedside cabinet. She pulled out a square photo frame and gazed at the charcoal drawing of a small child gently holding a dove. It was beginning to fade, and Hannah had promised herself when she was rich and famous, she would take it to a renowned restorer, and have it redrawn and enlarged into a large gilt picture frame. It would sit above the fireplace in one of the houses she used to work at in Kensington, a beautiful house that she would now own. Hannah held the photo close to her heart and closed her eyes. It was the only piece of her childhood she had left.

TEN

Marcie tried as much as possible to stick to her working from home schedule, but today she simply needed to escape. She had driven to Kylesku, the tiny fishing hamlet north of Ullapool, and hiked the four-kilometre trek to reach the impressive waterfall she now saw before her. She looked up, around, then across the water as it tumbled down from the top of the hill opposite. The Wailing Widow Falls at Loch na Gainmhich was a picnic spot like no other. The fifty-foot falls spilled out from the loch and over the cliff to let the water dance along the rocks of the narrow canyon below. She was still struggling to sleep. She had worrying dreams in the night, waking up in a cold sweat at least once a week and was sure if she had not been made a partner in her law firm, she would have been gently eased out of the door long before now.

She began the stroll back to her car after an extended time sitting contemplating her future and listening to the falls. She stopped to eat from her backpack and refresh her water bottle in the cool, clear, fresh water. She had spent too much time on her own, she knew, whether crouched over paperwork or taking herself out on long hikes into the desolate landscape beyond Tigh-na-Lochan and only snatched coffees or chats with Bella and Heather.

She drove back to the village, passing her own house on the way, and was surprised to find the Inn quiet. She ordered a skinny mocha and chatted while Heather made it in front of her.

'Don't suppose you've seen Dieter Frum?'

'Nah. He's away first thing, early supper, bed by nine,' replied Heather, referring to the guest who had certainly made the ladies in the restaurant give a second look over their morning paper. Heather shut the till and handed Marcie a pile of coins in change.

'Had a bus tour in. Sorry. No debit cards from anyone. Need to get rid of this.'

Marcie stared at the pile of one-pound coins and then back to Heather. Her friend was motioning to the large blinking monstrosity that had replaced the ancient one-armed bandit in the corner next to the equally aged jukebox. Heather looked busy, taking the time when the hotel was quiet to do all the little jobs that could easily pile up. Marcie wanted to talk over the Ruaridh situation with one of her best friends, but what could she say? *I've been given the exit letter by the man who was once the centre of my universe.* Instead, she strolled over to the fruit machine, still peering at the change in her hand, and decided a one-pound game of chance was worth the loss. She looked at the machine in front of her noisily inviting her to play.

'I have absolutely no idea how to work this,' she shouted to her friend still behind the bar when confronted with the giant machine in front of her, displaying four reels of designs like a video machine. Marcie dropped in the pound coin and rested a hand on each side of the giant box. 'Ha! Ha! Here we go!' she said as she suddenly felt someone invade her personal space to stand directly behind her.

'Why not let me show you how it's done?' said the soft voice she felt was just a little bit too close to her ear. She stood up straight as he closed in on her. His arms outstretched around her until his hands were just glancing hers on either side of the machine. 'Let's press this,' he said and pushed a button on the side until all the images started to spin. She could feel his breath on her neck, so close she could smell he was fresh from the shower.

'Hmmm,' he said, 'cherry, lucky seven, apple, lemon. Let's try again. Let's hold the cherry.' He pressed the hold button as she began to release her hands from the machine, but he rested his on hers, taking them back to the button on the side of the huge box.

'Now, this is your money. You've got to make the choice. Hold or spin?'

'Hold,' she said quietly as he did what she said and took her hand to press the button again. Two cherries remained on the screen as another lucky seven and an apple appeared. 'Spin?' she suggested. He leaned in close to her ear and she could feel his skin on hers.

'Now, I would have held there, but lady's choice. Spin all?' he asked and pressed the button.

The machine suddenly lit up, flashing fast and playing loud music, and the man leaned over her to press the button marked 'cash out'. Immediately, money started to flood out of the machine, spilling one-pound coins into Marcie's hands and into the small basin Heather had rushed over with to place in front of the money slot.

'Mossie McMosse, still got the magic touch,' said the familiar voice behind her, and she spun round with a mouth open in shock.

'Ross Balfour, as I live and breathe.' Marcie smiled up at him as he grabbed her in a tight hug, lifting her up and off her feet. 'What the actual?' she asked as she reached up and wiped a lipstick mark from his cheek while behind them Heather was now catching the money spilling out of the machine in a tea towel.

'I know!' mouthed Heather as she emptied her full cloth of money into the basin on the floor. 'Now, you know what to do. You buy everyone in the bar a drink because you know the old saying? *Money is like manure – it's not useful, unless it's spread around.*'

'You still pushing that old chestnut, H?' laughed the elder Balfour sibling as he took two coins from the basin and handed them back to Marcie.

'There you are. You've not lost a penny, Mossie, and even made a profit.' He smiled and walked over to the bar. 'I take it you want to splash the cash. Spread it around, as the lady says?' The three glanced around at the empty bar with not a single patron gracing its seats. 'Nothing for it, then, but this,' said Ross as he slotted the coins into the tall charity container on the counter which had a *Strathkin Mountain Rescue* sticker attached to the front. When it was impossible to fit another coin in, he simply crossed to the other side of the bar and did the same with the charity box for *Royal National Lifeboat Institution.*

Within moments, they sat nursing their drinks in the table at the window in the restaurant, sitting opposite each other on the banquette.

'Well, you being here makes me think the other side of the world isn't so far away,' joked Marcie to the handsome man across from her whose previous address had been in New Zealand. She leaned across the table and patted his hand, then took it in her own and squeezed it hard before letting it rest back on the table. They gazed at each other momentarily, these old school friends who had been out of touch for fifteen years. She leaned her elbow on the table, cupped her chin in her hand and smiled at him until he turned away. There was no mistaking he was related to Ruaridh Balfour with his tall, broad frame and well-trimmed stubble. He was slightly greyer at the temple than his younger brother and had the light tan of the outdoors worker from his job as a land agent. He had settled in well on the other side of the world, the mystery of his disappearance overnight from the family croft now lost in the mists of time. Known locally as the Strathkin Twins when they were younger, he and Ruaridh were both born in the same year, Ross in early January, several weeks late, and Ruaridh in December of the same year, several weeks early. With another two younger brothers in the family, *actual* twins, Gregor and Blair, both in Aberdeen, the Balfour family had enjoyed a long association with the village, all having married locally and gone on to provide Strathkin with a rising birth rate. Gregor and Blair would in time return with their young families as was the subject of much discussion at Dina's funeral, a life event not attended by Ross due to distance and work commitments and the sudden circumstances of her passing.

'It was impossible for me to drop everything at a moment's notice,' he explained when he felt Marcie was about to ask about his no show at the funeral. 'I had agreed to come over, but I thought it would be better to let things calm down and come back when I was likely more needed by the wee man.'

Marcie nodded in agreement.

'Are you staying at the croft? A bit tight unless you're in the guest room.'

'Nah, I'm staying in the salubrious surroundings of Strathkin's finest establishment.' He held his hands up and gestured around the empty room. 'Here!'

'Oh!'

'Heather gave me a good rate – I think it's because she stood me up at that last ceilidh the year before I left. Guilty conscience, if you ask me.'

'When *was* that?'

'Och, too long ago to be bothered about it.' Their reminiscing was interrupted by Heather bringing over a small sandwich tray of food and side plates.

'Scottish tapas,' she said, as she dropped napkins and sachets of mayonnaise on the table. 'Also known as "too much made at lunchtime".'

'Ah, haggis bon bons, the food of the Gods!' said Ross enthusiastically, eyeing the food in the same way as his younger brother. He started to pick up the small morsels greedily.

'Mossie, if you're not fast, you're last!' he joked, again using her school nickname.

'I'm fine. Tuck in.' She smiled and watched as he devoured his food with the eagerness of Ruaridh's children.

'I was hoping to rent somewhere but it's all booked up for the summer with the solstice coming up and all. Trying to get accommodation is a f... oh sorry, it's a nightmare with this new North Coast 500 palaver.'

She nodded as he held his palms up in apology.

'I know,' she agreed.

'Heather said you'd moved into Sweet Briar – don't suppose you want a lodger? I'll pay good money?'

'Well, I was. But I've moved out. Couldn't really bear being next to the big house.' She watched as he glanced over her shoulder to what had been her family home for so many years.

'Tragic,' he said with a shake of the head and a lick of each finger. He wiped his hands with a napkin. 'Would've been a great house to live in,' he mused.

'It was.' She followed his gaze across the water, shifting in her seat to look at her former home. When she turned around to speak, he had cast his gaze on her. They locked eyes for the briefest of seconds before he spoke again.

'So, Sweet Briar not up for a short-term rent then?'

'No.'

'Okay. I get your drift,' he conceded.

'I'm up at Tigh-na-Lochan.'

'Nice. Lovely views. Always liked it up there. Kinda hidden away from prying eyes.'

'And what were you up to that you have to say that?'

'Och, you must remember. We, well, me and the wee man, used to go up there to show off, try to impress the ladies who came up with their parents in the caravans. Worst offender? Jamie MacKay! He's the local *bobby* here now, I hear. I could fill his bosses in on a few stories that would make their hair curl! You remember we worked at his pa's garage? We used to tamper with all the cars...' Ross shut down, not wanting to remember the tragedy.

'Uh-huh?' she encouraged, leaning forward.

'Actually... nothing. You want a real drink?' he asked, pointing to the bar.

'No, not for me. Just a bit of a drive up the road,' she qualified by holding her hand across the top of her cup. 'Listen, if you're okay with slumming it, there are a couple of cottages on the estate that are currently empty. Don't know how long you're planning on staying?'

'Not sure. Got some loose ends I need to tie up. Are they habitable?'

'Oh, they're liveable. Been cleared out after the tenants, er, "left",' she said with air quotes.

'I'd be up for that, I'm handy with a toolbox. Beds? Kitchen?'

'Definitely all got a kitchen. Ruaridh made some of the kitchens, well, helped install them up at Stratheyre and

Lubnaig. Broomfield is probably more habitable, but we haven't used that since...'

'Oh, aye. I remember them. And the wee man told me about Broomfield. Listen, I'm happy to slum it. Lovely as this place is, it's a bit stifling – a bit too full of the locals, if you know what I mean. Strathkin thrives on gossip and the like but it's not really my scene. I'm well away from all the nosy parker stuff of small-town living.'

Marcie agreed, immediately relating to his situation.

'I have the keys at home...' she began.

'Home? So, you've definitely moved back to Strathkin, albeit not to...' He indicated to Swanfield through the window.

'Don't own it anymore, plus, I do hybrid working so it suits me fine.'

'Ah. Heather filled me in a bit on your personal situation.'

'I'm sure she did. Listen, if you want to head up for a gander... I mean, it'll be light for hours yet.'

He glanced at his watch. 'Aye, why not? Nothing else on the agenda for now.'

He placed a ten-pound note on the table under the side plate, and Marcie followed him out to where their two cars were parked side by side.

'You want to follow me? In case you decide to try it out for size tonight?' she asked innocently. He smiled at her. Then, in typical Balfour fashion, he raised his brows and gave her a suggestive wink. She shook her head, a smile dancing across her lips, and they pulled out of the car park in convoy. *So, a call from your brother has brought you halfway across the world. Is that all that has brought you back? Tying up loose ends could mean any number of things*, mused Marcie as she pulled the car on to the road that would take them to the edge of the Swanfield Estate and to Tigh-na-Lochan.

. . .

'Honest to gawd,' sighed Heather McLeod from her seat in the hotel's office, her desk covered in paperwork, her eyes on the CCTV. 'What kind of pheromones do these Balfour's have? And what does *she* have, for that matter?' she added aloud and picked up her phone. She glanced up at the photograph pinned on the noticeboard. She was with her three friends at their seat on the banquette, their usual table. Three friends without a care in the world, wide smiles and hands all clasped with red friendship bracelets on each one's wrist.

'Right, Dina, I'm going in,' she said, as she searched for Jamie MacKay's mobile number.

Ross Balfour stood outside the small white cottage, Tigh-na-Lochan, and gazed out to the hills as they rose up all around the lush glen and small stretch of water, today glistening a dark green.

'Stunning,' he said, 'like New Zealand in miniature.'

'You're comparing *this* to New Zealand?' Marcie shouted to him.

'Well, there's a reason it's called the New World,' was his response.

Marcie was standing on the threshold, arms folded as she observed him from behind. He was standing like Ruaridh, legs slightly apart in a firm stance and hands in his pockets. He was wearing a pair of expensive designer sunglasses, and she smiled to herself as she recalled Ruaridh in the same place, just a few days ago. He was in the same pose but in light blue plastic too-small sunglasses, presumably belonging to one of his sons. The brothers were so alike yet so different. Marcie wondered how long he was going to stay, what his plans were and decided not to spoil his moment of taking in the scenery glowing before him. Silently she watched him scan the hills. A bird squawked in the distance, and she observed as his eyes found and trailed it as it swooped low and slow along the lochan in front of them, searching for prey. When it sailed up and out of sight, its colour blending in like camouflage in the glen, he turned to her and smiled broadly. 'What does a guy have to do to get a girl to buy him a drink around here?'

She chuckled as he followed her and, like her previous guest only a few days before, he gasped loudly at the modernity of the interior of this small croft in such a rugged landscape. 'Well, I wasn't expecting this.' He took in the modern décor. 'It's not like any Highland cottage I remember when I was growing up. Splashed the cash here, Mossie, eh?'

'I wanted it to be comfortable,' she said as if in apology for how much the refurbishment had cost. The living room and kitchen, knocked into one large room, took him by surprise at the size. Large seascapes on the wall seemed to fit the room surprisingly well. He walked over to the long charcoal drawing of a wedding dress that hung in an alcove and then glanced back at her in silence. She was about to say, 'I should take it down.'

'Pictures are our memory prompts. Like coming across an unexpected photograph from school. A photograph that falls out from a letter. Takes you back. Makes you think. And your mind plays all its wee tricks, so you only remember the good times.' He continued to gaze at the drawing. She didn't recall Ross Balfour as being a particularly reflective character or as attractive as he now was. If he had memories or remembrances from school or from his travels around the world, she was sure he would tell her in his own good time. She had no idea how long he would be staying but it would be good to have another friendly face in their tight circle. Especially one who looked as good as he now did.

He turned quickly. 'Tour?' he suggested, and she led him into the small vestibule which had a cloakroom with a toilet and sink and then into her bedroom. Like the open living room next door, this was a room that had been knocked through to create a much larger space, two bedrooms now one large expanse.

'Wow!' he exclaimed at the sight of the super-king-sized four post bed with expensive bedding and a feature wall of William Morris wallpaper. Facing the bed at the far side of the room near the wall, a beautiful modern bathtub sat on its own on a small plinth. A basket of lotions and potions sat next to it on a small upcycled table. 'I'm a shower man myself,' was all he managed to say as he followed her to a door that led to an en-suite which had a toilet, sink and a step-in shower in stylish black. The blind on the window was the same as the wallpaper on the bedroom wall and was a splash of colour in the fashionable and on-trend black and white décor. 'Aye, that'll do,' he said as he peeked around the door beside her. 'I'm now looking forward to seeing what you've done to my new gaff!'

'I'm afraid they're a bit basic over the hill there,' she apologised, 'but in the future, who knows?'

'You've got an eye, that's for sure.'

'I'm afraid I'm not responsible. What you see here is the result of a Pinterest board I sent to Dina.'

'Aye, I see.'

'She had such a good eye for décor, understated elegance, "modern Scottish",' Marcie explained with air quotes.

'It is for sure,' he agreed as he glanced around. 'She was one in a million.'

'She helped Heather with the Inn and with Sweet Briar. It was lovely.'

'Was?' he asked as he followed her back into the kitchen area, leaning on the edge of the countertop. 'Didn't you say you stayed there?'

'Well, I still think it belongs to Callum. I moved in for a brief time – it's a fabulous place to live but I don't want to be there long term. I know he'll be back at some point.'

'Yeah, I heard all about it. It had some time of it, did wee

Strathkin, not to mention the people,' he began as Marcie opened the fridge and pointed to a Corona Cerveza.

'Don't mind if I do,' he said and held out his hand. 'Can I ask you something, Mossie?'

'Sure,' she said, deftly opening the bottle and handing it to him.

'How's the guy doing?'

'Callum?'

'No,' replied Ross and took a large gulp of beer, his eyes not leaving Marcie. She realised he meant his younger sibling.

'He has good days and bad days. It was so quick. I don't think any of us will ever get over it. I'm not sure how he would cope if it weren't for the boys and Mari.'

'I saw him last night,' confessed Ross.

'And what did you think?'

'Seriously? He's like half a man. He's not the wee brother I remember but there's been a wide sea between us for a long time.' It was an expression she'd heard Ruaridh use before when his brother's name had come up. A wide sea. A continent. An unimaginable distance. As well as an out-of-character disappearance.

'Seas can be crossed. Continents conquered,' she said as she found herself pouring the last of a bottle of rosé into a glass and pushing it under the dropper on the freezer, letting cubes of ice fall into it to create one of her favourite coolers – *Piscine*. He raised the bottle he was drinking in an open gesture. '*Slainte*,' he said and drank down the rest of the liquid.

'So, can you see you and him...' he began.

'Oh, no, no, no. That ship has sailed. It's definitely left the harbour.' Marcie smiled. Ruaridh had made his feelings clear to her, that was for certain. It was as if in the sudden freedom that had been forced upon them, they had been pushed in opposite directions and the words he had shared just days before had firmly drawn the line in the sand that she never wanted to see, never thought she would *ever* see.

'Sure?' Ross was asking, his eyes piercing her.

'Oh, yes. Absolutely.' Suddenly, she thumped her glass down on the counter without taking a sip. 'Come on. Enough of this chat. Let's get you a place to stay. Get a shizzle on, Balfour,' she said, as she grabbed his beer bottle, dropping it into the sink, and encouraged him out the door. He gave a long glance back into the house as she shot past him.

ELEVEN

Heather was sitting at table number one in her restaurant dining room at The Strathkin Inn. She had discussed a new menu with chef Adam and was bemoaning the continuing situation in her love life. Or lack of it. In her opinion, the online sites she had tried had continually thrown up misfits and the desperate. Now she found herself gazing out of the window across a shimmering loch, chin in hand, elbow on table, and mind elsewhere. Her strategically placed mirrors saw someone approach the bar next door and she slid out of the banquette and made her way to the man with his back to her, whom she failed to recognise at first.

'Jamie! Happy new haircut! Undercover?' she exclaimed and slapped Constable Jamie MacKay across the back, laughing at seeing him out of uniform for the first time in a long time.

'Off duty,' he replied and slipped his wallet out of his back pocket to retrieve his debit card as Heather pulled his favourite pint of stout and let it settle on the counter.

'My treat,' she said as the white foam lifted slowly to the top of the glass. 'Been a good month.' She wiped her hands on the cloth at the sink and then made her way back to the seat she had occupied for the past hour. Jamie took the pint and glanced around the empty bar.

'You did invite me to drop in next time I was off duty so can I cash that invite in now? Mind if I join you?' He wandered over to her, and she pointed to the empty space next to her.

'Sure! You're looking all trim and handsome!' she joked. 'Where were you?'

'Down south at a conference. Then the police college for a bit of training. Away from this,' he said as the pint of stout settled in front of him.

'Suits you,' she said and cradled her face in her hands, sighed and blew out her lips.

'Every time I see this table I think you must miss Dina,' he said after a moment of silence. All at school together and growing up in the village, the residents of Strathkin were a close-knit group. Jamie, the boy racer who turned his life around to driving fast cars with a yellow stripe and lights on them rather than his father's fleet in the garage at Strathdon. And Heather, who had gone to catering college only to return to the village to take over the reins of the local family-run Inn. They had mostly left to pursue their dreams, but the invisible thread of family and friendship had pulled them all in the same direction and caused all but one to return.

'I can't believe she's gone, Jamie,' Heather suddenly blurted out and felt a lump rise in her throat. It didn't go unnoticed to the police officer, and he reached out and rubbed her shoulder tenderly. 'It was all so unexpected and quick and... just unbelievable.' She shook her head then tilted it to one side, and her hair touched his hand that still rested on her shoulder. She glanced at him. He returned a knowing smile back. She felt his gaze rest on her for a moment longer than normal.

'I don't know how Ruaridh's coping,' he said and took a sip of his drink.

'I don't think he is,' she admitted. 'He puts on a brave face, but those poor boys, and wee Mari.' She felt her tears bubble up and then out they came unexpectedly like a raging torrent. Suddenly, she was swept up in a strong embrace by Jamie and she could feel his heartbeat against her, fast and loud in her ear. He sniffed loudly as if he, too, was fighting back tears. She clung to him for what felt like an age, and he didn't seem to want to let her go. When she finally released herself, he had pulled a packet of paper tissues from his pocket and handed them to her.

'No wonder you're in the police, you're always so prepared,' she joked and dabbed her eyes before blowing her nose loudly into the paper.

'Here, steady on! They're not the cheap ones!' he said, and she raised a smile, laughing at his throwaway line to her.

A bustle next door saw three people enter the bar, and she folded over the papers she had been working on with Adam some time before and leaned over to Jamie.

'Do I look presentable?' she asked, wiping under her eyes and hoping her waterproof mascara did what it said.

'Just brilliant. As ever,' he said to her, and she punched him playfully on the shoulder as she gathered up her detritus.

Making her way to the bar, she threw a glance over her shoulder and caught his eye. He winked and she gave a little giggle. He had continually come up on her dating site and she had constantly swiped his beaming smile off the screen. *Could it be that it was time to finally let nature take its course, after all, as Dina had suggested to her?*

TWELVE

At the curve of Strathkin Loch, just as the single-track road that ran alongside it split for Strath Aullt and Strathdon, the shingle and sand beach turned into a swathe of white sand before disappearing into a rocky outcrop and then into sheet cliffs. Strathkin had crept up on Hannah quite unexpectedly. This place, this distant village far away from the bustling town she had known all her life, had embraced her in a way she never thought possible. The hamlet and its people had captivated her from the moment she stepped off the bus from Inverness; a bus that had taken her through scenery she had only seen on television and in discarded magazines.

The journey that some found tedious had been a rapture to her, and she found herself gasping as valleys and glens gave way to a rocky moonscape then to shattering peaks reaching up into the clouds. And, here today, she was on a beach. An actual beach with water lapping at her feet and the feeling of soft white sand under her soles. She had sat on the jetty and then noticed this small patch of beach further along the shore. She had helped at the breakfast service in the hotel, Heather declaring her a *revelation*, whatever that meant. In return, she had made her a cheese and pickle sandwich with actual homemade brown bread, wrapped it in foil, and told her to go out and get some sun on her face. On the way out, she was going to reach around to the bar and take a bottle of water secretly, but instead asked the owner if it were okay if she could *borrow* one. Here, it seemed the right thing to do. She did not want to jeopardise her new life by being caught thieving.

Heather told her there was a sheet pinned up at the bar and just to jot her name down and put whatever she took against it. No need to pay, she had said, it was purely to keep her stocks right. She found herself ready to have her picnic, as she decided to call it, on the beach, but was disappointed to find a young boy was sitting in the sand with a magazine. She had wanted this to be her secret place and was annoyed to find someone already there. She watched him for a moment and then decided she would sit anyway but would not take off her jacket for obvious reasons. He closed his magazine and watched her; someone was invading *his* private beach. She sat down on the sand and glanced back and took her sandwich out of her pocket. She broke a tiny bit of bread off the corner, nibbling at it and casually trying to make it appear that she came here every day. She turned again and noticed he was gone, but then was quite taken aback to find he was in front of her, in the water up to his ankles, and silently staring at the cold still loch and the little cottages and crofts on the other side. Moments later, she saw him walk towards her, his bare feet kicking up the sand, until he was next to her. Her hands closed tight around her sandwich in protection as if he was going to steal it from her, but instead, he put his hand out and offered her the magazine he had been reading and had stuffed in his back pocket.

'I've finished this if you want it,' he said in a soft Highland lilt, and she shook her head. 'It's a magazine about planes, but it's a bit old.'

Hannah shook her head again, as if she had suddenly been struck dumb, her hand clutching her lunch tightly.

'I live over there,' he said and pointed to one of the little white cottages sitting at the water's edge on the other side of the loch. 'Are you the *new* girl?'

She nodded.

'My dad said there was someone new at the hotel. Do you have an English accent?'

She stayed silent.

'What's your name?'

'Hannah,' she said quickly as if it would disappear in the wind, and he wouldn't catch it.

'I'm Dax.' He held out his hand to take hers to shake it, and she was unsure of what to do, particularly now juice from her pickle had seeped into her hand. She held it up to face him by way of explanation and he made a face.

'Oh, yuck! I hate lumpy pickle. It's got *bits* in it!' he said, and then they both laughed.

'I like it. It's quite sweet,' she said and realised this boy in front of her was also quite sweet with a tumble of blond hair, piercing blue eyes and warm olive skin. She squinted in the sun, and he threw himself down on the sand beside her.

'My brother calls this Douglas Beach,' said Dax as he stretched out and crossed his long legs out of blue shorts, feet bare and still sandy.

'What's your brother called?' she asked, sneaking a tiny bit of sandwich into her mouth.

'Douglas,' he answered, before laughing again with her.

'Ah! Sorry! I didn't take it in.' She laughed at her own stupidity.

'Further up there is Dax Cove,' he stated with a nod up the loch.

'Ah, I see a pattern! Named after you, obviously!'

'Obviously!' He pointed to a small inlet with reeds and a

couple of swans gliding in the shadows. 'David's Den,' he stated. 'Donald doesn't have his own place yet. He likes books. He's an *inside* kind of guy.'

'How many brothers do you have?' she asked, astonished at these revelations.

'Three: Donald, David and Douglas.'

'Your mum and dad were fond of the Ds, eh?' she joked.

'My sister is called Mari,' he said, as if to break the spell, 'and my mum passed away.'

'Ah.' She sighed and took a large bite of the sandwich before hiding it back in the security of its foil and putting it in her pocket. She took the bottle of water out of her other pocket. She offered him a sip, but he shook his head.

'There's a stream up at the back there, better water than you'd get in any bottle,' he stated, and she swallowed her sandwich hard.

'What's it called? Willie's Well or Robbie's River?' she joked, and both burst out laughing. She felt her shoulders relax and began to take off her black leather jacket before swiftly pulling it back on again; her short-sleeved black top would make everything too obvious.

'Are you not hot?' he asked as he watched her struggle back into her jacket.

'It's not *that* warm,' she concluded, 'not as warm as Kent at this time of the year anyhow.'

'The Garden of England,' he said, with the keen knowledge of a fifteen-year-old. 'We read about it in school. All about the wine they make down there because the terroir is now the same as it was in France about two hundred years ago.'

'How do you know these things?' she asked, astonished at his knowledge while licking the sweet brown liquid off the end of each finger.

'I like school, I listen. Then I can wind up my little brothers.

Douglas and the twins still play with dinosaurs, and at their age, too,' he scoffed.

'Are these more brothers or the same brothers?' she joked, and he gave a little laugh at her delightful English accent.

'Donald and David. The middle two,' he explained and lay down, folding his arms behind him, turning his face towards the sun. She observed him, hopefully unnoticed, taking in his handsome, youthful face, a hint of soft fuzz appearing, and she suddenly found herself lying down next to him. She closed her eyes as the sun filtered through a cloud and gently warmed her face, her head nestling in the soft sand. She felt warm and content, her belly full of food, and reached her arms up behind her head, mimicking his movements, the back of her head resting on her open palms.

Dax turned slightly to gaze at her and her luscious hair. Thick dark waves curled over her shoulder. Her skin was a palette like he had never seen. He did not know what mixed race was, but her tawny complexion was enticing and rich like a fawn on the hills, a timid deer with eyes a vivid olive green. He was immediately entranced. Where her jacket had ridden up, he saw little marks on her skin like perfect little circles. He wanted to reach out to touch them but decided against it. He could tell she was slightly older than him, but Dax recalled the words of his father, *if you don't ask, you don't get*. And he thought to himself, *Hannah from Kent, I'm going to ask you to be my girlfriend.*

THIRTEEN

It was an early morning text message the following day which brought the three friends together. Just before lunch they sat at their usual window table at the Inn. These childhood friends were all still coming to terms with the fact the space for Dina Balfour had been taken up by the fragrant Maureen Berman, who both fitted into the group and frustrated the girls in equal measure. And it was Maureen this morning who was holding court, dressed head to toe in a zebra print playsuit which defied her years but suited her trim figure.

'So, I got this letter,' she began, flat hands resting on the long envelope sitting in front of her on the table. 'It's from Ange.'

'Ange?' asked Heather, mouth around a straw, and inhaling the last of her smoothie.

'Angelina,' qualified Maureen, 'Angelina San.'

'Oh, yes?' asked Marcie, suddenly interested in what she had to say.

'The police have caught up with the little *dwarf*.'

'You can't say things like that, Maureen,' corrected Marcie with a reprimanding tone.

'All right. All right. The little *squirt* – or is that *demeaning* to people who have problems with their waterworks?' asked Maureen indignantly.

Bella put her hand over her eyes for a moment then caught Marcie's gaze as if to say, *Yes, I live with this, twenty-four seven!*

'Anyhoo,' continued the older woman, 'now we've ruined the English language for anyone over seventy...'

'*Maureen...*' said Marcie, in a tone that sounded like a warning.

'I mean,' started Maureen, drifting off into another conversation, 'just the other day I was in your village store with that odd little man, the whassisname owner, I mean, he keeps giving me the eye, well, the one wot works anyway, and I just said to him—'

'Maureen!' came a call in unison.

'Oh, right, where was I...?'

'You received a letter from Angelina about her husband.'

'Yes, that little...' Maureen glanced around to test the water, 'Dutchman.'

They all sat back apart from Maureen, who leaned forward as if she were about to impart some delicate or secret information. She glanced around furtively.

'So, it turns out, the authorities have caught up with 'im.'

'Who?' asked Heather, distracted by her phone, her smoothie, and somehow late to the party.

'The slimy little... *Dutchman*,' qualified Maureen, gazing at the accusatory faces around the table.

'Oh, yes? How so?' asked Bella.

'Something that happened in Holland to do with money or washing money, whatsissname.'

'Money laundering?' asked Marcie. 'Wow!'

'That's the fella. What time is it? Is the sun past the yard arm yet?' Maureen went on with an exaggerated glance to her watch.

'And?' asked Bella encouragingly.

'And what?' asked Maureen, as if she, too, had just joined the conversation.

'And what has happened?' asked Bella, gesticulating with her hand to spur on the storyteller to continue the yarn.

'Yes. Well – he's banged up.'

'*Banged up?*' asked Heather.

'*Inside?*' asked Marcie.

'The slammer,' agreed Maureen.

'The big house?' Marcie continued.

Bella stood up and left the table just as Heather understood the phrase.

'Ah,' she said in realisation, 'the pokey! Why didn't you say?'

'Oh, I forgot, herself was in the old crowbar hotel,' said Maureen, with an apologetic face as she watched Bella head towards the toilets. Her eye was then drawn to the young girl who had headed down the main stairs and into the bar area leading to the kitchen.

'And what's going on with *that one?*' Maureen asked the owner sitting opposite her.

'Hannah? Oh, she's been a godsend,' replied Heather, 'quiet at first but coming out of her shell a little. The regulars love her. She has the most beautiful face when she smiles – it lights up. It's as if she's only just learned to smile. I'll miss her when she's gone.'

'Why? Where's she off to?' quizzed Maureen, looking at Hannah suspiciously.

'Well, it's all seasonal work up here, isn't it? I'm sure she'll be back down south once the summer crowds go home.'

'Hmmm, not so sure about that,' said Maureen quietly and watched as Hannah drifted up the stairs from the kitchen with a mug of tea.

'Bleeding 'eck, it's like King's Cross Station in 'ere,' Maureen continued as Ruaridh and Ross Balfour sauntered into the room, acknowledged the three women left at the table and headed to the bar area next door.

Heather got up from her seat, shrugged her shoulders, and headed to serve her only two customers, leaving Marcie and Maureen alone. Silence descended.

'Well, since you're the only one left,' she began, 'and I suppose it involved you the most.'

'Uh-huh?'

'Well, you see, Ange, she's a clever one,' began Maureen and waited for a moment before asking, ''ere, do you know, is the bar here open to non-residents? I mean, what time is it?'

Marcie hauled herself off the banquette, caught herself in the long mirror on the way out of the lounge, tucked her hair behind her ear and headed to the bar.

'Mars,' Ruaridh acknowledged as she approached them.

'Hey, Mossie! I was going to ring you, but I didn't get your number yesterday,' began Ross.

'Yesterday?' queried Ruaridh, handing over a banknote to the woman behind the bar.

'Yes, we met yesterday. Mossie here has donated one of the cottages to her old pal.'

'Cottages?'

'Lubnaig,' qualified Marcie and called to Heather, 'Any chance of a G&T for the zebra?'

'I thought you were staying here?' asked Ruaridh of his brother.

Ross picked up the two pints of dark stout and wandered over to the identical seat in the bar which mirrored the one in the dining and lounge area. He squeezed himself into the window seat and welcomed Marcie to join him, and she squeezed in from the other side. Ruaridh wandered up, counting what little change he had been given and squeezed in next to Marcie. Both men folded their arms with a sigh as the liquid in front of them settled, separating black from the white until it was still. Marcie sat back and looked at each of them in turn.

'Well, it's like the back of the school bus all over again,' she said, and they both replied in unison with an 'aye.'

'I just came over to see how you got on last night. Was it warm enough? Enough furniture?'

'Well, I didn't need a telly as I had the rodent family providing the entertainment,' responded Ross after a long sip of stout.

'Oh, I have them, too, really should get a cat. I have the humane mouse traps I empty every morning, but they think it's a game and come straight back in.' Marcie, short nails clicking on the table, imitated the sound of the mice who frequently invaded her house.

'Not staying here then?' asked Ruaridh, leaning around Marcie to question his brother. She leaned back as Ross responded in the same manner.

'Like being in a goldfish bowl here, bro. Just came back to collect my stuff. I'll take the bags up this afternoon and I'm heading to Inverness tomorrow.'

'Oh, aye. What's on there then?'

'Just catching up with people.'

'Need company?'

'No, you're okay,' replied Ross furtively.

'Hello!' interrupted Marcie from her space in the Balfour sandwich.

'Yeah, we know you're still here.'

Ruaridh gave her a friendly nudge with his elbow. She giggled a little and turned to speak to Ross, who was already looking at her, and it was she who turned away. She suddenly felt overwhelmingly hot, waving her hand across her face. 'I really need to get out of here,' she said and began to stand up before both brothers pulled her back down by the forearms,

Ross leaning over behind her to push open the casement window to let in fresh air.

Next door Maureen sat staring into space when Bella reappeared.

'Where is everyone?' Bella asked her.

'They've all buggered off. One behind the bar, one trapped in every woman's dream scenario,' Maureen said with a side glance to the scene next door, and Bella leaned back to witness her friend with her head on the table buried in crossed arms as the two brothers continued their conversation over her.

'And?'

'And what?' Maureen had a blank expression on her face.

'WHAT. WAS. IN. THE. LETTER?'

'Oh, something and nothing,' said Maureen and glanced at her watch again. 'It's eleven fifty-nine somewhere,' she added, referring to Bella's no drinking before noon rule and, with a heavy sigh, Bella hauled herself up just as Heather appeared with a large balloon glass filled with gin and tonic.

'I take it all back, she's not that bad,' muttered Maureen to herself as Bella and Heather simply shook their heads.

'So, the letter?' Bella asked again.

'I'll wait until herself comes back.'

'Och, she'll be ages,' sighed Heather and sat down in her still-warm seat.

'Hmmm,' said Maureen, after a long cool drink of the clear liquid, 'I have a feeling something is afoot.'

Heather and Bella exchanged a look that clearly said, *not again*.

FOURTEEN

Ross, like Marcie before him, was astonished at the changes in Inverness and the growth in the area since it had gained city status several years before. The whole town, as he still called it, had a cosmopolitan feel with its outdoor cafés and high-end restaurants dotted around the city centre. He ate at Rocpool, recommended by his brother as the last place he and Dina had had a dine and sleep without children, and was impressed with both the menu and surroundings. High quality local shellfish served with the freshest of vegetables was a hit on his palate and after a sample of a predinner wine flight, he had booked a room in the Rocpool Reserve Hotel, preferring not to drive after having even one alcoholic drink. That, combined with the fact a night in a supremely comfortable bed was more appealing than the long drive back to Strathkin to share the single bed and waterproof mattress with a family of rodents, was an easy decision to make. By the time he had finished a late breakfast and made his way fully refreshed to Farm and Household Supplies with his list, he had a spring in his step and a whistle on his tongue. His post-breakfast meeting at the family solicitors had gone well, better than expected, and he walked with purpose from aisle to aisle. Wandering around between the gardening equipment and before he went to the crockery and pots, he was thinking hard. He didn't have a plan, as such, he preferred to call it a *grievance*: something that he had been ruminating for such a long time; something that had started as a curiosity and ended up as a focus on those long, lonely nights away from his family on remote sheep farms and in distant glens on the other side of the world. And now it was going to be fixed. This was a secret he had held on to too long and if he was proven right, there was a high likelihood he would be back for good, even if it upended the status quo in the hamlet he had called home for nineteen years. His job as a land agent allowed him to travel all over Australia and New Zealand, and he had managed to build up a hefty sum in his bank account at the same time. He had started as a farm hand on a work visa in the Northern Territories at just nineteen years of age. He studied hard in the evenings and at weekends, shunning the heavy drinking culture of his friends and fellow students. As a result, Ross Balfour had earned a reputation for being an industrious and diligent worker, a quick thinker, and an astute negotiator in navigating the complex processes of buying and selling land. It was his tutors in Contracts and Legal who had got his mind turning and, suddenly, a buyer had whisked him off to New Zealand and he fell in love with the scenery and its people in the land of the long white cloud. The country's recent tourist campaign motto was right – *If you seek, it's here to find*.

He had sought out a life journey and, en-route, found a fellow traveller in bohemian Suzy, and for a while they travelled together. They flew to Australia, back to the Northern Territories and held a 'commitment ceremony' at Uluru, exchanging love tokens, handwritten poetry and ideals. A set of twins later, they were living in separate cities, ideas and plans for their futures pushing them in different directions. He missed his daughters, but the separation had been amicable, and he paid his fair share of what he called 'commitment cash' to ensure their lives would not be impacted by their parents' failure at love.

He thought of them today as he drove back to his own childhood home. When he saw the first sign for Strathkin he pulled into the layby and slipped out the car to gaze at the mountains in the distance and the valley floor that lay before him. He knew he would stop again at the high ridge and do the same thing. If he were to come back here and settle, this time it would be on his terms and with his future in mind. With obstacles in his path to be overcome, he'd more than likely have to deal with carnage on the way but overcome them he would. If he was, in fact, the rightful heir to Swanfield, he was going to prove it.

Despite the warm spring weather, the high sun and the fresh feel in the air, Marcie's table was covered with jars of varying sizes fresh from a sterilisation in the oven, and her house smelled like Christmas. She wanted to continue the kitchen table catch-ups of her grandmother, and when a gift of deep dark Barbadian sugar arrived from the Caribbean, sent by Callum, it was the nudge she needed to have a baking day. It was a world away from work, a world away from her imminent divorce and a step into the past for even just a couple of hours.

Aromas in her kitchen floated out the front door and made the nose twitch of the person coming up the path.

She wiped her apron and pulled open the door to be faced with a large box with holes in it.

'I don't remember ordering that much cardboard,' she joked as the box began to make its way into the house and she watched as it passed her. 'Not on the table!' she ordered as the person carrying it stumbled in, placing it on the coffee table. 'What on earth...?' Marcie began to a hot and bothered Ross Balfour.

'I've been to Inverness,' he explained.

'What did you bring back, polluted air? Bad move, it's escaping through the holes.' She leaned down to peer in just as he bent to open the box and lifted out a large and half-asleep tiger-striped cat.

'They didn't have a big enough carrier at the Cat and Dog Home, so I had to get this from Farm and Household,' he explained as he lay the sleeping animal over his shoulder.

'So, please tell me, this is a pit stop on your way to Lubnaig?' She stepped back, hands resting on hips.

'Well, you said you had mice?'

'And?'

'He's a mouser.'

'And?'

'It's a gift,' he explained, his face appearing hurt.

'Don't do animals, sorry!' She walked purposefully towards the still-open door and leaned against it, a movement of her hand indicating she was ushering him out.

'But you had cats growing up? You said you needed a cat,' he stated.

'Yes, we had them to keep down the vermin.'

'Exactly! And this is what Atlas is here to do, aren't you, buddy? Atlas, meet Mossie.' He patted the large sleeping beast over his shoulder, snoring loudly.

'Is it alive?' she asked, looking at the cat as he lifted his head slightly to gaze at her, gave out a squeak rather than a miaow, and closed his eyes.

'Well, the big fella is probably a tad tired. We had to give him a wee bit of a tranquiliser.'

'A tranquiliser? I hope you fired the dart from a long way away because he's going to be furious when he wakes up. He's massive!'

'Well, it's a long drive and I couldn't risk him escaping the box. He's like a flipping mountain lion, look at him.'

Ross moved his face back and the cat flopped slightly onto his cheek, purring. Marcie wandered back to them, stroked the soft fur of his head.

'How am I supposed to take care of a cat? I don't need something to tie me down – I still fly to London every few weeks, you know?'

'He's a mouser, Mossie. I'm told he's mostly an outdoor cat. Came from a farm. The owner went into hospital and the people in the Cat and Dog Home said the poor guy's been there a while. Everyone wants wee kittens nowadays.'

'A *wee* kitten he is not.'

Ross put the cat down on the floor at her feet and they both watched as he slightly wobbled his way around the room, sniffing at items in his path. Atlas rubbed a furry cheek over the sofa corners and then unsteadily plodded his way into the small hall.

'If that cat sprays anywhere,' she warned.

'Oh, no worries, I'm told he's been *taken care of*.' Ross made the statement in a hushed tone and with air quotes as if the cat were to hear.

'I can't keep him. You're going to have to take him to Lubnaig when you go. This thing will eat me out of house and home!'

'He'll eat the vermin,' assured the gift giver. 'He catches what he wants to eat.'

Marcie watched as the cat made his way on huge paws into her bedroom, and as she began to follow, she glanced around to where Ross was eating from the wooden spoon she had left in the filled cake pan. He winked at her as he chewed the soft fruits. She followed the cat to where he had found his new favourite spot and was immediately fast asleep on her bed, lying, belly up, gently purring on her expensive cashmere throw blanket. As she turned to go back to complain to Ross with a *nice thought but no thanks*, she heard his car pull away and she dropped her shoulders. 'I don't believe it,' she said to herself and made her way back into the bedroom and climbed up onto the bed. The cat immediately stretched out until he was lying along the length of her legs.

'Don't get comfy – you're not staying.' She drew her hand along his soft underbelly, and he opened his eyes and gave a soft croak as if in agreement. Within a moment Atlas was fast asleep, exhausted after his long journey and the number of tranquilisers injected to calm down a cat of such magnitude.

'I've only got tinned tuna so when you've had your fill of that, you'll be going on your holidays to Lubnaig Cottage, you two big fellas together, hmm?' She stroked the sleeping animal, and he gave another croaking miaow. She had to smile at Ross's thoughtfulness. Maybe she should keep him for a few days until he dealt with the mouse situation and then she could deliver him back to the visitor's cottage. She found herself stroking the cat's soft fur and then curled herself around a pillow watching him intently. Maybe this was the gift from Dina that she asked for, something to accompany her on her new journey forward. Still with a contented smile on her face in the warmth of the bed, suddenly she was fast sleep like the cat lying next to her and the mess in her kitchen, unusually, remained untouched.

As Ross pulled the car into a passing place on the single-track road, he looked back in his wing mirror at the little white house he had just left. He hoped Jamie would get to the mystery of the car crash that had haunted him for such a long time. And the other thing he had come here to finish? Well, it could end up making him a small fortune and then he'd have a big decision to make that could reshape the rest of his life and shake Strathkin to its core.

FIFTEEN

Maureen was running scenarios over in her mind as she sat on the blue painted bench outside Lochside Croft. It was a walk she was happy to make from the Trekking Centre as it took only moments, and it meant she could wear her sandals with the small kitten heels which showed off her shapely ankles. She had always been a fashionista and being this far north, in the glens and mountains, did not dissuade her from wearing her normal bright coloured, and mostly modern, animal print outfits. Her leopard print skirt today was a little longer than she remembered since its last outing, and she knew she had lost a bit of weight and shrunk a little. At eighty-three, that was considered perfectly normal, but Maureen had refused to believe her age when she had to write it down and believed your attitude to life and how you approached it was all in your head.

She sat up as Ruaridh handed her a cup of tea.

'I 'ope it's not builder's tea that her indoors makes,' Maureen complained.

'Ceylon,' was the response as Ruaridh sat down next to her.

'Don't suppose you've...' she began.

'Nope,' was the answer. 'No gin, no rum, no Scotch, no nothing. Dry house.'

'Pity.'

'I'm detoxing,' said Ruaridh as he sat next to her on the bench – the same woman he had dragged through a broken window from a burning house, surely saving her from certain death. He had roughly given her the kiss of life, although when he recalled the scenario in his head, his mind played tricks as if she was the one who had pulled him to her to extend the life-giving breath.

'So, to what do I owe the pleasure?' he asked Maureen, who was staring into her tea and trying to change it into gin by the power of thought alone.

'What was that?' she queried.

'You said you wanted a chat on the phone,' he reminded her.

'Oh, yes. I need you to pick someone up from the airport. I mean, I don't know when she's coming yet but I need you to be on standby.'

'Sure. Who and when?'

'Mrs San. *Mrs San*, you know her.'

'Mrs San?' He felt a bit confused, both knowing and not instantly recognising the name.

'Angelina San.'

'*Seriously*? Wow...' he said, sitting back. 'Angelina San,' he said aloud, thinking of the last time he saw her. Dressed head to toe in pink silk with a look of disdain, lording it over everyone at Swanfield before it became The Retreat. He gave a little whistle.

'Have you told the girls?' he asked.

'That lot? I can't get them all in the same place at once. Honest to God, *Roo*, it's like herding cats. One sits down, the other one leaves, they all sit down, then one of them is on the phone. It's a nightmare dealing with that bunch of women. I said to my Brian last night, I said, Bri, wait till they 'ear Ange is coming back, they'll form a coven.'

Ruaridh laughed at the suggestion, mainly because it was likely to be true, and the fact that the long-deceased Brian was addressed every day by Maureen as if he were sitting in the next room.

'She's got a proposal for them. Well, herself.'

'Marcie?'

'Who else.'

He waited as Maureen sipped her tea again and made a face. 'And?' he encouraged.

'And what?'

'And what is the proposal?'

'Oh, I can't go around gossiping.'

'Well, they'll tell me anyway,' he said with a nudge, trying to persuade her to disclose the information.

'But I really should tell them first because they're all in it together.'

'In what?'

'The coven.'

He shook his head and sat back, folding his arms and flipping his sunglasses from his head to cover his eyes.

'Do you want me to get them together on your behalf?' he suggested.

'Oh, that would be mustard. Why didn't I think of that?'

'When is she arriving, because you'll want to tell them before she appears like Banquo's Ghost?'

'Who's that then? Is your 'ouse 'aunted? Blimey.'

'It's Shakespeare. *Macbeth*.'

'Didn't do Shakespeare at my school. Not that I can remember anyhoo.'

'He was murdered by three assassins after Macbeth thought he was a threat.'

'Oh, really? Like the guy that was here. The "assassin",' she said, "'e disappeared right fast, didn't he? You think he'll come back?'

'Wouldn't have thought so,' confirmed Ruaridh of the man who had nearly brought Strathkin to its knees. They sat silently for a moment.

'So,' began Maureen, 'I'm gaspin', me. It's too warm for tea I shouldn't wonder.'

Ruaridh stood up, emptied his cup, and offered a hand, helping to ease her off the bench.

'You're a good man, Roo-ray. You and that brother of yours really do bring a smile to a girl's face.'

'There's another two of us,' he said, taking Maureen's cup and saucer.

'Blimey,' was Maureen's response, 'your poor mum. The size of you.'

'We weren't born this size, Mrs B!'

'I should think not! Come on, Roo, the sun is well past the yardarm.'

The Strathkin Inn was only a short walk away and he linked his arm through hers as they chatted on the brief stroll along the road. He knew he would have to pin Marcie down to tell her what Maureen had just imparted before she met with the other girls and before Angelina San had decided on the date of her visit back to Strathkin. His mind was racing. Does he tell the local police officer she was coming back, as he knew there had been trouble tracking down Angelina and husband, Louis De Groot, after the fire? Does he quiz Maureen more as to the real intention of San, since Maureen wasn't very forthcoming on the actual reason for the visit? His mind was full of thoughts he had been mulling over, but it was Ross who was at the forefront of his mind. They had talked but he felt Ross was evading the answers to some of his younger brother's questions. They had been thick as thieves growing up, but Ross was always on the edge, walking that thin tightrope between right and wrong.

He was back, but he was here, there and everywhere. Ruaridh knew that he probably came over as desperate on the phone and if that was the case, where was he? As if that wasn't enough to occupy him, in his mind's recipe book, he was trying to create a light supper that seemed interesting enough to plan a date with Arshia Brahmins but not basic enough for his guest to think he could not cook.

'Salmon,' he said aloud, and Maureen glanced up at him as they entered the front door.

'Well, I wasn't really after a lunch, but it'll save me eating later. Salmon it is,' said Maureen, as she and Ruaridh strolled into The Strathkin Inn, arm in arm.

SIXTEEN

Atlas settled quickly into Tigh-na-Lochan. Left to sleep most of the day and fed the best food Strathkin General Stores could sell, the cat had certainly landed very comfortably on his four furry feet.

'Seriously, I didn't know what I was going to do. I mean, I thought we'd be together for life, well, you do, don't you, when you're in the first flush?' Marcie said, busy in her kitchen. 'No one really prepares you for what's in front of you, do they?' Atlas was sitting on the counter at the sink, gazing at her intently as she chatted to him, close to his face. Sometimes he made a little noise as if in agreement. Sometimes, he left her gaze, looking out to the lochan in front of the house. Occasionally he would give a little rumble in his throat, baring his teeth, planning a future wildlife attack from the confines of his new surroundings in the cottage. 'And then *poof*! It's all over. Looking back, though, it was never really meant to be. You were the same, Atlas. There you were, living your lovely life with your owner and next thing, with no thought to your true feelings, you're shoved in a little carry cage never knowing if you're going to get out again, eh?' The cat miaowed in what she presumed was agreement. She continued with her task of decanting soaked fruit into jars to distribute as gifts until she was interrupted by her phone pinging with a message. She wiped her hands and went over to sit at the table. It was Ruaridh.

> Hiya Mossie, ha ha

'Ha ha indeed,' she said aloud.

> You know I've never liked that!

> I know, he does it to wind you up. Free later?

> Maybe... what are you offering?

She studied the message for a moment then pressed delete.

> Maybe...

> BBQ?

She felt deflated and turned to Atlas who was purring and watching her intently from the draining board. 'Why can't I say anything to him?' she asked of her furry therapist. 'Why is it not like before when we would tell each other everything? Is this what being an adult is all about, puss? Eh? We used to lie on the beach and talk for hours when we were younger, way back when I used to live here. And even when he married Dina, puss-puss, I would complain to him about work, and he would moan about the kids. It's what best friends do, isn't it? What happened to all of that? Hmmm?' She turned her phone over in her hands, thinking, then she raised her index finger and ran it over her lips.

Bored of the one-sided conversation, the cat jumped off the draining board with a thud onto the floor and, tail up, made his way back to the bedroom. She heard the small noise of him landing softly on the bed and knew he had found the only spot where the sun flooded in, with a shaft of light over the quilt. She followed him and there he was, in exactly the place she had predicted, belly up, paws dangling in the air.

'You certainly landed on your feet when you were brought here,' she said to the animal, who was already drifting into a second sleep of the morning, belly full of tuna.

The phone pinged again, and she went back to the table and sat down heavily on the chair, knowing she should really be working on the three major files she had brought from London on her last trip. But work was boring her, if she had to admit it, and the lives of her friends here seemed more important than what was going on in chambers. She picked up the phone.

> Still there? Get a better offer?

She was still pondering an answer when the phone rang, and she accepted the call.

'Well, I might get a better offer, I don't want to show my hand too soon...' she answered, expecting Ruaridh to come back with another quip.

'Hello?' asked an accented voice she did not immediately recognise. 'Marcella?'

'Yes,' she said and realised she had made the wrong comment.

'It's Dieter Frum.'

'Oh! I'm so sorry! I thought it was someone else!' she apologised. 'So how are you?' she asked with a shrug of the shoulders, not really knowing what to say to this man who had come into her life and disappeared just as fast.

'I am good, thank you. I'm just calling to ask if I may take you to dinner?'

She sat up suddenly.

'Ah... um...'

'There is no problem if you are not available.'

Marcie thought for a minute then asked, 'How do you feel about going to a barbecue?'

'At your house?'

'No, not at my place, at a friend's place in the village. Are you still staying at the Inn?'

'The Strathkin Inn? Yes.'

'Well, it's just along the road from there. I could meet you at the Inn and we can walk there. I see your number has come up so I can text you a time. When will you be here?'

'I have just arrived at The Stag and Thistle. I wanted to get wine to replace the good wine you shared with me.'

'Oh! Okay! Pretty close then!'

'Well, I will wait to hear from you,' he said, bringing the call to a close, 'and I'm really looking forward to meeting with you again.'

She was about to say the same, but he hung up quickly. She put the phone on the table and thought for a minute before her phone pinged again.

> You playing hard to get, Mossie?

She laughed.

> You can take away the leftovers for your furry pal...

The suggestion had a smiling cat emoji, and she laughed again.

> What time? I'm bringing a friend

This time she was the one who had to wait for the response. She tapped her fingers on the table as the response bubble appeared on screen then disappeared. 'Come on...' she said and waited until she couldn't wait any longer and then simply asked:

> What time?

> Five

This was the quick response, and she answered with a thumbs up then went back to her room to join the cat. She lay down on the bed just as Atlas was moving into the shaft of sunlight spreading over the quilt.

'Well, well, well, big fella. What is today going to bring?' she asked the purring cat, who, like Marcie, had no idea.

After a warm afternoon bled into an even balmier evening, Ross was chopping vegetables at the sink at Lochside Croft while his younger brother admired his knife skills. Mixed peppers were sliced, tomatoes quartered, and a raid had been made on the spice cupboard. A homemade mix was then deftly sprinkled over the vegetables on the tray, a liberal pouring of olive oil was drizzled over the mix and set aside. Still in plastic gloves, Ross chopped two red chillis and then attacked two garlic cloves with salt to soften them. He scooped the mix up and knifed it into a gallon-sized resealable bag, where he had already placed a kilo of lamb chops, more sliced onions, half a lemon and olive oil.

'I have to say,' began Ruaridh, watching closely, 'I'm impressed with your culinary prowess.'

'That's easy for you to say,' was the swift response.

'Mum didn't allow us to leave home without showing us how to cook but I don't remember this one,' continued Ruaridh, slurping noisily from a bottle of light beer.

'Well, when I first went full Antipodean, I had so many jobs. Best ones were in a café then a restaurant. You know what it's like – places wanted some muscle to cart the heavy stuff around, then I was asked if I could help in the kitchen on one section, then the other, and I just picked it up. Plus, it's a great way to charm the ladies.'

Once Ross had washed and scrubbed potatoes he put them in a gallon bag with another spice mix. Then, to complete his tasks, he washed everything down, counters and table, and suddenly the kitchen was clean again, everything prepared for the BBQ later, set out and arranged in order.

'I do miss watching someone cook,' sighed Ruaridh as he sipped from his bottle. A case of low alcohol beer had been brought in by Ross earlier in the morning so that he could at least assess what was being drunk. The last thing he wanted was his younger brother to be consumed by alcohol the way their father had been, and he had carefully planned the early evening BBQ around fun and not as an alcohol-fuelled party.

'I can't imagine what it must be like, bro,' said Ross as he turned and leaned against the countertop. 'I always thought you'd end up with Mossie, but then when you and Dina got together it was like you were always meant to be.' Ruaridh was sure he had got over the emotion of breaking down into floods of tears every time his wife's name was mentioned. Now he just kept it for quiet moments on his own – in their bedroom in the dark when demons invaded his mind about all the things he *didn't* do to save her. His mind playing tricks saying it was *all his fault*.

'It was so quick, bro. One minute she was here, next minute she's gone and I'm standing here in silence wondering what happened to my life.'

'What *has* happened to your life?'

'Went off the rails a bit...'

'Only natural,' was the big brother response.

'Still can't come to terms with it. Brave face, stiff upper lip, all that shite.'

Ross watched his brother as his face began to crumple in front of him and he took the few steps towards him to wrap him up in his arms. The last time they had hugged like that was after a winning shinty match in their teens when they were full of exuberant joy, way back when brotherly jostling and punching was the norm. And here they were, two giants in their own way, one shouldering more responsibility than most at this young age. Ruaridh, no longer embarrassed at, or by, his grief, cried like he had wanted to for more than a year. Tears flooded out, shoulders heaved in guilt-free sobbing, and the brothers, separated by space but not love, stood for an age until the tears dried and silence resumed. No words were exchanged – neither spoke. When they separated, Ross patted his younger brother's shoulder heavily, and Ruaridh pulled on a piece of kitchen paper, wiping his face and blowing his nose forcefully.

'So,' began Ruaridh in a change of subject, 'you and Suzy Sutherland?'

'Och, we just drifted apart,' was Ross's reply to the question about his life on the other side of the world. 'I mean, Starr and Skye are both absolute crackers, great wee girls and they're on all the socials with your team,' Ross continued, speaking openly about his two young daughters.

'Aye, cannae get them off sometimes. The time difference is a killer if it's a weekend, *man alive!*' agreed Ruaridh.

'I mean, though, FaceTime, Zoom, all this new stuff. What a godsend. I can see them anytime I want – the time difference? I know what you're saying. But at least you don't have to wait for a letter to see what is happening to your nearest and dearest.'

'Well, *you* stopped writing,' said Ruaridh suddenly.

'I stopped writing when Mum stopped replying.'

'No, she didn't,' responded Ruaridh in defence of his greatest cheerleader.

'Well, I stopped receiving anything.'

'You kept moving!'

'But you can pick up mail anywhere. It's normal there. Everyone is on the move.'

'Why didn't you email?'

'Well, Mum and Dad had a joint account, and *she* wanted them direct to her.'

'I posted plenty!'

'Did you?'

'Dad did.'

'Did he?' asked Ross firmly.

Ruaridh thought for a moment before recalling unposted mail in his father's pickup and being told they were being posted all together.

'Well, I think he did,' qualified Ruaridh.

'You know what thought did? *Pee'd the bed and blamed the blankets.*' For a moment there was silence until both burst out laughing at a phrase from their childhood. Suddenly their bond was renewed. Ross winked, took off the gloves he was wearing and walked past his younger brother, punching him lightly on the shoulder.

'Matches!' he shouted as he walked out the front door and headed to the BBQ that had been laid with a funnel to light the coals. He didn't even turn when his brother threw the matches, so instinctive was their closeness, and he reached out to catch them with his left hand, his eyes on the house across the water. He gazed at it for a long time.

'Stirring up a hornet's nest,' he muttered under his breath, and he wondered if that close bond they shared today would still be there when the truth came out.

Only steps away in the Trekking Centre, the usual argument about clothing was taking place. 'I don't know why we can't both get dressed up. I never go out. I'm always trudging around here through the slop in me 'eels, watching you in your wellies spilling mud all over the shop. I'm getting on my finery. I don't care if you want to wear your jeans and an old T-shirt like you've just finished work in a plumber's warehouse. I'm putting on my best frock and my best jewellery 'cause you never know *who* might be there and you never know *who* you might meet, so if I were you, I'd get dressed up in something nice.'

'Pardon?' asked Bella to Maureen. 'Did you just say something?'

'Why do I bother?' complained Maureen.

'It's a barbecue down the road. We're not going to The Ritz for a slap-up meal.'

'I went there once. It was tragic. Cold food on a big plate. 'ow long does it take to cut those vegetables into tiny little strips? I mean, how many servings of carrots can you get out of one big carrot? Forty? No wonder it's so blinking expensive, feeding the rich masses small portions so that they can *instergrammer* their nosh and get paid for it.'

'Instagram,' Bella corrected.

'That's wot I said.'

Bella was standing in the stable yard, stretching out her back while Maureen sat on the bench.

'Finished your rant?'

'Me? Rant? Oh, you'd not want to see me when I go on a rant. My Bri said I was like a whirling dervish when I went on a rant. *Stay out of her way*, he would shout to his staff when I went into his salon if someone had done me wrong. He said 'e knew by the way I pushed open the door what kind of mood I was in. And 'e wasn't wrong. Oh. No. My Bri was right about most things. Bless 'im.'

Bella waited as Maureen had a moment of reflection about her deceased husband.

'So... what *are* you wearing?' asked Maureen, and Bella raised her eyes to the sky.

'Jeans and a T-shirt,' she repeated as Maureen shook her head and stood up, moaning something about the 'youth of today' which Bella took as a compliment.

'Have you spoken to Marcie?'

'That one is too wrapped up in her head to have a decent conversation with, tried the other day and she went off with that pair of handsome buggers. I don't know what it is she's got – I can't see it meself. 'ere, is that doctor one going to the barbecue? You know, that woman doctor?'

'*That woman doctor*? Maurs, we're not in the nineteen fifties! Her name is Arshia. She's lovely. And after what she went through with "him", I thought you'd be on her side,' said Bella, with reference to the man who had wreaked havoc on their small village. The renegade Russian posing as the self-styled Brodie Nairn had caused devastation and carnage and then escaped into the night while she had had to suffer the consequences. A chill ran through her. Her time in a women's prison was not something she wanted to repeat or be reminded of. She had flushed it – and him – from her memory banks while Maureen continued on her matchmaking quest.

'I mean, I know that herself is fluttering around Ruaridh like a bee to a whatsisname, but I think Arshia—'

'You think she and Ruaridh have had their time?'

'Whatevs, it's just the more I think about it, the more I think they might be a lovely couple together. She's still young enough to have children.'

'I think the last thing on Ruaridh's mind will be how many *more* children he could have!'

'Well, keep your eye on them tonight. I might set myself up as a matchmaker if it all works out.'

Maureen sat back on the bench outside the stable and

folded her arms, making a little sound reflecting a job well done. Bella shook her shoulders out.

'Right! I'm off for a shower!' Bella said before Maureen started on another story from years gone by. 'And try to get a minute to sit down and talk to Marcie. She needs to know what was in the letter from Angelina San!'

Marcie was surprised at how happy she was to see Dieter Frum. He was dressed casually in a pale blue linen shirt and with Ray-Ban sunglasses perched casually on his short salt-and-pepper hair, and she admired his casual elegance. He gave her a welcoming smile in the reception area of The Strathkin Inn and kissed her on both cheeks. He was wearing a fresh and light cologne that reminded her of Callum, and she felt herself smiling widely back at him.

'It's so lovely to see you again!' he enthused, and she felt the same, pleased that she had invited him out on this beautiful late afternoon.

'I should keep in touch more – there is so much here to see I understand why my son loved it so. I apologise,' he said with his hand on his heart, and he gave her a little bow of regret which she found incredibly endearing.

'No need to apologise. We all have busy lives.'

'I have also been working on a bit of a plan. I have a man.'

She gave him a side glance, and he gave a little chuckle.

'Ah! I understand that may not have been what I meant to say. I have a man in Edinburgh doing a little bit of work for me.'

'Ah, that makes more sense!' She laughed as she felt him take her elbow and lead her into the bar area, where Heather gave a nod and a wink as she caught Marcie's eye in the large mirror.

'I imagine it's time for a gin and tonic?' he suggested as he led her gently to the table at the window that had the best view out across the loch.

'A gin-less tonic for me,' she suggested, before lifting her hands in front of her to simulate a steering wheel. 'Driving.'

'I'm sure you could have stayed here,' he suggested before backtracking. 'I'm sorry, I sound a bit presumptuous! I mean, I am sure your friend could have found you a spare bedroom. I don't believe the hotel is full.'

'No. Not at all,' she responded, glad of the explanation. 'It's a regular thing for all of us lucky enough to live in the country – you always need a designated driver. There's usually one or two of us on soft drinks if you go for a night out. It wasn't so bad earlier when I lived here but now that I'm out at Tigh-na-Lochan, it's a bit of a drive so better be on the safe side.'

'You lived here? In the village?'

She pointed to the house on the other side of the loch.

'I used to live there. I was brought up there when it was called Swanfield.'

'Ah,' he said and gazed across the still water. 'I remember reading about it, but I didn't put two and two together that you were the person. That you are, in fact, *the* Marcie.'

'The person? The Marcie? That makes me sound a bit grand!'

Drinks served, Marcie was happy that it was indeed a gin-less tonic and raised it to her lips before she was interrupted by her guest.

'You don't say *cheers*?' he asked, surprised.

'Oh, excuse me. How rude! We say *slainte*! To your health!'

'*Prost!*' he said, his eyes not leaving hers as he held up his glass before gently hitting it against hers. He savoured the flavour of the mix of that week's special, Raasay gin and elderflower tonic, and ran his tongue over his lips. 'A perfect combination.'

'So, this man of yours doing work in Edinburgh. Are you buying property or what?'

'Oh, no, no, no. My goodness, no!' He took another gulp of his drink.

She waited.

'I believe we have found him.'

'Uh-huh?'

'The man we are after.'

'We?' she queried.

'The man we would both like to see pay for his actions.'

She sat back, shocked.

'You've found Poytr Medvedev?' Her breath was taken from her for a moment.

'Yes.'

Marcie leaned forward in astonishment and placed her elbows on the table, her glass moved aside. 'Where?' she asked.

'I have paid a man, a private detective. I have paid him a considerable amount of money because I knew the police would never find him. He is, how they say, under the radar. He was living with a woman for a brief time, a woman called Victoria, and then she unfortunately died.'

'I bet she did.'

'And now he is living in a very expensive rented flat in Edinburgh, but I have been working on a plan, a plan I would like to see come to fruition. My man tells me he is running out of money, and he is frequenting places that, let me say, are less salubrious than normal.'

'Uh-huh?' encouraged Marcie.

'I understand from my man he led this woman into a trap.' *Sounds familiar*, Marcie said to herself. 'This is how he came across this woman he was living with. He was, as you would say, "flashing the cash" and he drew her in whereas, in fact, he had little to no money. He certainly likes the high life. Expensive watches, shirts, clothes. He looks the part of the wealthy young man about town.'

'I like your turn of phrase,' said Marcie, sitting up and suddenly wishing her non-alcoholic glass of liquid were filled with something more substantial.

'But whatever way she found out, he disposed of her before clearing out her bank accounts to which he had access. He is such a nasty piece of work. I am a doctor, I save people's lives if I can, try to help them to live a longer, more productive life. I do not want to share the same air as someone like him.'

Marcie looked at this man's handsome, open face with laughter lines around his blue eyes. She could imagine him holding a person's hand while he told them what he would do to make them whole again. She believed he would have a genuine and caring bedside manner. And yet here he was talking about taking a life. She felt uneasy at his suggestion.

'People like him will never be caught because they think like a cat – one step ahead of where they are going, always knowing where the escape route is. He will no doubt plan methodically to get where he wants to be. I don't think he is finished yet. People like that need to be stopped or they will continue to wreak havoc in other people's lives. Your life, my life. But, Marcie, I do not want him to *take* another life, *ruin* another family. I need someone to help me – you said you would, so will you still do that?'

Marcie glanced over to the bar where Heather and Ally were busy laying out a tray of cutlery and giving instructions to their latest recruit, Hannah, laughing and joking as if the three women did not have a care in the world. Then she turned around to her childhood home across the water, fire damaged and unliveable. Would that have happened if she had not sold her house to the highest bidder? Was she, in part, somehow to blame for some of this? Was she suffering from survivor's guilt? Marcie would never truly know.

'I don't know if I want to lower myself to his level,' was all she could say, barely audible, so that Dieter Frum had to lean in close to hear her.

'I'm not asking you to do it. I'm asking you to help *me*.'

She waited as the three girls between the bar and the office glanced over to where they were sitting. Ally made a comment, they all laughed, and Marcie noticed suddenly that Heather was right. When Hannah Hurley laughed, her whole face lit up. A flash of beautiful white teeth in her young, fresh, olive skin set off a chain reaction that made her eyes widen and she looked as if she belonged on the cover of an expensive magazine. A young girl on the verge of womanhood – what chance would she have if she came across someone like Medvedev?

'I really don't know. I've closed off that part of my life, Dieter. I can help you where I'm able but...' She wanted so much to agree to what he was suggesting but knew that what he was saying was a step too far. She encouraged him to drink down his cocktail and suggested they made their way to Lochside Croft. She needed to get away from any reminders of what went before, and a boisterous Balfour BBQ would be the right place to do it.

As Marcie casually strolled to where noise and laughter were permeating the fresh, cool springtime air, she was completely oblivious to the man on the scaffolding across the water at Swanfield. Binoculars covering his eyes, he could easily make out the people gathered in the garden. Poytr Medvedev knew them all. He wasn't close enough to absorb the delicious smells drifting from the coals or listen to the conversation but in his mind ran an English phrase that had become his raison d'etre: *revenge is a dish best served cold.*

· · ·

Spring, especially early in the season on the west coast of northern Scotland, was the ideal time to enjoy outside eating, long before the midges made their annual appearance to suck the blood out of tourists and locals alike. The twins, Donald and David, were splashing about in the water at the end of the lush green lawn as it bled into the shingle and sand beach, and the small guest list of people were making their presence known with howls of laughter, mostly at Ruaridh's expense. Maureen was sitting in a large wicker chair under a branded parasol from the Inn. A vision in white linen, it was as if she had the lead part in a film of her life. A trestle table was near the bench seat in front of the house, slightly in the shade, and where various foodstuffs and bottles were laid out. Heather and Bella were chatting to Ross who oversaw the barbecue, sizzling lamb chops wafting a delicious aroma around the garden. Marcie had introduced her guest to both Ruaridh and Ross, and Dieter Frum had joined the host in a bottle of beer.

Maureen was giving strange nods to Marcie who was deep in conversation with Dax about the benefits of a legal profession for the young boy who had set out his case for a career in land management despite still being at high school. When Hannah appeared with a tray of cutlery to place on the table groaning with food, she had not expected to see Maureen, who pointed a finger at her and motioned with a curling of her index finger for her to come and speak to her.

Hannah scanned the garden and noticed everyone was busy talking and chatting and that there was no escape. She strolled as casually as she could over to where the woman sat, as if holding court. She was half facing the water, half facing the garden, strategically placed with her back to the sun to save her pale, translucent skin from receiving even the merest hint of UVA.

'You're the new girl at the Inn?' asked Maureen with a smile as fake as her glasses.

'Yes,' responded Hannah as her eyes widened in fear.

'I'm Maureen,' she offered and held out her hand.

When their hands met, Maureen jerked Hannah forward, and Maureen quickly pushed up the sleeve of the black jumper, noticing the scars and marks on the girl's wrists and arms. 'Are you who I think you are?'

The young girl of barely seventeen recoiled backwards in fear and straight into the body of Dax, who had left Marcie's side when he noticed Hannah's unexpected arrival.

'Whoa!' he said as she clattered into him but not out of alarm, more surprised at the fact that she had touched him. 'I didn't know you were coming.' He smiled at her from behind his uncle's expensive sunglasses.

'I'm not. I'm just dropping stuff off. I need to go,' she said, in such a flurry that Dax was left startled.

'I'll walk you back to the hotel,' said the ever-growing Dax. Even now, just before his sixteenth birthday, he was heading to the six feet plus that was his father's height.

'No, it's okay,' she pleaded, and he reached out to take her hand.

'I'd like to. You look like a horse that's been spooked. Is everything okay?' asked the oldest of the four Balfour boys as they walked out of Lochside Croft to head along the narrow road that would take them to The Strathkin Inn.

'I- I just got a bit of a fright,' she tried to explain. 'This is all new to me.'

'What?'

She waited for a moment to try to figure out the right answer before deciding to tell the truth.

'Being with people.'

'Being with people? What are you, an alien?' he laughed, seeming quite impressed at his comedic answer, until she pulled her hand out of his grasp.

'I'm not really a sociable person,' she said by way of explanation.

'We might just be too loud for you?' he suggested by way of his *own* explanation. 'You'll get used to us. Balfours are normally known as the life and soul of the party.'

Hannah tried not to stare. He had a fine bone structure to his face, she thought. He was still in the process of transitioning from boyhood to manhood, and she realised he would be as handsome as his father in a few years. She had planned to be long gone by then, of course. She felt a strange feeling coming over her, as if she wanted to protect him, as he seemed to want to protect her. It was a feeling she was unfamiliar with and so she stood, her face still, as she surveyed him and his surroundings. The strong and silent type, Dax was doing the same to her. He leaned in to give her a clumsy kiss, which was awkward at first before becoming soft and gentle. It was he who pulled away first, which surprised her. The whole world seemed to stop as they looked at each other. She took his hand again and they continued their walk to the Inn, a few steps away. When the couple reached the back entrance to the offices and store, she turned again and pulled him towards her. She could still hear the noise from the barbecue and the laughter of the guests caught in the light breeze. The aroma from the hot coals hung in the air.

'You'd better get back. They'll be searching for their waiter,' she joked, 'which is why I came back here. I'm helping Ally.'

'I'm sure I can stay,' he lied, to try and convince himself he would not be missed in the small gathering.

'I'm not going anywhere.' She smiled at him.

'Tomorrow?' he asked urgently.

'We'll see,' she replied and leaned over to kiss him briefly on the lips before turning and disappearing back into the Inn.

. . .

Wandering back up the single-track road, heading straight to Lochside Croft, Dax was grinning like a Cheshire cat. He stopped at the overgrown verge and picked up a long piece of fallen branch and trailed it behind him, something he had been doing since childhood. Each of the four Balfour children had their own little quirks and traits that endeared them to family and friends alike. Then he suddenly thought, *I'm acting like my youngest brother Douglas; I'm acting like a child* and immediately threw the branch over the hedgerow and marched with purpose back to the barbecue at his home. *I'm almost a man*, he thought, *so I need to start acting like one*. A loud 'whoop' behind him made him turn sharply to see a police car creeping slowly up on his tail.

'Good afternoon, young man,' greeted Jamie MacKay, leaning out of the driver's window.

'Aye, aye,' replied Dax to the uniformed man he had known since childhood and not in the slightest fazed by the man dressed entirely in black.

'Nice looking woman you've got there, Daxy, my man!' joked Jamie.

'She's just a friend,' stated Dax, embarrassed. *What if he spied me kissing her and tells my dad?* he thought to himself and felt his face flush.

'Well, she looks like a lovely friend to have, Dax, and well done on her snagging Strathkin's most eligible bachelor. Want a lift? Hop in?'

'It's only up there!' said Dax, pointing to the croft only metres away.

'Aye, you're growin' up, Daxy. I remember when you were a wee lad, you couldn't wait to jump in the police car and show off to your pals!' joked the police officer, but Dax had no recollection of any of this happening and now, on the cusp of manhood, he didn't want to be reminded of his innocent childhood days.

'Race you,' suggested Jamie and put his foot down so that the car, wheels burning, took the last few metres at a breakneck speed. Dax, oblivious to Jamie's previous life as a boy racer, simply shook his head and meandered up the road to where the car was parked outside his house.

Once out of the car, Jamie checked himself in several of the mirrors, affixed his chequered hat and prepared to make his entrance. People were scattered around the garden, some standing with drinks in hand, some sitting on kitchen chairs and two people on the long, painted blue seat. Jamie spotted Heather speaking to the lady sitting in the chair like some minor royal and gave a wave. Heather waved back enthusiastically to the uniformed man with a wide smile. When Jamie saw Ross at the barbecue, carefully turning spiced lamb chops, he made his way up to where he was talking with his younger brother. Ross was first to spot Jamie and gave out a 'Whoa, man!' to their uniformed friend.

'Aw, pal,' he said and embraced the man that stood in front of him, 'never thought I'd believe it until I saw it.' He stood back and took in the friend he hadn't seen in so many years.

'Poacher turned gamekeeper, right enough,' Ross went on as Jamie stood, sharp like a new pin, in his highly pressed uniform.

'Aye, times change, eh?'

They were tearaways together and known as 'The Naughty Boys', always up to something and always getting caught. But it was never anything serious, and never anything to cause anyone much concern – two boys from good families who were just bored with their remote Highland life and filling in their time until they finally grew up. And when they did, one stayed and one escaped. Texts and communications drifted off until they were non-existent, and both men grew up and got on with their lives, sensibility taking over as the years flew by.

'Gawd...' Ross drawled. 'Nearly twenty years, man.'

'More like fifteen,' corrected Jamie.

'Aye, you always were a stickler for the facts!' joked Ross and handed his friend a bottle of beer, which was declined with a palm up hand.

'So, how long are you here for?' asked the police officer.

'Och, dunno. Just had a hankering to come back, you know. Didn't make it back for the funeral, of course. A few calls with the big man over there and I knew he wasn't doing so well, so I thought I'd better make the trip. I'm on an open ticket.'

Ross drank down the rest of his beer and tossed the empty bottle into a big drum next to the flaming BBQ. It was almost full, but Jamie noticed most of the bottles were of the zero per cent alcohol variety. He realised the benefit of having his big brother around must have shocked Ruaridh back to his senses.

'We must try and get a wee night out together. Catch up. Reminisce.'

'Aye, not too much reminiscing or we'll just get maudlin',' laughed Ross and watched as Jamie's eyes, even behind his aviator sunglasses, drifted over to the two women talking animatedly on the lawn.

'No romance on the cards for you yet?' asked Ross. 'I was told you're still free.'

'Och, always on the lookout, you know me,' was Jamie's response as he watched Heather tossing her hair back, exposing her smooth neck, in a hearty laugh.

'Funny how far we've all come, eh?' asked Ross, watching Jamie gaze at a girl he had teased at school.

'Aye,' sighed Jamie and then turned back to the chef, 'there was a time I thought the only way we'd leave here was in a *hurry up wagon* and straight to a cell in the big city. Way back then, eh?' The men stared at the sizzling meat on the grill, silently watching as the flames rose and fell with each turning of the chops. Time ticked slowly past as they were transported to another age.

'I used to wake up in the night,' said Ross quietly to the man standing at his side, 'playing it over and over in my head. Just wondering, you know?'

'Aye, deep down I sometimes wonder if it's why I ended up like this.' Jamie gestured to his uniform, slowly absorbing the smells of the charring supper. 'Sometimes I wonder if I can resolve the past, and also think, what if someone were to find out?'

'What are you two getting all moody and serious about?' asked Marcie as she slapped both Ross and Jamie on the back and then stood back. Both men appeared slightly startled, brought quickly back to reality. 'Oh, gosh, could that be police assault?' she joked and grabbed Jamie's arm, hooking it around hers. Both men studied each other for a moment, their reminiscences of dark days interrupted. Ross gave a very brief, almost unnoticed, shake of the head to Jamie.

'I'll let you off with it this time!' warned Jamie, jokingly, and said, 'Back in a jiffy.' He left them and made his way over to Heather.

'This all smells delicious,' said Marcie to Ross, sniffing the air and watching as he piled the meat on a long platter. He leaned over, brushing against her slightly, to hand it to one of the twins who placed it on the long trestle table that was already groaning with food. 'How's Atlas?' asked the chef as he placed the rest of the marinated chops on the grill.

'That monster? I confess, he's great company. He's a good listener. Oh, escapee!' said Marcie and pinched a potato wedge that had strayed from the plate, dipping it in a spiced mayo mix before biting it in half.

'Who invited Grandpa?' asked Ross with a nod to Dieter

Frum who was deep in conversation with his younger brother. Marcie laughed slightly and nudged him until he nudged back, and they began a back and forth in front of the grill like naughty children waiting to be scolded.

'Cheeky! He's lovely. Don't let the white hair fool you, he's not that old. He's the father of one of the boys who died on the hill a few years ago. He's making a kind of pilgrimage.'

'Oh, aye?'

'He's staying at the Inn. He's off hiking every day. His wife had a bit of a breakdown.'

'And are you the tour guide or the nanny?'

'Whatever do you mean?'

'You seemed quite cosy when I saw you earlier.'

'He's a lovely guy. Surgeon. German.'

'He a "potential" for you then?' asked Ross, only half joking, taking what was left of the potato wedge from Marcie's hand and popping it into his mouth.

Marcie was surprised at his action, but she knew the old Ross Balfour well; she knew he was flirting outrageously.

'Jealous?' she joked and then when she caught his eyes, she realised there was a powerful and dominant look about him. She looked away quickly, cast her eyes over to Dieter and then back to Ross. Their eyes locked in a brief second and Marcie felt something run through her. She turned and walked to join the guests and then glanced back to the barbecue where she noticed Ross' eyes were following her every move. She breathed out heavily.

'Friday? Or is earlier in the week better for you?' asked Jamie to Heather when he finally broke her free from the conversational grip of Maureen.

'It doesn't really matter. I have this new girl helping so it's an extra pair of hands around the place. What do you have in mind? Please don't say let's go for dinner...'

'We can go for a drive, pick up something en-route. You probably want to get away from the stifling eyes of Strathkin,' suggested Jamie, glancing around at the people gathered on the lawn.

'That would be bliss,' sighed Heather. 'Anywhere!'

'How about I pick you up late morning? We can be away all day?'

Heather smiled and closed her eyes. The thought of escaping from her life – lovely as it was – and a change of scene for even a few hours was something she had dreamed about for a long time. She loved her job – she loved her hotel – she loved her guests – she loved the fact that every day she was meeting new people. But lately as profits had begun to rise and people from all over the world were now descending on her doorstep, her job and her life had become all-consuming. She longed to disappear even for a short time to another view and some different chat. Jamie, it would appear, had stepped into her life at just the right time.

'Let me work on a plan,' he suggested and then leaned over and kissed her cheek. 'I'll see you Friday,' he said and left her to go back to Ross on his own once more at the hot grill.

Heather placed her hand on her cheek and glanced around. It had seemed to go unnoticed, and she thought, *you were right, Dina, at last, something for me.*

'Catch up, big man?' Jamie suggested to Ross as he pulled his phone out of his pocket and within a second, numbers were exchanged. Jamie gave his friend a final hug and disappeared back to his car and back to work. Ross observed the scene playing out in the garden. Children scattered around, the right amount of people of varying ages which he always felt was a good mix, most standing, some sitting, all laughing. Music was playing and he noticed it was the same music that the group often played at the Inn – it must be a Spotify playlist, he thought, a mix of old and new and just the right kind of music for such a relaxed and outdoor event such as this. He noticed a woman had appeared that he hadn't seen before. Small, and delicate, she had a thick mane of long dark hair and was engaged in an animated conversation with his younger brother, but his eyes fixed on Marcie. He watched as she held Dieter Frum's gaze while she talked wildly with hand gestures to exaggerate her points. He observed her unnoticed for a long time, his eyes taking her all in. Her hair had escaped a clip that was holding it up and he watched as she unclipped it, gathered her hair up and reattached it without breaking her stride in the conversation. He blew out a long stream of air. He turned back to his cooking and glanced at his phone and Jamie's number. A plan was forming in his head.

SEVENTEEN

Like the rest of the village, the next morning The Strathkin Inn was quiet save the regulars' table with the same four women gathered around it.

'I've never really cared for a barbecue, me. Too much meat. Too much of that smell of cooking flesh. I would quite happily survive on a pill once a day that rested in your belly like a three course Sunday roast that you didn't 'ave to eat but you fooled your tum-tum into thinking it had stuffed your face. My Brian always said...'

'Oh, give it a rest, Maurs,' sighed Bella. 'You stuffed your face at Lochside Croft so don't deny you didn't enjoy yourself!'

Maureen pulled her pink linen dress over her swollen stomach. 'Look what it's left me. This! I'll 'ave to starve meself to get my figure back. That big Roo-ray one kept feeding me those chops. Or was it the other one, Roddy?'

'Ross.'

'Whatevs,' said Maureen, with a roll of the eyes and a thought of when it might be twelve o'clock somewhere. 'I went to see that young doctor lady when I 'ad a problem recently with me...' She checked for listening ears. Together they glanced around the empty restaurant at The Strathkin Inn, waiting for what was next to come out of Maureen's mouth. 'Waterworks,' she said in a stage whisper.

Bella leaned forward on the table, resting her forehead in her open palm.

'And she said I was a wonderful specimen for my age. In fact, when she gave me all me test results, she said *Perfecto! Perfecto! Perfecto!*' Maureen began ticking imaginary boxes on an imaginary sheet on her small hand.

'Will we ever get to finish a conversation that you start?' suggested Bella, trying to bring Maureen back to the reason they were all sitting at their usual table.

'Right, where was I? So, Angie is coming back,' she began.

'How many times have we heard this?' started Marcie. 'For all we know, she could have been and gone in the time we've been here waiting for this story to finish.'

'Well, I can't 'elp it if you're all 'ere one minute then gone the next? You're like Will o' the Wisp, the lot of you. Especially you,' said Maureen, eyes rigidly fixed on Marcie.

'Me?' asked Marcie, pointing her finger to her chest.

'As soon as one of those Balfour boys appears, you're off like a...'

'Like a...?'

The three women waited to see the resulting fireworks if Maureen continued in her line of one-sided conversation.

'Like a...?' Marcie asked again.

'Where was I...?' started Maureen, eager to move the conversation on to what she really wanted to talk about.

'Angelina,' sighed Heather with a glance at her watch and a stifled yawn.

'Oh, yes, did we not discuss this last time we met?'

'MAUREEN!' said an exasperated Bella. 'Get to the point.'

'Why are you so annoyed all the time? You sound so aggressive. I know what you need, and it doesn't come in a tin... with ice. Any chance of a...?'

'Give me strength,' sighed Bella and sat back, raising her eyes to the ceiling.

'She's coming back with a proposal.'

They waited.

'Have you stopped doing that free homemade shortbread with morning coffee? I'm ravenous, me. You see, I'm fine if I don't eat, but once I start it's like opening the floodgates to me stomach.'

Marcie laid her elbows on the table, rested her hands in her palms covering her face and sighed. 'I drove all the way from Tigh-na-Lochan for this. I'm supposed to be working. This is like drawing teeth.'

'I can only go as fast as me brain... who's that then? I saw him last night.'

'Brain like a butterfly,' sighed Bella as she saw Dieter Frum enter the room and try to catch Marcie's eye.

Heather, sitting next to Marcie, nudged her friend, who excused herself from the table.

'What does she 'ave for her breakfast of a morning? It's all that unnatural horsey muesli stuff, innit? Bet it gives 'er that inner glow that we ladies can't see,' said Maureen with a shake of her head.

As Marcie approached Dieter, she caught sight of Hannah prepping the room for service. After a nod from Hannah, she gave Dieter a signal that she was going to speak to the younger woman.

'Hi, Hannah.'

Hannah looked up and returned the greeting with a wide-open smile, her face, as described by Heather, lighting up.

'Have you got a minute?' she asked.

Marcie nodded.

Still holding the cutlery, she made her way outside to the seat at the front of the hotel, bathed in light and looking out over the loch.

'Nice to get away from Maureen's stories!' Marcie joked as she took a seat next to the girl who looked fidgety and nervous.

Hannah knew from Dax that Marcie was a lawyer. She was enjoying her *new* life in the Highlands but there were so many unknowns in it.

'How are you settling in?' Marcie asked when she saw that Hannah was slightly distracted.

'Fine.'

'Making lots of new friends?'

'Yeah, I guess.' Hannah shrugged.

'Planning on staying a while?'

'You're a lawyer?' asked Hannah, ignoring the question that had been fired her way.

'Of sorts, yeah,' replied Marcie with a shake of her head.

'Do you defend people in court? Do you go to the Old Bailey?'

'Well, a while ago, yes, but—' began Marcie.

'But you *are* a real lawyer?'

'Last time I looked! Of course.'

'Can I talk to you? Like, in confidence?'

'In confidence? Absolutely.' Marcie looked down as Hannah reached out her hand, grasped hers and tears began to well up in her eyes.

'I think I killed my boyfriend.'

It was the last thing Marcie expected to come out of this young woman's mouth, and it was all she could answer when she said, 'Oh?'

Hannah had started to shake slightly after her revelation, and Marcie held her hands tightly.

'You don't have to tell me if you don't want to, but I'm sure I can help you.'

'I had to get away. He wanted me to do things, and I said no. He just wouldn't stop hitting me.'

This revelation shocked Marcie but she knew there had to be more than just a simple runaway story.

'So, what did you do?'

'Nothing. But I got up in the middle of the night, and he was at the bottom of the stairs. I just left him. I didn't want that life anymore and I just left. I took advantage and ran.'

'Uh-huh?'

'I didn't mind running his drugs, but...' she said quietly.

Marcie leaned over and took the girl to her, wrapping her arms around her and pulling her in tight. Hannah began sobbing, quietly at first then more vocally while Marcie soothed her. Hannah didn't flinch when Marcie pulled up her sleeves over her wrists to reveal what were clearly cigarette burns, and self-harm slashes across her wrists. Hannah opened her mouth to speak but Marcie held her hands up.

'There's no need,' she said softly. 'We both know what's happened here.'

Marcie's soft tone was a comfort. Hannah had always seen her as quite loud and formidable, and she suddenly felt reassured, reassured enough to pull up her black jumper to reveal several similar burns across her flat stomach.

Marcie gently pulled the top down and took Hannah's hands in hers.

'We'll find out what happened, and I will help you, don't worry. You're in the right place.'

'I just wished he would stop. I prayed that he would die. Is that enough to kill someone?'

Marcie shook her head. She pulled the girl towards her once more and hugged her harder this time, wishing she could transfer her strength to the frightened young woman in front of her.

'Let's take it one step at a time. Start at the beginning and tell me all about it.'

EIGHTEEN

There had been a time when Ruaridh relished his job as a chauffeur, driving visitors back and forth from Strathkin to the airport at Inverness. A time to decompress. Thinking time. Planning time. A little bit of extra money in the Balfour Bank. But since Dina's death, he had made more time for his home life and the trips had all but fizzled out. Occasionally, like today, Heather would ask him to pick up a guest, but they rarely saw the old chatty, self-effacing and funny Ruaridh. Instead, they mostly found they had been gifted the reticent Highlander, stoic and silent with an occasional reference to a viewpoint or area of historical significance. Answers to tourists' eager questions now seemed to be mostly swallowed up by his beard. Unusually, he was glad of the silence. On more than one occasion, on a return trip, someone would offer their condolences having been told of their driver's background while staying in the hotel. He did *not* appreciate it. The last thing Ruaridh needed was to be reminded of his life without his wife in it. He saw her every day in his children's eyes, their smiles, their window gazing and their happy paddling and laughing in front of the house they had so happily shared. He saw her in their daughter's face as she gazed up to him in wonder. This was a journey he had loved – a journey that brought people to his home. But now it was laced with sadness as there was no one to share the chatter and the excitement with at the end of the long road. No one to chat through the visitors' questions with. No one to share the endless summer nights with, and no one to share what was left of his love once he had showered his children with cuddles, hugs, and kisses.

He had tentatively broached the subject of a coffee or a drink with his local doctor on the pretence of thanking her for helping him through some dark times, but he was unsure who was to make the first step. She had been receptive, but he was unsure of how to move it on. He had discussed food with her and they had joked about it, but that elusive first date still seemed far away. And then, of course, there was Marcie. She was preoccupied, as Marcie always was helping here, sticking her nose in there, trying to solve everyone's problems while dealing with her own devastating separation. There was a time they could talk about anything. A time when they would share hopes and dreams but now, they had grown apart. She was fluttering like a butterfly around a guest at the hotel, and even his brother Ross had asked him about her *situation*, as he so delicately put it.

Ruaridh was lost. The road map of his life's plan had gone missing and even though he was the only one who could find it, he was not sure if he really wanted to. He was brought back to reality on more than one occasion by his passenger telling him he had taken the wrong road. Frequently, at the junction, he had taken the road to Swanfield instead of turning right into the village. He would apologise and pull the car to a stop ready to instigate a nine-point turn on the narrow single-track road to take them back into Strathkin, but often, he would drop them off at the Inn and drive himself over to the big house and gaze at the building that had dominated his childhood. It was now covered in scaffolding with *Keep Out – Dangerous* signs pinned on every other pole. Sometimes, he'd slip out of the car, push his hands into his pockets and wander up to get a better view. The signs that had been put in place by both the council and the Fire and Rescue Service were now faded and weatherbeaten and blowing faintly in the slight breeze as they peeled from the windows. Each time he visited, Ruaridh took in the facade and felt it was a metaphor for his life – *all things crumble and turn to dust, some long before their time.* Today he took his passenger straight to the hotel, helped her with the luggage and glanced at his watch. Mari was with her grandmother, and the boys were not yet due in from school. He sat the luggage down beside the visitor, who shook his hand with a polymer note passed in the exchange, and he gave Heather a nod of recognition. He glanced into the dining room where two young couples were enjoying an afternoon tea in the banquette by the window.

The *regular's* table.

The *reserved* table.

As Ruaridh looked at them chattering, he blinked the sight of his wife away. In his mind's eye, it was she who was there, sitting with her girlfriends laughing at some joke at his expense. Then she turned from her friends and gave a look she reserved only for him – eyes blinking slowly, wide mouth smiling with her tongue resting between her teeth, her head moving coquettishly to one side. He became aware of someone talking and it was only when he turned, he saw his bother Ross suddenly stop mid-conversation.

'You okay, bro?' he asked, concern etched on his face.

'Aye, aye, fine.'

'You look like you've just seen a ghost.'

Ross made the statement and looked as if he immediately

regretted what he had said, knowing everywhere in Strathkin had memories of his sister-in-law engrained into the walls and the very air of the small village. Unconsciously, he pulled his brother close to him and bear-hugged him like they were still children.

Ruaridh felt a wave of emotion well up in him, but his new coping mechanism pushed it back to hold it in check until he could release it later at home in the company of his own solitude.

'I'm meeting Jamie. You want to stay for a pint?'

'No, no. Thanks, though. D's mum has the wee one and is doing tea for the boys when they get back. I'll need to get home and relieve her of granny duties.'

'No probs,' said Ross and gave his brother a firm grip of the hand before heading into the bar where Jamie was paying Ally behind the counter for their order.

As he glanced back, he watched his brother leave, a distant look in his eye and his shoulders slightly hunched. He gave a sigh as he sat down with his childhood friend at a corner table, gave a *cheers*, and both downed half of the drink with a smack of the lips before sitting back.

'Boy, I needed that today,' said Jamie.

'One of those days?' asked Ross as he wiped the beer foam from his trimmed stubble with the back of his hand.

'Nah, not really, nothing much doing. Quiet week, to be honest. Helped an old biddy who'd got stuck up at the burial ground the other day. Parked on the verge and couldn't get back on to the road. Up from Inverness laying flowers for a friend. I told her she should stay the night up here; I know there were a few rooms available, but she was determined to get back to the big smoke. Long time since I've been in such an old car. Small, too – a wee Ford Fiesta. Cracking condition, I have to say. Well looked after – one lady owner, I imagine.' He laughed. 'So, that's been the sum of my week so far. Took me back, mind you, to all those wee Ford Fiestas I used to, like, *borrow*, if you know what I mean.'

'Oh, I know what you mean!' Ross laughed, he, too, downing his beer and remembering Jamie's previous life as Strathkin's very own boy racer. They exchanged glances.

'So, you still wonder?' asked the policeman. 'About what you were saying the other day?'

'Sometimes I do, you know. Wonder if it was us – well, you. Well, we were *both* fiddling about in it, were we not?' queried Ross, trying in his mind to justify the actions of a long time ago. 'I can't deny it used to keep me up at night,' he continued in almost a whisper. 'I was sure you'd call me at some point saying you'd found evidence, and the feds were on my tail.'

'I hardly think we have the *feds* up here,' replied Jamie, trying to make a joke out of what had been, for a long time, a desperate situation.

'Your mind plays tricks when you're on the other side of the world,' stated Ross. 'Seriously.' He stared into his beer.

'What brought you back then?' asked Jamie, his index finger running around the top of the glass.

Ross had always considered Jamie his best friend, even with oceans between them; apart from his brothers, he thought often of his youth and them both discovering the joy of growing up together.

'Do you think you could find out?' asked Ross.

Jamie appeared a little worried at his friend's suggestion.

'I'm up for promotion, Ross. I need to be dead careful, pal.'

'How difficult can it be?'

'Well, it's no' easy,' replied Jamie in the vernacular and took a small sip from what was left of his beer. 'It was a long time ago. Everything's centralised now. Not held locally, if you know what I mean.'

'Just a favour for a friend,' suggested Ross.

Jamie pondered and breathed out hard. 'I'll see what I can do,' he said to Ross and sat back, clearly beginning to regret his friend's return.

NINETEEN

Not for the first time that week, Marcie was surrounded by papers. Papers with notes. Papers she had printed off. And then actual pieces from newspapers she had found online. A call to one of her friends in the same legal firm and who, like Hannah, lived in Maidstone, had not yielded much by way of information, but the *Kent Messenger* had produced a few lines about the body of a local drug dealer found at home. 'Believed to have died while his girlfriend was visiting her grandmother', read the scant report. There were no suspicious circumstances mentioned after the post-mortem. Years of substance abuse and poor life choices had finally caught up with twenty-two-year-old Chester Walker. A grainy picture taken from an old Facebook account was all that was left of the man who had claimed Hannah as his own and then tried to sell her off. She had made the right decision in leaving, thought Marcie, as she investigated the young woman's life.

Marcie's own life was divided into black or white, right or wrong. This was a somewhat grey area, but Marcie liked Hannah and knew *she* had lived a life of privilege that few could achieve if their place of birth simply dealt them the wrong hand.

'What would you do?' she asked of the large cat sitting on a pile of legal books at the end of the table, paws tucked beneath him like a closed envelope, eyes firmly shut and gently purring. She poured another glass of dark red liquid from the carafe next to her and took a long gulp. Watching the cat made her drowsy, so she picked up her phone and turned up the music. This so disturbed Atlas that he let out an angry *yam*, gave her a look of disdain and took himself off to his box by the fireplace, the empty wood-burner gently glowing with string lights. The song was a dance tune from long ago, a favourite on the jukebox at The Strathkin Inn and now transferred to Heather's Spotify 'old school hit list' to be occasionally played on a locals' lock-in. Marcie washed up her dinner plate and put the leftovers in plastic tubs for the fridge later while dancing to the music. Atlas curled up, covering his eyes with huge paws. She poured another large glass from the carafe and closed her eyes, hoping the music would take her back to a place where she was still young, as young as Hannah, with no worries and time on her side. A time when work, *real* work, was still far away in the future and every weekend at this time of the year was a beach party in her little lochside village.

The sound of a car horn outside made her jump. The cat looked up, looked at her, then turned towards the door. From the kitchen window she watched Ross whistle his way to the door, which she eagerly opened.

'To what do I owe the pleasure? Can I help you?' he asked, as he stood on the doorstep and watched as a puzzled expression appeared on her face.

'But I...' she began, indicating that it was he who had knocked on her door.

He burst out laughing. 'Your face! I do this to my two all the time – it confuses the hell out of them!' He made his way in carrying a small package and leaned on the worktop by the sink, still chuckling at his joke.

He caught the cat's eyes, gave a whistle and without so much as a stretch, Atlas was out of his bed and bounding over to Ross who was tapping his chest. In one leap, the cat flew up and was gathered into a bundle.

Marcie watched and shook her head.

'Seriously, you two. You need to move in together. It'll only take me five minutes to get his things packed.'

'Nah. Look how settled he is here. Eh, fella?' The cat was purring loudly, headbutting Ross and snuggling into his neck before leaning back, nose twitching.

Marcie watched as Ross pulled a piece of kitchen towel out of its holder and laid it on the worktop. He unwrapped the small parcel one-handed, taking out freshly poached salmon, which the cat started to snatch from his hand before he could place it on the paper towel. 'Hey, big guy! Mossie here not feeding you? You'll fade away to a baby mountain lion at this rate!' He laughed while stroking the cat, and Marcie caught how his eyes crinkled up at the side when he smiled.

She looked away to the cat as he turned.

'That's a big glass for a work night. I presume it is work?' He indicated to her table littered with paper and the carafe and large glass of red liquid beside it.

'It's juice, if you must know. I got it in for your nephew's next picnic but it's a bit addictive.'

'Sugar.'

'I know. I forgot how delicious it is.'

He walked over, after giving his hands a quick run under the tap and wiping with a fresh towel. He picked up the glass and sniffed.

'Jeez, it even smells sweet! Not for me. I'm more of a ginger tea kinda guy.'

'Seriously?'

'Don't really do sugar. Don't really do caffeine.'

'Are you sure you're a Balfour? That whole house down the road runs on sugar.'

'Well, they need their energy, but they'll grow out of it. Dina's a great wholesome cook. I know she slips the veggies in unnoticed and takes out the sugar and replaces it with...' He started to drift off. '*Was*,' he said, correcting himself.

Marcie let out a little gasp, raised her palm to her mouth to cover it and bit her lip. She glanced at the letter propped up on her desk. This sudden jolt back to reality didn't go unnoticed by Ross, and he made his way to her and gave her a hug which caught her by surprise. Surprise at how he had quickly sensed the change in mood and surprise at how engaged with her feelings he appeared to be.

'I'm sorry, it sometimes just catches you.'

She realised he had wrapped her up so quickly and so fast that her arms remained pinned at her sides. She wanted to wriggle out, not to have him release her, but so that she could return this moment by wrapping her arms around him in thanks. *Just thanks?* This was a different hug than from Ruaridh, and she felt herself leaning her head on his chest. She closed her eyes.

'I should have come so much sooner, I realise that now, but I had so much to sort before I...'

She was only half listening. He pulled back, hands on her shoulders and holding her out to look down at her.

'You okay?' he asked, and she nodded, looking up at his concerned face and those eyes. 'Sure?'

She smiled, and he released her, watching as she made her way round to her seat at the table, paperwork strewn across the top. He pulled a seat out opposite her.

'Busy woman,' he observed as his eyes took in the paperwork. 'Work, I take it, nothing to do with the estate?'

'Work, yeah.' She puffed her cheeks out. 'Richard really

deals with everything to do with the estate. I think Cal was glad to leave it behind, to be honest. It's hard going. Even after the sale we still had a lot of land left, and it's all got to be looked after, repairs made, animal considerations. I'm sure I don't have to tell you.' She began sorting the paperwork into piles, coloured sticky notes on top of each one.

'Please do.'

'Well, the new fencing alone costs thousands. Running an estate, these days is like painting the Forth Bridge.'

'A job for Ruaridh?'

'What do you mean?'

'Estate manager.'

'I don't think he's got the time.'

'He'd be better at that than changing bedsheets in those pods he has at the back of the house.'

'Well, looking after the children is a full-time job, and the pods were only to give him and D a bit of extra cash. Plus, there's a lot of facts and figures to keep on top of, not to mention land management, new legislation – keeping on top of *that* is a full-time job, so we...'

'We?'

'Well, me and Cal.'

'And you want to keep it in the family?'

'Well, yes, of course. I think we were too hasty selling Swanfield, particularly now that we know what happened.' She watched as he put his elbows on the table, hands together, fingers entwining.

'What would have happened if it *had* been taken away from you?'

'I don't know what you mean?'

'Well, this other guy and the deal he made with Callum. What if you'd lost everything?'

'I still have my own assets. Things left by my parents that can never be taken away. Ever.'

'Like memories?'

His face was now resting in his hand, a dimpled chin placed on an open palm.

'I don't have many memories of them left.' When she responded, she realised she was mirroring him. Accidental or intentional? While their eyes were locked on one another, she was aware of his shoulders moving up and down and each time they sank she was sure he was going to say something, but he remained silent. This intimate moment was interrupted by the sight of a huge cat leaping onto the table and sliding on paperwork, only to be rescued by Ross as he grabbed it and pulled Atlas towards him before planting a huge kiss on the cat's head with a noisy 'mwah.'

'You're a liability, big fella!' he joked as the cat snuggled into him, parading up and down in front of him, teasing him to get petted once more.

She watched Ross. So alike his brother but so different. There seemed to be a calmness about him that reminded her of Dina. He began to talk to her about animals, the peace they brought him. How he enjoyed practising meditation. How he was no stranger to a yoga or Pilates class when he first moved to the other side of the world, and that he would cause a stir walking into an all-woman session; this big, bearded Scotsman who was clearly in touch with his feminine side. He was still young when he left and needed to find himself, ground himself in a new country. She was fascinated. Ruaridh, surrounded by noise and boys and chaos. And Ross, surrounded by nature and greenery and fascinated by the cosmos.

When he left, after standing at the table and having a one-sided conversation with the cat who looked up at him adoringly, she found herself standing on the threshold, gazing up at the moon. Thousands of stars were visible and shimmering like diamonds on a black velvet sky with no light pollution to dull their dazzling brilliance. *Why had he come back? Why now? Why such an interest in Swanfield out of the blue?* She closed the door, double locked it and left the table strewn with work and research. The cat was sitting on the end of the bed, legs tucked under making him look like a small furry sphynx. She sat down next to him.

'Well, well, well, Atlas,' she said to the cat who remained impassive, clearly already missing his best friend. 'Things are heating up between us and it could go either way. And, of course, I'm meaning you.'

The cat *yammed* in agreement and fell onto his side to sleep.

The next morning, Marcie was only half listening to what was going on around the table in the dining room of The Strathkin Inn. She was unusually fidgety and distant, something that had not gone unnoticed by her friends. She had positioned herself so that she could see the main door on the off chance either Balfour brother might come in. She was tapping her fingers on the table until a glare from Bella made her cease. The four women sat silently, and then Marcie saw three sets of eyes on her. The only problem in that scenario, thought Marcie, was that she had not been listening to a single thing that anyone had said for the past twenty minutes. Her mind was very much distracted, and she took her finger and ran it over her lips. Everyone waited for the response to the question she had failed to hear.

'I'm just going to refresh myself,' she stated, finger in the air, and slid her way out of the banquette, making her way quickly to the ladies' bathroom.

In the mirror, the face reflected at her was one that had hardly slept a wink. *What was happening to her?* She had the concentration of a toddler; her focus was non-existent and when people spoke to her, she watched their mouths as if they were talking in slow motion. She splashed some water on her make-up free skin and made her way back out to the vestibule, where Hannah was standing with a note, ticking things off.

'Hi!' greeted Marcie with a smile, and Hannah returned it. It was clear her normal look of panic had subsided slightly. 'Everything okay?'

Hannah nodded and bent to pick up an open cardboard box that was filled with sandwiches and snacks. She placed it at the back door and re-entered the hotel. Marcie quickly glanced back to see her friends were still engaged in conversation.

'Listen, Hannah, I did a bit of digging last night.'

'Is that what lawyers do?'

'Yes, well, we deal in facts and, well, whatever. Listen, I don't think you have anything to worry about. I got some information about Chester, and I think everything is going to be okay. The police aren't searching for anyone in connection with whatever happened; you're not to blame.'

Hannah stared forward, clearly thinking back on what trauma had befallen her young life.

'Are you okay?' asked Marcie, reaching out to touch her arm. Marcie noticed she was wearing a long-sleeved white T-shirt. She had only ever seen her in black and the light colour suited her beautiful complexion. 'Do you need to contact someone? Did you have a best friend? Just to let them know you're okay?'

Hannah remained quiet.

'I can do it if you like. Say I'm a friend and you're staying with me or something?'

'I can do it. As long as no one is coming after me.'

'No one is coming after you, Hannah. You're fine. I'm sure Heather will want you here if *you* want to stay.'

Hannah was staring into space.

'Will your best friend be worried, do you think?' continued Marcie to the girl who was in a world of her own.

'She's probably not worried,' Hannah conceded.

'What's her name?' Marcie probed.

'Hmm?'

'Your best friend, what's her name?' quizzed Marcie.

Hannah took a moment. 'Claire, Claire McEndoe.'

'Well, why not give Claire a call, say you're okay and then she can pass it on in case anyone is concerned about you? You don't need to say where you are.'

Hannah smiled weakly, folded the piece of paper she had been working with, and put it in the back pocket of her black jeans.

'Thanks,' she said to Marcie and turned to head up the stairs to the staff quarters, throwing her a brief glance as she reached the top.

Marcie turned to look at the glass cabinet behind her, where Hannah had been staring, and the photographs of awards and recognitions in the small village. There was the picture of Heather handing over the Women's Institute Cup to the best baker at last year's village show. And there, centre stage, was Claire McEndoe, holding up her winning Victoria sponge. Marcie glanced up the stairs to where the young woman had been seconds before.

'And what's *your* real name, Hannah Hurley?' she said quietly to herself.

'Aye, aye!' shouted the voice in front of Marcie. Ross was holding up the food-filled cardboard box that had just been left by Hannah at the door. She watched as he loaded it into the open trunk of his Subaru Forrester. Marcie walked out to join him and watched him manoeuvre things around the space where folded chairs were spilling out.

'Off somewhere nice?'

'Taking the boys up to Achmelvich. Dina's mum has taken the wee one. Himself has got some guests arriving at the pods again this weekend so he needs a bit of time to get organised. Is that wee lassie still here? Think she could do with some extra dosh? He's great at the heavy stuff but a bit clumsy around the girlie stuff, if you know what I mean? You know, the wee touches that make a return visit more likely.' Ross slammed the door shut firmly, and a nod of the head let his sunglasses slide from his forehead back down over his eyes. 'The big fella's settling in, I see?' he stated, leaning against the car door.

'My only complaint about the guy? Place is awash with dead animals, so I think he's paying his way.'

'Must pay him another visit. Man-to-man chat,' he joked, and Marcie laughed as she watched his mouth open in a wide smile. She felt her tongue run over her lips.

'You're welcome anytime, just give me a bit of notice so that I can get something in. A vegan platter washed down with gallons of hibiscus tea! But really, thanks for coming up, I think I just needed a bit of company.'

'Nah, You're okay. And forget the food, you've always got cake in that freezer. That's what we Balfours had as our first solids! Here, Mossie, just a thought. I think I've outgrown Lubnaig,' he said, about the cottage he had been gifted as free accommodation by his childhood friend.

'Outgrown?' she quizzed.

'Any chance I could move to Marchwood?'

'Well, of course, but it's more rundown and a bit further away... didn't your dad live there at one point when he was working that far out on the estate? I suppose it's okay.'

'Listen, I said in lieu of rent I'm happy to do any of the work. I've already fixed the fireplace at Lubnaig. Full of old bird's nests. Had a great fire going the other night. I could steal a couple of bits of the furniture from Stratheyre, too, and do a wee bit of repair work.'

'When were you up at Stratheyre?' she asked, thinking it quite odd he hadn't mentioned it to her the previous night when he seemed so engrossed with the current events surrounding the wider Swanfield Estate.

'I was just out for a run in the car. When I get back down the road, I'll have a good look around, eh?'

'Sure thing,' she agreed, and she saw beneath his sunglasses he gave her an exaggerated wink. *You're so Balfour. Your father and grandfather in their younger days must have been absolute charmers*, she thought, and wandered back into the hotel where she met Maureen heading to the dining room.

'Don't see it meself,' she said just a little bit too loud as she gave Marcie a glance.

Marcie shook her head. *Me neither*, said her internal voice as a seed of suspicion was planted in her mind while her heart was beating faster than a drum.

TWENTY

Heather was as thrilled as she could be to escape the confines of the hotel, the stifling nature of small village life. Her drive with Jamie had been full of laughter and reminiscences, both knowing each other so well. He had packed a picnic and, as they drove through the spectacular scenery near the sea, she had no idea where they were headed. He had turned off at Ullapool and took plenty of stops at the passing places before reaching the secluded beach of Gruinard Bay. With the Coigach Hills to one side and Gruinard Island in front of them, she had forgotten this secluded part of the coast – not too far, but far enough, from Strathkin. He had a backpack and a cool box and grasped her hand as they climbed to the top of the dunes that led down onto fine white sand and to the crystal-clear waters of the ocean. It was a beautiful cloud-free sky that sat above them. Jamie spread out the picnic before he sat down on a folding chair as Heather lay down on the blanket, letting the sun warm her pale skin.

'Aw, this is amazing,' she sighed, 'utter bliss.' Far away from the prying eyes of The Strathkin Inn, they could have been on a deserted Greek island, so isolated they were from prying eyes and so warm was the sun above them.

'Do you want to go for a walk?'

'Nope,' came the answer.

'A swim?'

'Not a chance.'

'Something else to eat?'

'I just want to wallow in the fact that I'm not on my feet listening to Fraser MacRae talk about that house he's doing up over at Strath Aullt. Honestly, you think Maureen repeats herself, I've heard his story a million times. I just want quiet and solitude. Just the sound of the sea.'

'I'm going for a dip,' stated Jamie, standing up and peeling off his light fleece, revealing a pale but firm body already dressed in swim shorts. Heather opened her eyes and cast them over her *date*. She was pleasantly surprised at what lay beneath the dark uniform she was used to seeing him in. She purred. He ran down to the water, over the cool powder sand and dived in as the waves hit the shore. The Caribbean Sea this was not, and it took him some moments to adjust to the icy water that engulfed him, then wallowing in the fact it was only slightly colder than Loch Strathkin. She leaned up on her elbows watching Jamie swim out and then float back in, and part of her wished she had slipped into her wild water swimming costume – well, wetsuit – while she debated her last-minute outfit. She had settled on a floaty maxi-dress, as she knew Jamie would be used to seeing her in her workwear outfit of jeans and a T-shirt or occasional sweater. She leaned into the backpack and took out a microfibre towel when she eventually saw him make his way back to the dunes. She stood up and wrapped him in it while he tried to splash her with water, and this time it was Heather who took to the chair while he lay down on the towel and wool blanket to dry himself off in the warmth of the sun.

They waited for a moment in silence, the sound of the Atlantic Ocean beyond mesmerising them for a while.

'Nice seeing Ross back, isn't it?'

'Hmm,' sighed Jamie.

'Must be a great comfort to Ruaridh to have his big brother around,' she went on.

'Aye.'

'I keep thinking, imagine just upping sticks at such a young age – I mean, he was still a teenager – never knowing if you're going to see your family again. There were all sorts of rumours, of course, you must remember them. His father told him to leave; do you remember that one? We never did find out. Could be that he just wanted to get away, all that *bright lights, big city* stuff.'

Jamie ignored the suggestion.

'So much village gossip, as per,' said Heather.

'I think it was always his intention to come back at some point,' stated Jamie, in defence of his friend.

'Why now, though? Is he here to make amends or rekindle old friendships? Is he here for good? Have you asked him?'

Jamie chose not to answer.

'And why not for the funeral?' pondered Heather.

'Some people can't get last minute time off,' replied Jamie, rolling over on to his stomach to prop himself up on his elbows.

'Well, I mean, it wasn't as though it was unexpected,' stated Heather, and then, shocked, she raised her hand to her mouth, aghast at what she had just said. 'I don't believe I just said that.' She sat up in the chair. 'What was I thinking? What a horrible thing to say,' she went on, her hand over her mouth as if it would take the words, scrunch them up, and throw them into the wind for them to never be repeated.

Jamie hauled himself up and stood in front of her, urging her to do the same, and she did so. He wrapped his arms around her, hoping that he could squeeze the pain of her friend's loss out of her. She wanted to cry but she also wanted this moment to go on. She had always thought of Jamie as nothing more than a good and dependable friend, and here he was showing her he was, in fact, her knight in shining armour. When he released her slightly, it was Heather who leaned in for a kiss. They stood in the dunes of a beautiful beach, wrapped in each other's arms and with all thoughts of nosy, gossipy, village chatter a lifetime away. And it was Heather again who gently started to pull a still-wet Jamie down onto the damp blanket to warm him up.

It was Heather who initiated the hand holding on the drive back, hair full of sand and a head full of memories of wasted time and promises to come. They laughed about what they had done and reminisced about their childhood. It was the best day Heather could remember in a long time and although she wanted desperately to share it with her girlfriends, part of her wanted to keep this new romance with Jamie a secret for just a little while more so that they could nurture their private moments together. In the driver's seat of the Ascot Grey BMW X-5, Jamie was only half listening to Heather and wondering when he should tell her of his imminent promotion to sergeant that might pull him away from Strathkin and from her. He also knew there was something he had to do that night before suggesting if he could stay over at the Inn. He just hoped it would work out as planned.

While joy was breaking out as a car sped to the beach further west, two women were chatting animatedly outside the stables in Strathkin.

'I knew it was something!' said Bella, hands wrapped around a chipped cup of tea. 'It was as if she deliberately wanted to come here, didn't I say that? I mean, nobody pulls out a map and sticks a pin in here!'

She and Marcie were sitting on the bench that overlooked

Strathkin Loch at the end of the stable yard, well wrapped in fleeces as a cool wind blew. 'Don't say anything, don't let on,' encouraged Marcie after she had disclosed information about Hannah. But not everything, obviously. 'She's clearly still in shock about what has gone on before, her boyfriend deciding he'd make more money out of her as an OnlyFans model, not that I even know what it all means. But I think she and Dax have a wee thing going on, which is lovely to see. D would be delighted.'

'So, what about Ross being back?' asked Bella. 'What's all that about?'

'Dunno, kind of out of the blue.' Marcie picked up the mug again as a distraction and busied herself with the tea leaves, swirling them around.

'Nothing Ross Balfour ever did was out of the blue. He was always a planner, unless he's had a complete change of personality.'

'That's a bit harsh!'

'Did you say he was staying at Lubnaig?'

Marcie nodded a response.

'I was out with Pebbles. Saw him up near Broomfield.'

'He's a bit of a walker and a runner... very fit.' Marcie was aware she was beginning to make excuses, but her mind began to wonder why Ross was visiting all the cottages and crofts on the estate like he was in a modern-day version of *Goldilocks and the Three Bears*. Her finger moved to outline her lips. 'I think he was on a hunt for furniture and stuff.'

'Hmmm.'

'It's great for Ruaridh having him here. He's a lot more his old self.'

'Hmmm.'

Marcie looked at Bella and a thought flashed through her mind. *A potential.* Bella was looking out to the loch and thinking hard. *You're thinking of asking him out*, thought Marcie.

'I wonder how long he's planning on staying,' Bella mused, and Marcie was about to speak when she heard someone shout behind them. Heather was walking up to her friends, swinging her basket bag, and smiling broadly.

'What am I missing?' she asked, beaming.

'Just talking about the old days,' said Bella by way of diversion. 'How was the big day out?'

'Great, we went up to Gruinard.'

Marcie stood up and crossed her arms in front of her as if she were repelling her friend.

'I hope you've been decontaminated!' she joked, referring to the biological weapons testing that took place on the island of Gruinard, effectively making the stunning area a no-go zone for almost eighty years.

'She might have been decontaminated, but it's left her with a stupid grin on her face,' said Bella, noticing her friend's suddenly very sunny demeanour. Heather walked around them and sat down on a large, flat-topped rock in front of the bench and sighed.

'It was lovely. You know the best bit?'

'Oh, do tell?' said Bella, eyebrows raised.

'Just getting away from here! Knowing that no one is going to see you and then it is all around the village like wildfire. Sometimes it's like living in a goldfish bowl in wee Strathkin. I'm not surprised Ross left, to be honest.'

'Tru dat,' said Bella and emptied out what was left of her tea on to the grass.

'That's why I'm not sure it's going to work,' continued Heather.

'Not sure what's going to work?' asked Marcie.

'You might be right,' agreed Bella.

'I don't know what you're talking about.'

'What Angelina is proposing in her letter?' said Heather, turning to her friend who had returned to sit on the bench. Marcie shrugged her shoulders.

'What is *wrong* with you?' asked Bella. 'We were all there. Mrs B read out the letter!'

'I'm just a bit distracted.'

'You do know Maureen has a name for it?' said Bella, sitting back, arm over the back of the bench.

'A name for what?'

'For what you've got?'

'Pray tell,' sighed Marcie.

'Balfouritis.'

'*Balfouritis?*'

'Yup. I think she's right. I'm in two minds about which one it is...'

'What *are* you on about?'

'Oh, yes!' agreed Heather, nodding. 'I can see where that's coming from.'

'Mostly Lochside Croft if you ask me,' said Bella, with a knowing nod to Heather.

'I do not have *Balfouritis*! Ruaridh and I have always had an understanding.'

'About which buttons to press?' asked Heather jokingly and waited for Bella to join in.

'Moving on...' began Marcie, keen to change the subject before she was drawn in to revealing the true state of her relationship with Ruaridh.

'Well, the Angelina stuff is quite apposite, no?'

'I honestly wasn't listening. I've no idea what she's proposing in her letter,' confessed Marcie.

Both Heather and Bella made a tunnel with their hands over their mouth and whispered the word *Balfouritis* to each other.

'Honestly, you two are acting like children. Get over it!'

'Women's refuge,' stated Bella. 'She wants to rebuild Swanfield, well, The Retreat, make it a women's refuge.'

'Seriously?'

'You really were zoned out,' stated Bella with a shake of the head to her friend.

'Well, Maureen starts a conversation then drifts off into a past life and was doodling little flowers and you didn't even stop her droning on.'

'You do know she was trafficked?'

Marcie shook her head at Heather's statement and was about to ask *who?* before she realised that there was only one person they could have been talking about. Her thoughts were preoccupied with matters of the heart when they should have focused, like her friends, on the fears and concerns shared by women worldwide.

'Modern slavery? Heard of that?' suggested Bella sarcastically, and Marcie made a face at her friend. 'She was a sex worker in the Philippines when she met *Shrimp de Groot* and he took her back to Amsterdam. Instead of putting her to work, he put her into recruitment. Turns out he was making a fortune running all over Amsterdam before he decided to go into the despatching market.'

It was true that Louis de Groot, Angelina's husband, had seen a gap in the market for a swift despatch to a better life elsewhere that could be a lucrative way to make a vast income. The provision being only if you could afford it and sign over vast parts of your wealth to ensure you had the most perfect of happy endings. But shrewd as she was, Angelina put most of the property and profit into her name, telling the good doctor that if anything untoward was ever found, he could not be seen to be profiting from it in any way. It was in trust and overseas shell companies where double invoicing was the norm. Whilst some of the money did come from legitimate business and property investments, Angelina had made sure that a careful skimming of the enormous profits was going to be put away and, at some point, put to good use. And, as Angelina had detailed in her letter, in this case the perfect escape for those in desperate need like she had been years before.

Marcie stared at her friend in astonishment.

'What were we talking about earlier?' she asked of Bella with reference to their conversation about Hannah.

'Exactly,' she agreed, 'and clearly you weren't listening to a thing that had gone before.'

Marcie admitted she had been distracted and had paid no attention to the conversation at the Inn.

'She's got an architect, plans, the lot.'

'Crikey,' said Heather in astonishment.

'You were there, too! What is *wrong* with you guys?' asked Bella.

'Got a lot on my mind,' apologised Heather as Bella stood up, leaned over to Heather and pulled something from her hair.

'Seaweed?' she queried, and Heather appeared embarrassed. She covered her mouth with her hand and gave a small giggle.

'You didn't?' asked Marcie to her friend who let out another stifled chuckle before nodding.

'Spill!' demanded Bella with a pointed finger.

'Lovely!' beamed Heather, her face glowing a tinge of pink.

'What did I tell you when he kept coming up on Plenty of Fish? I told you to take a chance... all this time you've wasted?' stated Bella.

'Well, it wasn't exactly wasted,' Heather responded. 'Sometimes we get a nice guest.'

The three women grinned at each other before bursting out laughing at the statement, and for a moment Marcie thought about throwing her discussion with Ruaridh into the mix before deciding to keep her own counsel and tuck it away in the compartment of her mind that she kept only for herself.

'Dina kept telling me to make the first move, so, finally I did.' Heather was smiling like the cat who had got the cream.

Marcie gazed at her friend and the look of joy on her face. *Dina Balfour, what else have you got up your heavenly sleeve?*

Jamie was pleased with himself when he dropped off Heather at the stables for her catch-up with her friends. It had taken a long time to get to where they ended up today, but it was well worth it. He had pursued her relentlessly at a distance and while he was resolute in his work life, his personal life had always been in disarray. Failed relationships that did not last because his mind was only ever on one prize, and now that he had reached his goal, he metaphorically patted himself on the back at his achievement.

Heather McLeod had made him dizzy from their first day at school, but he was shy and hid behind the bravado of the Balfour boys as he grew up. During his school days, if he wasn't out on his quad bike from morning until noon, it was only because he was sitting next to Ross as he drove his father's tractor. The two were inseparable. Shy Jamie looked up to cocky Ross like the big brother he never had, and they would do anything for each other. Anything.

Which was why Jamie found himself at the police office searching for information on something that happened long, long ago. He noted things down on a piece of paper he had taken from the printer, and when he had finished, he folded the paper away. It had taken an age to scroll through dates and times, but he was confident in what he had found and felt relieved when he traced what he had been searching for. He had erased it from his mind a long time ago when he had decided to pursue a career in the police force – something that came as a surprise to his family and friends, except maybe for Ross. Jamie had stolen cars, wrecked cars and souped up cars in equal measure. It was only a visit from the local community constable for a sit-down reprimand in the presence of his mother and father and, worse, *his granny*, that made Jamie decide to change his ways. If you want to drive cars at excessive speed and not be arrested there was only one thing to do, said the local bobby – join the police, and particularly the road policing department. Jamie pursued his dream, made the grade in every respect, and found himself on the A9, patrolling in the fastest cars he could imagine, and detecting people doing exactly what he had done in his formative years. Once out of his system and considering himself a grown-up, he asked to be sent to the place of his birth, to be their community constable, where he could protect and look after the very people he had driven to distraction in his younger days. He was an exemplary officer, about to be promoted, and with that was the very worst thing imaginable in Jamie's mind – to be posted somewhere else. What if he was posted to a big city, a violent city, a city with no moral compass? A place where he was not cock of the walk but another frazzled police officer running from job to job and in danger of not solving anything. It did not fill him with joy, more like dread. But if he wanted to succeed and show his new girl-friend that he had a future, that *they* had a future, he had to, as his tutor at college recently told him, suck it up.

He left the police office, switched the alarm back on and made his way out to the car parked outside, so caught up in his future romantic endeavours, he hadn't realised that each keystroke of his computer had recorded his every move. And when he had switched off the alarm – the CCTV both inside and outside the office was whirring away in the background and sending every image back to a central depository where it could be scrutinised and audited at the touch of a button.

TWENTY-ONE

When Marcie finally made it home, fed the cat and sat down at her kitchen table, she thought about the secrets that she kept tucked away and hidden. She poured a glass of *real* wine this time and sat with her feet on the empty cat basket. Atlas was now comfortable enough to venture out to explore his new surroundings on his own and enjoy himself by catching anything that crawled, flew, or mistakenly ambled into his path. She opened the wide door of the tall wooden wardrobe and reached into the back to take out a new black tin box that had *personal* engraved on the front. Climbing up onto the bed, she began to sift through the contents. In it she found her birth certificate and wedding certificate, which she ran her fingers across and folded neatly back into its envelope then took out other paperwork. The plans for Swanfield were next and then another envelope with another birth certificate. She carefully opened the paper as she had done before and pushed the pillows high up against the headboard to get more comfortable. Once again, she ran her finger across the name and studied it carefully.

'Secrets and lies,' she said to herself, but still could not make out clearly what had been written between the lines on the long piece of paper. She set it to one side and picked up another that was the sale of Lochside Croft to the Balfours. It was for a few hundred pounds, and she remembered the last time she saw it, thinking of the cost of the croft now and what it would have been then. She slipped off the bed and went through to the living room where her laptop was sitting on a small table in the corner. She picked it up and returned to the bedroom once again, shuffling herself up to sit against the pillows, and searched for house prices in the Highlands in 1969, the year of the transfer of the house. Clearly everyone was friends and neighbours but still the house was sold for considerably less than its market value. She pondered this while running her finger over her lips.

'Why would they do that?' she asked herself. 'There must have been a compulsive reason?' The paperwork in the tin had been carefully sorted. It even held the fake marriage certificate of her Uncle Callum, and she quickly glanced at her watch for today's date – she would call him tomorrow. It was so easy for days and dates to blend into one another when you were not confined by a work diary. She was tapping on her laptop, fingers rapping, when she started concocting a plan. She would see Ruaridh in the morning. He had an *empty*, a Scottish term for no adults at home, when the children of the house would run riot at a party. This time it was the opposite way around. She would visit asking about some long-lost information. He would be on his own. Quiet solitude. She would even take breakfast. She gathered up the paperwork carefully, except the one piece of paperwork she was trying to decipher. She needed something to see it more clearly. She had a lightbulb moment. She needed a magnifying glass, and she knew exactly where she would get one of them – out of the toy box at Lochside Croft.

. . .

The morning brought open doors and open windows at Tigh-na-Lochan. Warm smells were meandering out to the cat with the twitching nose sitting on the armrest of the Adirondak chair situated near the small pond of water. Marcie was not exactly known for her cooking skills, but baking was another matter. Brought up from a small age at the apron of her grandmother, she could pull together the most delicious scones and cakes with next to no ingredients. And bread was one of her most favourite things to bake due to the fact she could knead and knead and knead a loaf to get her frustrations out after a heavy week at work. Weekends were her favourite times to bake, and she had now mastered the no knead, no prove bread that could be thrown together in no time at all with just four ingredients: flour, water, yeast and salt. This morning was no exception. She let the bread prove for the briefest time while she showered and baked it just before she left so that when she arrived at Lochside Croft it would still be warm. While it was in the oven, she searched her pantry for homemade jam, settling on blackcurrant, and put a slab of Orkney butter in the basket. Now inside, Atlas watched this gathering of goods take place from his new position on top of a pile of books at the end of the long wooden table. 'Have I forgotten anything?' she asked in his general direction, and he *yammed* back at her. 'No, I don't want to put in a bottle of Prosecco – we're over that, Atlas, that door has firmly closed,' she replied to the furry butler. Once everything was ready, she put a large red and white napkin over the basket and checked herself in the mirror at the door.

'Don't wait up,' she shouted to the cat as she pulled the door shut and placed the basket into the back seat of the car for the journey back down the single-track road and into Strathkin. She drove very slowly, telling herself that it was precious cargo in the back, and then realised she would have to drive around the back of the Trekking Centre, hoping that Bella would still be in the tack room or, as it was still relatively early, be breakfasting with her unexpectedly permanent houseguest, Maureen.

She parked next to Ruaridh's Land Rover and glanced over the water to Swanfield. She took a deep breath, steeling herself for the moment that lay ahead, and approached the door, noticing a wool blanket still lying on the blue bench that sat beneath the living room window. She knocked twice and then turned the handle.

Nothing.

She tried the handle again.

Nothing.

The house that was always open, suddenly had a locked door.

She stepped back, basket over her arm, and peered up to the bedroom window. It was slightly ajar as it always was, so she approached the door again just as it opened with a sharp pull. It was unclear who got the bigger fright – Marcie at the sight of Arshia Brahmins or the doctor at the sight of a woman dressed up and in full make-up at barely nine thirty on a Saturday morning.

'Oh,' they both said simultaneously.

'I'm so sorry,' apologised Arshia, 'I couldn't find the key.'

She beamed a broad smile while the early morning visitor continued to stand on the step with a gaping mouth in shock until Arshia pulled the door back.

'Do come in,' she offered, and Marcie tentatively stepped into Lochside Croft. Remnants of the previous evening's meal were scattered around with a full wine glass on the table in front of the sofa and an empty one on the draining board next to a freshly made French press of rich smelling coffee from the artisan coffee roasters in Beauly. A basket of crackers was still in the centre of the coffee table, and a block of parmesan was slowly sweating on the dining table with a cheese slice atop it.

Marcie was speechless.

She heard a noise upstairs and immediately thought of an excuse to leave as Arshia closed the door behind her.

'I've just made coffee.' She smiled and turned to push down the plunger on the cafetière while Marcie noticed she was wearing a plaid shirt of Ruaridh's.

She stood aghast and was at a loss of what to say, her mind working quickly to think of a reason for the early morning visit.

'I just stopped by to drop these off. Did a bit of overbaking so I'm delivering around the village this morning,' Marcie lied with a fake smile and with the only excuse she could come up with at such short notice. She heard the stairs creaking behind her and didn't want to turn around. She was still thinking of something to say when Ruaridh appeared at her side.

'Morning, Mars,' he said calmly as he moved past her, a vision in a tight pink fluffy nightgown, a favourite of his late wife. 'Are you staying for coffee?'

She was astounded at his casualness in the circumstances and declined his offer.

'I'm on my way to Bella's – just dropping something off,' she said by way of an excuse.

'Didn't you drive past hers to get to here?'

'Meant to say Heather...' she corrected and reached out with the basket, and he took it from her, pulling back the gingham napkin to reveal its contents.

'Blackcurrant! My favourite.' He smiled, holding up the jar to show Arshia.

'Ooh, homemade!' squealed Arshia, and they then stood like three statues in the kitchen for a moment.

'Well, better get a move on! I'm like the Salvation Army this morning!' Marcie pulled the door open and pretended she was busily feeding the village. 'Enjoy, people!' she joked and made her way out to the car with Ruaridh and Arshia both shouting their thanks for the breakfast delivery.

. . .

Marcie sat in the car for a moment, gathering her thoughts, then drove back to the Trekking Centre, where Bella was in the middle of the courtyard directing Rosie, her stable girl, to tack up ponies for a Saturday morning trek with guests coming from the Inn. She was astonished to see Marcie so early, so well dressed and so made-up.

'Are you just arriving back from a night out or on your way somewhere?' asked Bella with a chuckle.

'Gawd, I need a drink!'

'What's up, doll?' asked Bella of her startled-looking friend.

'I've just been at Lochside,' Marcie said as she followed Bella into the office, and where she switched on the kettle.

'What a dawg!' said Bella, nudging her friend as she gathered up two mugs, sniffed both, and sat them next to the kettle. 'I want every gory detail!'

'Oh no, no, no.'

Marcie watched as Bella poured the water and sank a tea bag into one of the mugs for a moment before rescuing it and plunging it into the second mug. 'Economy drive,' she stated by way of an excuse. She took both mugs to the bench outside the office facing the courtyard and handed Marcie the weaker of the two.

'Oh, and there's no milk,' offered Bella as Marcie blew on the black tea. 'Right, let's get down to the nitty gritty – how long has it been and was it as good? No holds barred.'

Marcie sat the mug on the arm of the bench.

'I went over this morning...'

'Ooh, *thexy*, what are you wearing under that expensive Barbour jacket?' joked Bella with eyes opened wide.

'He wasn't alone.'

'Ross there?' Bella raised her eyebrows and made a face.

'Nopes.'

'Ah...' sighed Bella and took a sip of tea. 'Arshia?'

Marcie sat back. 'Now how in the heck did you know that?'

'Maureen. She's trying to set them up. Thinks of herself as a bit of a Strathkin Dolly Levy.'

'What?' asked Marcie as Bella put her arm on the arm rest and rested her face in her palm.

'To be frank, Mars, I thought you were over Ruaridh.'

'Well, he's certainly over me.' She stood up and walked into the stable yard, pacing, before coming back to her friend. 'Oh, I don't know. It's like I'm lost, Bells. It's like I'm lurching from one thing to another. My life is being stretched in so many directions I've no idea where I'm going to end up. I mean, he did come over the other day...'

'Spill.'

'Well, we had the *breakup chat*, but I don't know what it is. It's like as soon as someone says I can't have something, I need to have it.'

'I know the feeling. I'm the same with Maltesers.'

'I'm not being funny, Bells!'

'Neither am I!' Bella giggled and then realised that Marcie was being very serious. 'Soz.'

'It's okay. Just didn't think he'd move on so quickly, that's all. Hashtag miffed.' Marcie was trying to make light of the situation but miffed didn't even cover how she was feeling. She'd always thought that at some point she and Ruaridh would either couple up or close that door, and it was clear that door was now firmly shut. Deep down, however, she knew she didn't want that finality. But what exactly was happening to her? Was she keeping Ruaridh in the forefront of her mind because she didn't want to admit what was actually happening to her? *The spark when they first touched. The holding of a gaze. Circling each other like animals.* She shook her head to bring her back to reality.

'Maybe D told him to move on, and it's only just registered. You know how Roo doesn't like change.'

'Roo?' queried Marcie.

'Och, it's Mrs B's pet name for him. They get on like a house on fire, that pair. Ever since he saved her life... which I hear about on an almost daily basis.' Bella raised her eyes to the sky. 'And H and I thought you had moved on.'

'Hmmm.'

'I mean, you're fluttering about that German guest like a needy butterfly.'

'A what?'

'I don't know why you can't just settle. I mean, now Simon's out of the picture... he is, isn't he?'

'Definitely.'

'Just give yourself some time to come to terms with it. It's a big loss in your life so soon after D.'

'D said I was mean to him.'

'When? Well, you must admit you were a bit tough.'

'Last time we had a proper chat. She questioned why I married him.'

'Well, we all did, to be fair?'

'What? Why am I hearing this now?'

'I mean, don't get me wrong, we all thought Simon was a nice guy, but he always seemed a bit...'

Marcie waited while Bella searched for the right words that were not going to end the conversation in a shouting match.

'Compliant.'

'Compliant?'

'You know what I mean. You like a good debate and are so interested in everyone and everything that's going on and Simon, well, he just seemed to agree and go along for...'

'An easy ride?'

'I was going to say a quiet life.'

Annoyed as she was, Marcie knew that Bella was right. Simon settled in for a quiet life too early in the relationship, and whilst at the start he loved her strong and determined nature, his persuasive Italian mother told him that it was not how she expected her daughter-in-law to act. *Give her a child*, was the answer to all his woes according to his mother, but according to Marcie that was the last thing on her mind at that moment in time. They had grown apart quickly after their marriage, and their regular Sunday mornings of loving and laughing and walking and ending up in a local pub, quickly moved into a monthly routine then the routine stopped altogether. She threw herself into work and him into his gastro pub. He began to say she was spending too much money, not spending enough time at home, spending too much time in the office, didn't see his parents enough, they needed to go to his home in Yorkshire to visit more. Then he began to complain that she only changed into the Marcie he fell in love with when she was back in the Highlands. And finally, when he was nearly killed at the hands of Poytr Medvedev, his mother blamed her for his breakdown. He was too sensitive for her, complained the only Mrs Grainger who really mattered in his life before *she* was shut out. Then Marcie began to question if she ever truly loved him. She wanted to look after him and protect him, but was it really love or just a keen fondness that had got out of hand because everyone else was getting married and she had to be seen to be doing the right thing? She did not want people to think she had hurt him or, as Dina had said, had been mean to him. But she did want people to know that theirs had been a two-way process, and she simply hadn't discarded him like an old piece of unloved clothing.

'I'd better get going, see to the cat.' Marcie stood up, stretched and handed Bella her mug.

'Cat? When did you get a cat?'

'Ross got him for me.'

'Ross Balfour?' queried Bella.

'Of course. How many Ross's do you know?'

'Quite a few actually. Ross McFarland, Ross Harkins, Ross Lipscombe. They were all at school with us! But you only had eyes for one at school and I don't remember it being anyone called Ross.' Marcie had a little giggle at Bella's comment, red in the face.

'*Balfouritis.*' Bella laughed out loud at Marcie's expense, and she was about to come down with a classic put down when they were interrupted.

'Keep the noise down, you two, would ya?' Maureen complained as she came out of the house in a black velour dressing gown and black and white leopard print pyjama bottoms, feet in fluffy slippers.

'Mars has just found out about Ruaridh and Arshia,' sighed Bella.

'Oh, right, sorry about that, love,' said Maureen as Marcie raised her eyes skywards. 'But you know, my Brian always said "what's for you won't"—'

'Go past you,' finished Bella, silently mouthing 'help me!'

'No, I don't think that's it. "What's for you…" What's that old sayin' – it's on the tip of me tongue?'

'I'm outta here!' said Marcie and turned, heading back to her car and the drive to Tigh-na-Lochan.

It was on the drive there that she decided to detour and head to Lubnaig Cottage. On arrival, it appeared empty and deserted, as she expected. When she parked outside and peered in the windows, it was clearly unlived in. The front door was locked but the back door, as usual, was open – what she referred to as the Strathkin phenomenon. She wandered around, taking in the uprooted floorboards and peeled walls and realised that Ross must have made a start on repairs as promised before he decided on the move to Marchwood across the glen. She checked all the rooms, noticing some of the furniture had clearly been removed and decided instead to make her way to the other croft.

It was on the other side of the long road, and she was both pleased and surprised when she noticed Ross's car parked outside Marchwood. *Back from Achmelvich so soon,* she thought. A fresh pile of logs had been cut and were stacked at the side of the house in a newly built log store. An old dressing table and two chairs from Lubnaig sat perched against the wall, stripped and sanded and awaiting either painting or rewaxing. She nodded her approval and knocked the door. There was no answer. She peered through the window and knocked again. When there was no answer a second time, she tried the handle, and the door opened effortlessly. Like the other croft, the floors had been uprooted, and the old wood piled up against the wall in two groups – one clearly for disposal and ones for saving. Sheets of old plasterboard lay across the wide-open spaces for people to walk carefully across, and pallets of new wood were laid out in a corner. An ancient armchair sat by the open fire which had been cleaned and emptied ready for a new fire to be built when required. A distressed pine table was in front of the long kitchen, if it could be called a kitchen, with the sink being held up by two posts and a bedside table with a basin upturned next to it. A new packet of paper kitchen towels sat in their plastic alongside a camping stove with an old pot. As there was no electricity to the house and barely running water, this was clearly how Ross was cooking and living. Having not been this far into the old Swanfield Estate for such a long time, she was shocked at how the place had been left to go to rack and ruin, and as she walked through the empty house, her mind was ticking over. She leaned on the door lintel and looked back into the room. Her mind drifted back to the long conversations with Dina as mood boards and colour charts would be laid out on the long table at Sweet Briar. Each property was to be similar, but individual, and a colour palette was agreed for each croft. Soft muted teal and blue here, earthy brown and gold there. They had visited each place in turn and at different times of the day to see the casting of the light and the way the shadows fell. On their evening visits, Dina would gaze up at the sky and tell Marcie about the people who would visit and the special time they would share with loved ones, creating memories to look back on. Now it was different but if Angelina was determined to spend her money wisely and take young and not so young women out of disastrous and abusive marriages and relationships filled with hidden violence and coercive control, it could be that these derelict cottages on what was land and property that she still owned, could be put to good use as well as the big house. When she had toured the property, she wished, once again, that Dina was with her, filling her head with ideas and plans about how the house could look with an injection of cash and her keen eye for design. The house would not be flashy but comfortable and restful with a vegetable patch outside and an address very few would know. She now leaned on the only part of the kitchen that was held together with an old piece of rotting worktop and glanced to the old battered black tin that was closed and next to her. She opened it with some caution and trepidation and with a sideways glance in case some rodent or worse slithered out. Inside were old pieces of paperwork, yellow newspaper clippings and letters. She picked one up and saw it was addressed to Flora Balfour, Ross's and Ruaridh's mother, which she thought was quite odd. Sifting through the box she saw that many of them were all similarly addressed, except for those addressed to Ross Balfour at an address first in Australia's Northern Territories and then at Post Box numbers in New Zealand. 'How odd,' she heard herself say aloud and wondered both why they were there and why they were sitting out in a distant cottage that very few knew about. Nosiness or curiosity or both took over and she opened a random envelope. It was obvious it had already been opened and read, so she simply absorbed the information it contained: mundane chatter between mother and son. What was happening on the farm that ran adjacent to Lochside Croft and what Ross's brothers had been up to since he left. It was a regular letter until the end which had a plea to come home and to please write. The next letter contained similar information and ended the same way. General chitchat about who had passed away, who had moved on and who had moved in. This letter was mostly recalling a small electrical fire at The Strathkin Inn which was put out by those patrons still at the bar during a *lock*-in and the luck that three of the customers were members of the retained Fire Service, so it was put out in swift time and festivities resumed immediately. Marcie laughed – it was so like Strathkin, she said to herself. The next letter was from Ross. Again, general words and text about his move to New Zealand having been offered a job on the South Island and not to worry if he did not write for a few weeks or so, he would be busy. She swiftly went through the rest of the box. 'Really odd,' she felt herself saying aloud again and picked up a handful of letters, closed the box and moved to the seat by the fire. She was disturbed by the sound of someone outside scraping boots and, in a panic, she shoved the letters she had taken from the box into her back pocket. She had no idea why she had done this except for a sudden fear about being found somewhere remote without an invitation and going through someone's personal property. She hurriedly went to the door to the small hall and bathroom so that when the person came into the room, it would appear as if she had just come from the back of the house.

'Ah!' greeted Ross. 'Thought that was your car outside.'

'Just arrived!' said Marcie a little bit too hurriedly.

'Oh, aye...' he said, eyeing her with some suspicion.

'I was down in the village and just decided to pay you a visit on the way back.'

'Bit early for a welfare check,' he said, glancing at his watch. 'It's not yet eleven.'

'I was up really, really early. Did a bit of baking, made some deliveries.'

'Great! I'm starving,' said Ross and made his way over to the camping stove.

'Sorry, I didn't bring anything. Delivered to the village!'

'Oh,' he sighed, disappointed, and held up a tea bag and a sachet of coffee, 'because this is all I have here. If you're on the hunt for anything to eat, you're a day too late.'

'I might have something,' said Marcie quickly and made her way gingerly through the mess, edging her way to the front door and outside to where her car was parked, carefully walking with her face to him so that he could not see the letters she had stuffed into her back pocket. She opened the boot where there was a box of provisions she had collected on her last trip to Inverness and which she had kept in the car for just this type of emergency. Tea bags, a jar of expensive coffee, UHT milk, and a packet of a supermarket's *Finest* chocolate cookies. She gathered them up in one hand and with the other had removed the letters and placed them in her box of shopping bags so that they would be hidden and unseen. She took her booty back into the house with a broad smile, and Ross returned it as she gifted him the haul.

'Well, this will keep me going until at least September!' he joked and filled up the old pot with water from the very dodgy, loose tap. He held up the box of tea bags and the jar of coffee. She pointed to the coffee, and his eyes searched around in vain for a spare cup.

'Got another solution!' Marcie quickly said and ran back to the car where she kept her reusable coffee cup which, as usual, had been cleaned and washed since its last use. She helped him make the coffee and opened the packet of luxury chocolate cookies which were her guilty pleasure.

'I'd invite you to take a seat but there is only one, as you can see.'

'It's nice outside?' she suggested.

She glanced at the tin box, as did Ross, and they made their way to the old rickety bench seat that had been placed underneath the living room window. They gazed out to the mountain range that sat like a perfect painting in front of them.

'Not sure if it'll take the two of us, but we can try,' he said as they gingerly sat down on the bench that creaked a little but held them both. They drank their coffee in silence, him sitting close enough that his forearm rested temptingly against hers, their eyes drawn to the vista displayed in glorious technicolour in front of them. Ross sat the open pack of cookies between his knees, after Marcie declined his offer, and he munched on them one by one. When they eventually both spoke, they opened their mouths together and then laughed.

'Ladies first,' offered Ross, 'as always.'

Marcie felt herself blushing. 'I was just going to ask, why now? What brought you back?'

'Just the right time. Was worried about the wee man.' She found it funny that Ross called his brother the *wee man*, only because he was younger as they were both tall, broad and anything but small. 'Didn't get back for the funeral obviously, so now was the right time, as I said.'

'Didn't think about bringing the girls?'

'Oh, they're with their mum. Too long a journey for them when I'm not sure how long I'll be staying myself once I've...' Ross reached behind himself, laid his arm across the back of the bench and moved closer to her.

She didn't move but listened worriedly to the groaning of the bench beneath them. He fished out his wallet from a back pocket and opened it to reveal a photograph of two beautiful blonde, blue-eyed girls not too dissimilar to his brother's children.

'Gorgeous,' sighed Marcie as she took the wallet from him and took in the open, smiling faces of Starr and Skye Sutherland.

'I'm sure they'll come over at some point when they're

older. The big trip to the old country, as they call it. New Zealand is full of MacLeods and McKenzies and MacRaes. It's a wonder there's anyone left in Scotland. They took their mum's name, though – still a Scottish name, mind you – not sure if or when they'll become Balfours.' He pushed the wallet back into his pocket and was oblivious to the piece of card that fell out, floated beneath them, and landed under the bench.

'You fancy going for dinner some time?' he asked her unexpectedly, and she surprised herself by nodding in agreement. 'I'd offer to cook for you here, but my kitchen is a wee bit basic at the minute.'

She smiled at his joke and poured the rest of the dregs of the coffee out to her side.

'Sure, I don't have to be in London for a week or so – could I ask you to look in on Atlas as a return favour?'

'Deal,' he agreed and stood up and wandered down to see the view from just steps away from the cottage.

Marcie leaned down and picked up the card.

MacInnes Solicitors, Inverness

She turned it over and a number was scrawled below the name of Gus McSporran and, for some unknown reason, she hastily placed the card back where she found it.

'I hope you don't mind, Mossie, but I took the liberty of drawing up some plans,' he said suddenly as he turned to come back up the small hill to stand in front of her.

'Oh?' she asked, surprised. '*Plans*?'

'Thought I could replicate it on all the crofts around the estate. Well, *we* could... well, *you* could...'

She gave him a look at this odd suggestion but, if Angelina's plans worked out, maybe this could be a bigger venture; add the cottages on the estate in addition to Swanfield and therefore provide more accommodation for the clientele. Maybe she could stick to Dina's original designs, strip back a little from a luxury property to something more standard but certainly inviting. Her brain was ticking over. There was a mountain of opportunities ahead and she could see Angelina's plan now as possibly the start of what a *new* Swanfield Estate might become. In addition, having Ross do the hard graft might work out for the best for both quality and cost. *But where had this idea come from?* It struck her as rather odd for someone who had come back so suddenly and with ideas seemingly out of nowhere. He made his way back into the house and she followed him with a glance to the tin as he picked up some folded sheets of A1 paper that had been placed behind an old clock on the lopsided oak mantel that was barely holding up. He pulled them open and rested them on the old table. Marchwood had been drawn out and designed as a two-bedroom cottage, similar to her own at Tigh-na-Lochan, with an added deck outside to take in the magnificent view. She observed him as he talked over layout and presentation and wondered if she had not ventured out today, when he would have shared this information? He spoke excitedly about the plan and had gone as far as suggesting that each cottage on the estate could look the same and made available to holidaymakers and rented year-round to visitors. She was surprised and let out a little surprised '*oh*' to accompany her expression. It wasn't exactly what she was thinking about, but she let it go for the time being. She was leaning over the plans and as she turned to express her surprise to him, she realised his face was only inches away from hers. She looked at him, his eyes, his profile, his open mouth. The kiss was unexpected and soft and as she pulled away, she let out another little '*oh*' then realised this was not a situation she wanted to find herself in. Not right now. She struggled to find a word and felt his hand close over her arm, but she pulled away. He sensed her shock.

'I'm sorry, wow, so sorry. I don't know what came over me.'

She watched as the hand that had rested on her arm, moved

to cover his heart. 'Forgive me.'

She held her hands up by way of her own apology.

'Please, please, no need. My fault entirely,' she said but knew she really had nothing to apologise for. She could have stepped away when she realised what was about to happen but instead had closed her eyes in anticipation. Was Maureen Berman right? Was she suffering from *Balfouritis?* They stood awkwardly for some moments before she hastily apologised once more and helped him fold up the plans. Hurriedly, she said she had work to catch up on and made her way out to the car, smiling and waving as she pulled away, but inside her heart was racing.

She made it back to Tigh-na-Lochan at breakneck speed and once inside leaned on the back of the front door, sighing heavily.

'*What on earth?*' she said and went straight to her bedroom where Atlas was yawning himself awake from his third snooze of the morning. She started pacing the room, back and forth, only stopping to run her hands over her face and breathe out loudly. She found herself in the living room, then back in the bedroom. She climbed onto the bed and the cat came up to snuggle her and headbutt her his welcome.

'It's not even eleven, Atlas, and the day has already gone to biscuits.'

The cat *yammed* in agreement. 'And talking of biscuits, he ate the lot.' She plumped up her pillows and sat back. She felt her hands cover her face again, and she shook her head. She had been up so early and had achieved nothing but revelations. Her mind was racing but she felt more than alive due to everything that was going on around her. The cat lay down next to her and like Atlas, she closed her eyes and drifted off, but not before her fingers traced the outline of her lips which had been kissed so gently. 'Oh, Dina,' she said aloud, 'Dina, Dina, Dina.'

When she woke some hours later, it was still only early afternoon, and the cat had gone out on a prowl. She checked her phone – no messages – then made her way out to the car. She glanced around furtively, as if anyone could see her or be in such a remote location. She opened the boot to take out the letters she had effectively stolen from the box at Marchwood. She was confused as to where the box had come from and why Ross would have it – *did he carry it about with him*? Surely not. *Did he go there purposefully to find it?* She made her way into the house and poured a large glass of water and realised she was starving – despite making a beautiful loaf of freshly baked crusty bread earlier that she thought she would be sharing, none of that plan had worked out. She had a bowl of fruit that she began to dissect and took outside. She sat the fruit plate on the arm of one chair while she perched on the other. She opened the first letter, read the contents, carefully put it back in the envelope and read the next. She had seven letters in total – one from not long after Ross had left to one more recent – four years ago.

She couldn't really make out or decipher the contents or what they were trying to say: 'people forget', 'memories fade', 'bygones', 'the village has moved on'.

Each letter had more of the same from Flora Balfour and each ending with a plea for her son to return. Each letter from Ross never addressed any of the pleas from his mother but one did say he had sought forgiveness for what he had done. Marcie slowly ate her way through the fruit while trying to piece together this mother and son relationship and what had clearly gone on before, but without the whole of the circumstances around it – it was impossible. Ross had upped sticks in the middle of the night – disappeared. There were many discussions about it after it happened so suddenly:

It was a gap year.

It was visiting a sick relative abroad (one Ruaridh didn't seem to know about).

It was itchy feet like his grandfather and the desperate need for travel.

Then after six months, then a year, then two years, Ross was never really talked about and there came a point where he was only ever discussed when there was a family event. She was curious, inquisitive, and perplexed all at once. She watched as Atlas came strolling towards her, tail up, meandering slowly to run his fur across her legs then roll about in front of her before leaping on the chair beside her and surveying the scene that surrounded them.

'What exactly is going on?' she asked the cat, who paid absolutely no attention but continued to watch a little field mouse disappear into the shrubland. 'I might not go back to London next week, I might just stay and see what unfolds.' Atlas glanced up at her then turned away and Marcie followed his gaze to the hills. 'I just wish I knew what this mystery is,' she muttered and sorted the pile of letters resting in her lap. Deep down, she wondered if the man she was clearly falling for could be trusted.

TWENTY-TWO

The Aizle was busy, and Ruaridh walked around with his tray to the seat he had agreed with Ruthie Gillespie. She waved from a distance, and he found her at an outside table amidst the chattering tourists showing off shop purchases and pictures in their phones.

'Bit of a nightmare getting parked, Ruthie, sorry I'm late,' Ruaridh apologised as he sat down, moving crockery around the cluttered table until he found a place for his tea and fruit scone.

Ruthie smiled at him as he expertly piled the used plates and cups onto a tray.

'Everything okay?' she asked, observing his annoyed face.

He shrugged slightly. 'Just a lot going on. Decided to rent out the pods again this summer and I could have rented them out a dozen times over – everyone wants to come to the Highlands. Spent the last few hours airing them and making sure they were fit for guests,' he explained.

Ruthie raised her arm and with her hand displayed the spectacular mountain scenery all around them.

'Made your point.' He smiled and leaned forward. 'Have you met the wee girl at the Inn? I'm thinking of maybe asking her to take on some of the changeover days. It's all getting a bit too much. Every time I go into the pods, I'm just...' he began, and he felt Ruthie reach out and place her hand on top of his.

'I know, son,' she said, aware he was going to say that they reminded him of his wife.

'When will it stop, Ruthie?' he asked, begging for the answer he had been searching for, for what seemed like months and months and months.

Her hand closed around his as her gaze caught his, the tears in his eyes clearly visible.

'It won't. There's no point in pretending you're going to wake up one day and everything has gone back to normal. We just learn to allow our built-in coping mechanism to step in and do the heavy lifting, for want of a better expression, love,' she tried to reassure him.

'I keep trying to get back to normal...'

'We have to accept it's the *new* normal, Ruaridh.'

'I, er...' he began.

'Uh-huh?'

'I invited Doctor Brahmins over for dinner. Kids are away.'

'Oh, that is lovely, that's a big step. I was so sorry I couldn't make the barbecue, but I'm sure that went well, what with Ross being back and all. I've got a lot going on myself, you see.'

'How are you? Everything good?'

'I'm thinking of going to visit my sister in Canada.'

'I didn't know you had a sister in Canada?'

'It's not that I've kept her hidden! I'd have to go and get a passport and all that palaver. I sometimes wonder if it's worth it. All that nonsense just to leave here to come back.' He nodded at her suggestion, knowing what she meant. He had briefly thought about moving himself when Ross invited him to New Zealand, but it was nothing more than a flashing thought and he was glad it had never moved beyond the discussion stage. He was not a man for change, he freely admitted.

'So, you? Dr Brahmins? That's a big step. How did that go?'

'Well, I plucked up the courage to ask her over. Fu...' He was about to swear then stopped himself as she waited for him to continue. 'Apologies. Utter shambles. I had a bit too much to drink, spilled a whole glass of wine over her. Had to give her one of my shirts. She had had a couple of drinks so had no way of getting home. I took myself off to bed and she slept in the guest room. It was hardly my finest hour. I'm sure she thinks I'm a bumbling idiot.'

'I'm sure she wasn't bothered one bit. I bet she was secretly delighted that someone made her dinner.' Ruthie smiled, trying to make light of the situation.

'Then Marcie turned up in the middle of the chaos with breakfast.'

'Oh?'

'I mean, just after I'd told her we were now in different places and had to move on with our own lives independently, she sees me with someone else and probably thinks I've moved on at the speed of Usain Bolt.' He held up his hand in a stopping motion.

'We all have our moments, Ruaridh; we are nothing if not fallible human beings.'

'I'd agree if I knew what that meant.'

'We all make mistakes. We're human. We do stupid things. Mostly to the people we love.'

He leaned his elbow on the table and gazed into his tea.

'Ross enjoying being back?'

'Think so. He's up at Achmelvich with the boys. Hopefully, they'll come back exhausted.'

'And Mari?'

'Dina's mum has her. She's been a real godsend, she's a belter.' He smiled and for a second his face lit up.

'Is it a help or a hindrance?'

'Hmmm?'

'Ross being back.'

'Ross always has an agenda,' said Ruaridh and moved his scone away to the other side of the table.

'Strathkin is full of secrets.'

'What do you mean?'

'Och, it's small village life, isn't it, son? Grudges and bad blood always resurface. People put old grievances to bed then they resurface at the most inopportune times.'

He scratched his head and ran his hand over his beard before he shrugged, unsure of what she meant.

'Ross wouldn't just turn up unannounced if you ask me. Ask him why he's *really* here.' Ruthie made the statement then sat back in her chair.

He ran her words over in his mind as a woman behind him interrupted them to ask about their table.

'Well, I did invite him.'

'And he drops everything? Really? You don't think Ross has just turned up because it has suited Ross?'

'I don't suppose we could sit here?' asked the tourist of the two empty seats at their table of four.

'Absolutely, we were just leaving.' Ruthie smiled. 'Are you eating that?' She pointed to the scone that Ruaridh had discarded to the other side of the table. She opened her handbag, took out a well-used zip-lock bag and dropped the uneaten fruit scone inside. 'Waste not, want not.' She winked at him.

'You're a one, Ruthie Gillespie!' he joked and helped her weave her way out of the busy restaurant.

Outside, cars were struggling to find spaces in between motorbikes and camper vans.

'Getting too busy for my taste,' said the older woman as people jostled past and into the long white building behind them.

'What do you mean about Ross?' Ruaridh asked as he

pushed his hands into his pockets while they stood near to her car.

'People don't just up-sticks for no reason, Ruaridh. And certainly not teenage boys, torn away from their family. Especially their mother.'

'He was nearly twenty,' qualified Ruaridh.

'Still a boy,' said Ruthie and pointed to her cheek. Ruaridh kissed her quickly, his stubble grazing her soft powdered skin.

'Ask him,' repeated Ruthie, 'and when he spins you a yarn, ask him again.'

He watched as she pulled the small car out of the car park and on to the main road that would take her down into the Glen of Strathpine then the narrow single-track road that would lead her to Strathkin.

Two women, disgorged from a tour bus, giggled as they looked Ruaridh up and down approvingly and made their way across the car park. They stopped to take a selfie with Ruaridh in the background and continued to whisper as they made their way to the gift shop. He stood there for some moments, lost in his thoughts and oblivious to their gaze. He was the second person that day to think – *curiouser and curiouser*.

The man with the baseball hat who was watching them while leaning casually on the fence decided he was wasting his time watching the man who had given him the scar on the side of his body. It was his old girlfriend he was after. So Poytr Medvedev slipped back into his hired Lexus and meandered down the valley before Ruaridh Balfour had even made it to his car.

TWENTY-THREE

It's all gone quiet, thought Marcie, *and I don't want to upset the apple cart*. She was thinking about Dieter Frum and his plan for the man who had brought so much chaos to their small Highland village. She had thought long and hard and had made up her mind that she wanted nothing more to do with it; she wanted to close that chapter of her life and try to move on from all that had happened. She had also been thinking about Simon. A lot, it would appear, after she had written her own letter to Dina. Her husband, whose breakdown had not come as a shock to her, caught up as he was in the awful days that came with the fire that almost destroyed Swanfield. He was of fragile mind, she had known that when they married, but she blamed them both for their separation so soon after their commitment to each other. His mother, overprotective of her only son, had shut her out. Text messages went unanswered, phone calls cut off, letters returned. An unannounced visit to their house in Dore in Yorkshire had village curtains twitching, so she had left, looking back at the house for the last time where she knew her husband was closeted, enveloped in his mother's claws. They had never got on. An only son adored by a fierce Italian mother and who, in her eyes, could do no wrong. Mirella's unwavering support for her only son drew Marcie's ire and she had been a thorn in Marcie's side from their first meeting. His mother's comments about his wife continuing with her legal career post wedding were laughed off by Simon. However, the affection she showed him was not extended to the woman who had replaced his mother as the new focus in his life. She had planned an extravagant wedding for her *patatino* whereas Marcie wanted an intimate event in her village hall. The Grainger guest list was extensive and unworkable and presented to Marcie as a fait accompli. By the time the bride said no to the extended family invitations, cracks had begun to show and the planned honeymoon trip to the Far East was curtailed. To bring *Mama* back onside, a train journey through Italy was arranged where Marcie was displayed to Simon's family like a prize animal at a county show. She had closed the door firmly behind her, knowing she would never see Mirella again and walked away with her head held high. Maybe it was all for a reason, though? Inside, she felt different – something was changing. She had a strength inside her that came from the past few years; almost losing Callum and most certainly losing Dina. The man who had taken so much from the village had pulled people together like never before.

Initially, she had started by thinking, like Dieter, she would hunt down this man and make him pay for her husband's condition and almost killing her uncle, her only family, but had concluded, finally, that someone else would find him once he pushed them too far and that person was not going to be her. She had made her mind up that she could start to live freely, so sure in herself that he would never set foot in Strathkin ever again. Dieter was now where she was before she had come to terms with her future without Simon in it, and, it would appear, without Ruaridh in it. Just as Dieter was realising his wife would and could not return to him as the same person, Marcie had a dawning realisation that as she moved forward, she, like Ruaridh, had to close the door to enable her to open another. One, it would appear, she was very keen to open. A text brought her back to life, and it was one that made her smile. It simply said:

> Where are you taking me this year, lass?

'Chasing the sun,' she said aloud as the calendar turned swiftly forward to the longest day, and summer could officially begin. The summer solstice, a time when her uncle had vowed to return to spend time with his only niece, with time for reminiscing and planning their future. She quickly texted back.

> Surprise!

And remembered she had written down some places on a pad that she had to revisit sooner rather than later. When Callum had told her he wanted to spend what was left of his life in the warmth of a constant sun he could not find in his native Scotland, after the initial shock, she had actively encouraged him to spread his wings in the Indian Ocean, the Gold Coast in Australia and, recently, the clear white sand beaches of the Caribbean. He had island hopped, before settling for the new republic of Barbados where he found the casual living suited his new relaxed temperament. The Scotland District satisfied his craving for greenery and hills, resembling, as the name suggested, the rolling lush habitation of his homeland. She knew that he was in no rush to return to the land of his birth, not just yet – a frequent discussion in their FaceTime calls. He and Marcie had agreed on their 'chasing the sun' yearly visit to watch the sun as it almost set on remote beaches and far-flung villages in the north of Scotland years before. It had come about not long after Marcie had lost both parents in a road accident on a trip south without their tempestuous young daughter, and they had kept it up religiously since. It was something they both cherished, and she knew that Callum's flight home for this visit was booked, she just did not yet know the date. She had researched, found a perfect getaway, and could not wait for his short visit and reconnecting with him in person rather than simply on screen. It made her warm inside.

She was also very much aware that she had not shared with him some of the things she had found at Swanfield, ill as he was then, and she didn't want to add to his health burdens now. She would be glad to speak to him about the return of Ross Balfour and his penchant for flitting from croft to croft as if he was searching for something. Callum would certainly want to find the underlying cause of *that* mystery. Marcie sat up in her chair at the dining table, paperwork spread out all around her. Of course that's what it was. He *was* looking for something. She knew that his father, working the far end of the estate, had sometimes stayed at Marchwood, so why not say to her that that was his intention – hunting for and finding some lost family heirloom?

Unless...

Unless of course that something was already in her possession. A thought struck her. Was his affection misplaced? Was he teasing her, knowing she had what he was more than likely looking for? If he kept her onside, would she admit to having it? Hand it over without a thought? A finger ran along the outside of her lips. That kiss was surely not contrived. It was spontaneous. Licking her lips unconsciously, she leapt up from the chair and made her way quickly into the bedroom, to the tall wardrobe and into the back of it behind boxes of shoes. She pulled out the black tin box and took out the long piece of old yellowing paper she had found previously at the back of the wardrobe in Swanfield, in Lisanne's room. The one she had taken to Lochside Croft, to try and see it more clearly with the aid of one of the children's toys. When she looked this time, the name was clear as day – no need for a magnifying glass. *Why hadn't she seen it before?* This name, this scrawled name on top of something blanked out with Tippex. She spread the paper on the bed. Taking the phone from her back pocket, she quickly took a photograph then enlarged it on screen. Of course! Her finger automatically went to the outline of her lips, and she traced a line around them, again. Like the letters she had taken from the box at Marchwood, she knew she had to remove this paper from her possession and put it somewhere safe. It was clearly an original and not a copy, so she quickly made her way back into the living room and to her makeshift desk in the corner where her laptop and a printer sat side by side. She put the paper in the printer to scan but she realised that the familiar writing was so faded that it didn't scan clear enough for it to be legible. She would have to keep the photo on the phone if she needed the evidence.

'Blast,' she said aloud. She pulled a large envelope from her stationery pile and put the original inside, writing *Personal* on the front of the envelope and *Birth Certificate* beneath it. She made a phone call to the offices of Richard MacInnes, Solicitors, and left a message on the answering service to make an urgent appointment to see Richard as soon as possible. She then stood with the envelope and searched around for a place to put it – to hide it.

'Where, oh where?' she muttered to herself and then focused on Atlas's bed. She pulled out the fleece throw that she had folded up for the cat and put the envelope inside before refolding it and placing it back in the cat bed. *Who in their right mind would look there for anything?* she said to herself, confident in the knowledge that only she knew where this precious piece of paper would reside until she took it to Richard

MacInnes to ask – what does this mean, and can we just dispose of it before it causes any more grief?

In Marchwood, Ross Balfour stared at his uprooted floor and leaned on a brush that was of no use in the *burrach* that was his current home. He had no doubts that Marcie had looked through the box of unread letters from him to his mum and his mum to him. It was a meeting he had feared from the moment he had stepped on the plane in Christchurch, but the first sight of his mother at Hillview Croft on his second day back had melted the years away. It was obvious to him from that initial warm hug and the tears that followed that his father had intervened, and that Flora Balfour had been none the wiser to her husband's suppression of loving words and pleas. And here he stood with another woman on his mind, a woman who was occupying his thoughts more and more. *Had she found anything else?* He was missing one vital piece of evidence. *Was it just a myth?* Another mystery of Strathkin that never really existed, or was there something that could prove what he had known all along? Words he had overheard so long ago. Only time would tell. But he was determined not to give in until he claimed what he believed was rightly his: Swanfield.

Just over an hour later, when Marcie opened the door at Tigh-na-Lochan, she was greeted by a huge bunch of flowers, so large it covered the gift giver's face. She knew it had to be one of two people by the stance, the height and the build.

'I come bearing gifts by way of an apology.' Ross lowered the flowers and gave Marcie a pleading look as she opened the door wide. As he stepped in, she took the flowers from him and headed to the sink.

'Seriously, I don't know what that was all about, Mossie,' he began.

'It's okay. We can all get caught up in the heat of the moment,' she said as she began disassembling the tied bouquet, 'but thank you, these are certainly not from the village store.'

He made a conciliatory gesture and joined her at the sink.

'I'm not normally the kind of guy that gets turned on by architectural plans, to be honest!' he joked, and she leaned over and slapped his arm.

He was distracted by the cat wandering in from the bedroom, who began wrapping himself around his legs, weaving in and out, tail raised high. Ross bent down and picked up the large cat and heaved him over his shoulder, stroking him gently. 'And what about you, big boy? What are you saying to all this?' The cat purred gently, rubbing his face against Ross's cheek.

Marcie patted the cat's head then started to dissect a large plastic water bottle, cutting her knife through it to create a makeshift container for the large spray.

'There was no need for these, but they are beautiful. The Aizle?'

'Yeah, it was heaving... let me put you down, you weigh a ton, big fella.'

Marcie glanced around as Ross took the cat over to his bed, and she breathed in sharply as she watched him lean down and pat the fleece blanket before gently encouraging the cat into his box. He kneeled and petted the cat until Atlas settled down, and Marcie blew her cheeks out, watching wide-eyed. *Close call*, she said to herself. Ross wandered back to where the flower arranging was still going on, and she pointed to the fridge.

'You can raid it if you want,' she suggested, and he pulled the door of the fridge open to reveal plastic tubs of leftovers and bags of salad and fruit. He opened a container, sniffed it and made a face before kicking the door of the fridge shut. He took a fork from a pile of cutlery on the worktop and began to devour the food.

'I thought you were supposed to be up at Achmelvich?' she asked, continuing with her floral art. 'Did you come down and plan on heading back?'

'I left the boys there with one of their friends' parents. They were in the lodge next door with their gang. I'll pick them up tomorrow. Didn't tell Ruaridh as this way I get to do a bit of my own work in peace and quiet. I know what he means, they're a handful.' He leaned on the worktop. 'Girls are so much easier. I would just sit on the sofa while they painted my nails and put make-up on me. We'd have a spa day with facials and watch a romcom with popcorn. That's my idea of looking after children, to be honest. I do miss a mani-pedi.'

Marcie smiled, shook her head, picked the makeshift vase up and moved it to the edge of her small cream TV unit, standing back to admire her handiwork and the fact she had chosen the perfect spot.

'Nice work, Mossie,' he said as he shovelled cold pesto pasta into his mouth. 'So, what did you think of the plans?'

'Well, you did spring that on me a bit. I don't know what to think. You've clearly thought about it long and hard. I mean, I'd have to apply for planning permission and building warrants and the like, that's going to take forever. And discuss it all with Callum. It all depends on how long you're going to be staying, obviously.' She knew what answer she wanted.

'Well, I haven't any of my own plans made so far. May stay. May go. Depends.'

She turned around to face him on the other side of the room.

'Plus, I forgot how much I liked the scenery here.' He leaned back to place the empty container on the sink drainer and shoved his hands in his pockets. He set his gaze on her and she recognised it as the same look Ruaridh used to give her a long time ago. She held up her left hand, palm facing her, her ring finger clearly visible to him.

'Oh, yeah, and how is that going?' he asked.

She pulled the ring off her finger and placed it into the dish on the table that already contained her watch and a silver bracelet with a heart attached to it. She would sit in the evening, surrounded by paperwork, and rub cream into her hands at the table but had rarely taken off her wedding ring. For whatever reason, she realised it was now time.

'Let's just say, not as well as expected,' she replied and sat down on a dining chair while he remained leaning on the worktop opposite her.

'Divorce on the cards?' he queried.

'Yup.' She leaned her elbows on the table and rested her chin in her hands.

'Never met him.'

'Never likely to,' she responded.

'Does he have a claim on any of this?'

She thought it was a strange question to ask. 'Wouldn't have thought so. He has plenty of his own.'

'Surrey?'

'Yorkshire.'

'Monied?'

'Loaded.'

'Love him?'

She hesitated and thought before responding. 'I suppose I still do, in my own way. Yes.'

'Alcohol?'

'Breakdown.'

'Ah.'

'Fragile,' she said, and even as she said it, she regretted it. She couldn't think of the word to describe Simon. A breakdown was certainly what happened after he was chased through this Highland landscape by a killer and nearly killed. He had nightmares, panic attacks, anxiety, all brought on by one man who was now in Dieter Frum's sights. In a daydream of sorts of her past, Marcie suddenly turned to the man in front of her who was watching her closely.

'Why do *you* want to do all this? All that stuff you showed me earlier.'

'Hmmm?' asked Ross as he took a seat opposite her. 'Deep down, I suppose I want to come back. I just don't know yet. I'd need something to do. I'd need something to occupy myself and city living hasn't ever appealed to me. I'm not a drinker. Not a party animal. I never ran with the cool kids.'

'You and Jamie *were* the cool kids,' Marcie corrected.

'Nah,' he disagreed, 'we were just bored teenagers.'

'Why did you leave?'

'Why did *you* leave?' he shot back.

'Touché.' She smiled.

'There's an invisible thread, Mossie, that pulls you back to Strathkin. No matter where you go, there's always a tug to remind you where home is. Isn't that why you're here?'

They sat in silence, looking at each other as if they were checking each other out – which, of course, they were. Her eyes settled on the cleft in his chin. His eyes watched as she then studied her ring in the dish. Her phone pinged in front of her, next to the dish. Ross could see the name. It was his brother.

'Oh, the wee guy is on the prowl. Don't tell him I'm here. He thinks I'm up the road,' he said to her, referring to the trip to the beach with his boys.

She picked up the phone and glanced at the message without opening it.

> Picking up Callum – possibly week on Wednesday

She smiled.

'Dinner invite?' quizzed Ross, keen to know what Ruaridh was asking.

'That ship has sailed, left the harbour,' she said and placed the phone face down on the table.

'Interesting, Mossie,' he said and leaned back just as the huge cat leapt up from the floor to land on his chest and climb up onto his shoulder.

'Jeezo, big fella! Could have shouted a warning!' he joked as the cat nuzzled into him.

Marcie watched him from her seat at the table. *Ross Balfour,* she thought to herself, *what exactly are you up to?*

TWENTY-FOUR

She was in the shower when the call came in from Richard MacInnes. His message left on voicemail said that he could see her that afternoon. If, however, she didn't want to come to the office, they could pencil in a video call. She was in the mood for a visit to the city, as she could pick up provisions for Callum's arrival in the next few days, so opted for a face to face. She had worked late the evening before, so a treat of lunch 'in town', as she still called it, was appealing.

The drive was uneventful save for the many tourists still unable to understand how passing places worked, preferring to park up in them in their camper vans. As a result, she arrived with hardly any time to visit the shops for her groceries. She whizzed quickly around the supermarket throwing things into a trolley and had no time to lunch at one of the lovely restaurants near his office. She rushed up the stairs of the old converted Victorian villa and got to the main door just as Margaret Tulloch was opening it wide.

'Mrs Grainger.'

She smiled, still not used to her married name when it was

likely she would be resorting to her previous name sooner rather than later.

'Tea?' asked the woman as she led Marcie straight into Richard's office. Thinking of the previous offerings from parsimonious Margaret, she politely declined. Margaret closed the door as Marcie was greeted warmly by her solicitor, but left it slightly ajar, listening in while pretending to look through her large black ledger.

They exchanged pleasantries about the weather, the state of the economy, and the tourist season, which would be in full swing in a few weeks and when a table at local eateries would be like hen's teeth.

'So, I can't say I'm surprised to see you,' began the solicitor.

'No?' queried Marcie.

'Hmm,' said Richard, settling back into his chair and entwining his fingers over his corpulent middle.

'Can I ask you one thing before we start? Do you know anyone in planning or building in the area? I'd like to enquire about timescales for building warrants and the like. Of course, I should have mentioned this to you before because I was thinking about dropping in to the offices in Dingwall on the way back.'

'What are you thinking about?'

'Oh, nothing really, well, something and nothing. Just wondering if redoing some of the houses on the estate would be worth it. Just something I've been thinking about. Just pondering.'

'Bit out of the blue?'

'Hmmm.' Marcie smiled, not wanting to give the game away too soon. Richard was by no means a gossip, but Marcie was always one to keep her powder dry until the last possible moment.

'And?' he continued as she bent down to the bag at her feet and took out the envelope she had been nursing in close sight.

'I need to check something with you. Obviously, I don't need to tell you to keep it between us.'

'Undoubtedly,' replied Richard, trying not to sound peeved.

'I have something in my possession,' she began.

'And I have something in *my* possession,' Richard replied, and outside Margaret Tulloch leaned in a little bit further to the open door.

Marcie stood outside the main door of Richard MacInnes's offices and for a moment watched the fast-flowing River Ness in front of her. When she explained to him *what* she had found, what she had been keeping a secret and asked what her options were, he simply nodded. He told her he needed to do a bit more exploring but didn't seem to want to do a bit more explaining. It was not like him. *What was he keeping from her?* He had a look like suddenly one of them knew too much, and she was perplexed. He was a study in concentration as she explained everything to him, and he made some sounds of agreement and then moved the conversation on. When she left the office, agreeing to a further meeting soon, Margaret Tulloch fell in the door as she opened it. Marcie presumed she was there to take away files or Richard's perennially empty coffee cup, but she simply apologised and went back to the main office. Outside, Marcie stood, her eyes on the restaurant across the river in front of her, wondering whether to stay for lunch or start the long drive back to Strathkin. She checked her phone for messages and noticed she had missed a call from Dieter Frum, but she had realised she no longer wanted to follow his plan of revenge and put the phone back in her bag. She made her way to the Greig Street Bridge, the old suspension bridge that would take her across the river and back into the centre of the city. It was busy with pedestrians and youngsters jumping halfway along the footbridge, which caused it to wave and sway. Locals named it *The Bouncy Bridge.* She was only halfway along when she saw Heather coming towards her.

'What the...?' she said in surprise to her smiling friend. 'You're a long way from home!'

'I know! We escaped!' Heather grinned enthusiastically.

'*We?*' queried Marcie.

'Me and Jamie.'

'Oh, I see...'

Heather grabbed Marcie's arm, spun her around, and began walking with her in the opposite direction to where she was going.

'Jamie had to come down for a meeting. He's up at the Police HQ just now. Don't say but I think he's about to get promoted. He's passed all his exams, and we came down last night and stayed at The Townhouse. We're here until tomorrow. Isn't it exciting?' Marcie saw the beaming face of her friend and was at once touched and delighted for her. She gave her a hug and a squeeze, and they giggled like schoolgirls as they walked along Huntly Street until it came to the junction with Tomnahurich Street and Ness Walk. Across from them was Rocpool, one of the city's premier Scottish restaurants.

'Ooh! Ross told me all about this place! I've never been, it's supposed to be sublime!' said Heather, gazing at the restaurant on the corner opposite them with a look of whimsy on her face.

'C'mon, you! I get the hint,' said Marcie and dragged her friend across the road, hoping they would be able to get a table while the lunch service was still on. They did, were seated quickly at the window and drinks orders were swiftly taken.

'So, what are you doing in the big city?' asked Heather, perusing the small but highly prized modern Scottish menu.

'I had to see Richard about something and also get some extra bits and pieces in, as Callum's back this week.'

'Ooh. Chasing the sun! Doesn't that come round quicker every year? When Jamie and I went to Gruinard Bay, I said to him we should come back here and start a tradition like Marcie and Callum, but Jamie said we should also think about going further north into Norway, you know, land of the midnight sun and all that? Jamie is truly knowledgeable about these things...'

Marcie laughed.

'What is it?' asked Heather.

'Nothing,' replied her friend and buried her face in the menu.

'I'm doing it, aren't I? Talking incessantly about a new guy? I never thought of Jamie as a potential, and here I am, doing what I always complain about.' Heather raised her brows and sighed. 'Always said I wouldn't be the one to do that.'

'You deserve it!' encouraged Marcie. 'It's just kinda funny that it's Jamie you're talking about when he's been in everyone's orbit for so long.'

They ordered and shared a plate of hand-dived scallops with a spring onion crème fraiche and homemade bread to dip in the lemon garlic and parsley butter, which they ate with gusto. Then, instead of a simple coffee, they each had an affogato with Marcie taking only the expresso, declining the offer of a coffee liqueur poured over the vanilla ice cream. Her phone vibrated in her handbag, and she ignored it as she and Heather caught up.

'The issue, you see, is if he gets his promotion, he might be posted somewhere else, like one of the big cities in the Central Belt, but he'd apply again for promotion and ask to be posted back here. I mean, if he got Inverness that would be amazing.'

'How long would he be away?'

'I'm not sure but he'll find out all that today and maybe then we can talk about the future.'

'So, there *is* a future?' asked Marcie, draining her coffee cup of ice cream.

'Well,' said Heather shyly, 'we'll see.'

'I'm really sorry,' apologised Marcie as she dug out her

phone to see that she had missed several calls and had a new pile of both messages and WhatsApps. Most of the missed calls came from The Strathkin Inn's number and Ally, Heather's right-hand woman. The first message she opened was from Ally, asking if she knew where Heather was staying as her phone was off. There was even a missed call and a message from Hannah, which Marcie saw as a great turning point, but her message only said:

> Marsy, can you call me ASAP HH

'Is your phone switched off?' Marcie asked of Heather sitting opposite her.

'I switched it off last night. I don't think I put it back on; Jamie's probably looking for me.'

'The whole world is looking for you!' She held up her phone for Heather to see the list of missed calls.

'Oh jeez, I bet they've burned the hotel down. I can't catch a break,' she complained and began to search in her bag for her phone to nervously switch it on. Marcie, in the meantime, had called Ally back on her number and it was answered immediately.

'We're still trying to track down Heather,' was her opening line.

'She's with me here – is everything okay?'

'Not really. It's Adam, he's not well. Really not well. We don't know what to do tonight! Is she there? I need to speak to her urgently!'

'It's Ally – Adam's not well,' said Marcie across the table to her friend.

'He was fine yesterday. There is a big dinner tonight. It's for the Mountain Rescue Team and some of the families. He'd better not be shirking off!'

Marcie passed her phone to Heather who listened intently

with a lot of uh-huhs and okays as she watched the colour drain from her friend's previously joyous face.

'Ally, you'll need to give me a minute to think about this. I'm just trying to process it. But most things are prepped, yeah?' Heather's face took on a pained expression and shook her head.

'What is it?' Marcie mouthed.

Heather simply shook her head and rested it in her palm, elbow on the table, while in her other hand, she held up the phone close to her ear and tapped on it absentmindedly.

'I'll call you back in five,' she said, and turned to Marcie. 'Can we get the bill? I need to go back up the road.'

'What's happened?'

'Adam has taken ill. He was complaining the other day, and we were laughing it off. Ally says he's really ill and has taken to bed.'

'Ill? In what way?'

'Well, let's just say, all over the gent's toilet ill. And Monica and Jonesy, my two casuals, have the same thing.' She held up her phone. 'They've called off. No waiting staff either!'

'Oh, not good!' said Marcie, making a face of horror and then signalling to their own waiter for the bill.

'I'll need to get back up the road,' said Heather, fumbling in her bag, searching for an elusive pen and notebook.

'Wait, wait, wait. Why do you need to rush back? You've got Jamie to consider, too. I mean, Adam is ill, but Ally is perfectly capable.'

'Ally's not a chef.'

'Neither are you.'

'Yes, but I can wing it.'

'What needs to be done?' queried Marcie. 'We can step in.'

'He did a lot of prep yesterday or was preparing to when I left. I have a sit down for thirty or so this evening – Lachie and the MRT. And some of the relatives are over. It's all been bought and paid for. I can hardly cancel, can I? Where is that bill?' Heather complained while raising her hand to attract the attention of a passing waiter again.

Marcie reached out and pulled Heather's hand back down.

'Listen. Let's think this through logically and with our sensible heads on. You and Jamie need to stay here. I'll head back up the road and throw myself right into it. We can ask Bella for help, too; she's no stranger to a buffet. Remember Nosebag? Remember when you guys ran that catering company? *We* worked our asses off in the shooting season. Fair to say our asses were more ample at the end of it, the amount of food we scoffed!' said Marcie, puffing her cheeks out to make her face fatter. Heather gave a little laugh at the thought of her previous catering company and how all her friends helped out, uncomplainingly, when needed.

'I'm not sure. This is a showcase supper.'

'You're saying we're not up to it? The cheek of it!' joked Marcie.

'I just don't want to...'

'We won't let you down,' said Marcie, simultaneously picking up her phone and pressing keys while handing a waiter her credit card to scan.

'Bells, it's me. All hands to the pump. We're doing a shift at the Inn. Heather's got a big group in and Adam has taken ill.' Marcie was suddenly in control, her favourite place to be.

Heather listened as the person on the other side fired back instructions.

Marcie covered the phone. 'Do we need anything else from here?' she asked. 'I can go to any of the shops, and we can fake it if need be?'

Heather shook her head to Marcie's suggestion.

'Look the part? I know. Do you have a white shirt and black trousers? I can run into one of the supermarkets. No, I'm in Inverness. Deal.' The phone call finished quickly. Marcie smiled at a worried Heather. 'All sorted. You take yourself off to that hotel and I'll get a shizzle on back to Toy Town. We'll send you pictures!'

'I really don't think...'

'Don't you trust us?'

'It's not that...'

Marcie's phone pinged and the message was from Ross Balfour.

> I'm with Bella. Tell H I'm no stranger to a kitchen. Relax. It's all under control

She held the phone up to Heather.

'Apparently, the cavalry has arrived,' she said as Heather scanned the text.

'Well, his lamb at the barbecue was delicious. He told me he'd scavenged his way around Australia and New Zealand in kitchens to make a buck.'

'All sorted then,' said Marcie. 'Just one more thing, can I make a deal that anything uneaten I can take back for Cal as an extra treat?'

'Deal.'

Within minutes they were out on the street, hugging and promising photographs and perfect plates.

After a detour to buy a new white shirt, Marcie was on her way back to the west coast with a car full of food and goodies for Callum's return, and a head full of questions for the next time she met up with Richard MacInnes.

TWENTY-FIVE

By the time Marcie entered the kitchen at The Strathkin Inn, she was not in the least surprised to see Ross holding court as he ran through the menu with Ally and Hannah listening intently to his every word. Bella arrived moments later in the requisite uniform of white shirt and black trousers, and Marcie gazed at them admiringly – they had all stepped up and she was delighted. This was friendship writ large.

'Okay, division of labour. I need two servers, one at the bar, one helping me in the kitchen and one in charge of dishwasher stacking and emptying.'

Marcie pondered the numbers Ross was suggesting as she looked around – they didn't add up.

'Can we do with one less?' she suggested as she scrambled in her bag for her new shirt.

'Not if we want an efficient kitchen,' was the response from Ross as he folded his arms across his chest and leaned on the sink.

'Um,' began Marcie. They all stood looking at each other.

'I have an idea! Can I have a minute?' Hannah put down

the menu that Ross had asked her to memorise and rushed out the back door.

'Well, I hope she's planning on coming back,' sighed Ally and held up her own menu to look at.

'What are we serving?' asked Marcie, pulling the tags off her new supermarket-bought plain white shirt. Ross ran through a delicious sounding menu of locally sourced ingredients, and she looked at him in awe. 'That sounds delicious.' She leaned on the stainless-steel counter.

'Good,' agreed Ross, 'here's the dessert menu. Get cracking.'

'Wha…?'

'Bit of a cheat. Adam told us to go up to The Aizle and buy all their freshly baked meringues so it's really an assembly job. Made for you,' he said as he walked past, slapped her with the menu and made his way into the staff room off the kitchen.

Bella shrugged her shoulders, and Ally said, 'Bags the bar,' quickly, heading out to make sure all the tables were set, the bar was full and the place ready to greet guests.

Marcie raced after Ross and when she walked into the staff room, she found him with his shirt off and about to put on one of Adam's chef's jackets. She turned her back to him and found herself facing the mirror, Ross's reflection clearly visible in front of her.

'I'm really not up for this; I'm better as a server.' She found her eyes gaping at him as he changed shirts. Over his left shoulder to the centre of his chest was intricate body art that reached down to his arm and just above his elbow. It appeared to be a Māori design with dots and feathers before it blended into a Celtic knot. As he turned slightly, she saw the dark blue-black design stretch down part of his shoulder and onto his back.

'Every day's a school day, Mossie,' he shouted.

Certainly is, she thought to herself.

'I'm just hopeless at that type of fancy schmancy arrangement. I'll completely mess it up. I don't want to let Heather down. I'm better as a dishwasher stacker, to be honest,' she said by way of an excuse, her eyes still transfixed on his body and the ink that covered it, her hand now pulling at a stray strand that had escaped from her hair clip.

'You won't mess anything up if you're *my* sous chef,' he said and watched back in the mirror as he buttoned up his top. He walked over to her. 'Now, it's your turn to get your kit off,' he said in her ear, and she opened her mouth with a gasp to respond. 'Get into your new clothes and meet me in the kitchen in two minutes for a demonstration, then you're on your own.'

She caught herself in the mirror as he left, her face flushed and her heart beating a little too fast. She started taking off her blouse and then unbuttoning the new shirt as Bella walked in.

'Phew, I'm beginning to see him in a new light, eh? What's the word – *masterful*?'

Marcie tried to ignore her as she fumbled with the buttons on her shirt. 'Can we swap? I'm really regretting this!' she pleaded as Bella took the shirt from her, unbuttoned the top five buttons then pulled the top over her head.

'You're a bit red in the face, are you okay?' she asked, and Marcie nodded, blowing out air as Bella helped her button up the too-large blouse.

'So, guess where Methuselah is tonight? Only coming to this fancy tea!'

'How come?'

'Dieter Frum was trying to get you today and when he couldn't, he walked up to the stables and invited *Leopard Print Lucy*. Me? Oh no, I don't get an offer. I'm standing there like the cat dragged me in, covered in horse dung and with half-eaten hay in my hair. He took one look and heaved. So, he invited herself. Done up to the nines, she is.'

Bella was standing behind Marcie, and pulled the new shirt

down over her shoulders to ensure it sat well. She unbuttoned one of the buttons to show off a bit more cleavage.

'I don't think so! Not tonight!' complained Marcie and immediately did it up again.

'Suit yourself... Mossie!' joked Bella with a knowing look and slapped Marcie's bottom as she headed out the door.

In the dining room, Hannah was walking hand in hand with Dax, showing him the table settings and instructing him on how to be a waiter. Marcie noticed he was in what was clearly his school uniform, dark trousers and white shirt, which were the only *formal* clothes he owned. She listened as Hannah instructed him on how to lift and set down plates and how to take orders for drinks. As he stared at her in amazement and with a slight feeling of shock, she decided that this was one task too many. She told him she would be the one taking drinks orders, as the thought of teaching him at this late stage the art of tray etiquette was a step too far.

Marcie watched this other young love blossoming and smiled, thinking of what Dina would say as she saw her eldest son suddenly growing up. She felt someone at her shoulder, and expected when she turned to see Ross complaining about her not being in the kitchen for her own instructions. It was his brother.

'Hi, Mars,' said Ruaridh quietly beside her, hands in his pockets. 'Love's young dream, eh?'

'I think it's delightful.' She smiled and turned to go back into the kitchen to be instructed in the fine art of soft fruit maceration. Ruaridh took her forearm but for some reason, she couldn't bring herself to look up at him.

'Listen, about, er, the other day with Arshia.'

'It's okay. I've forgotten about it.'

'Oh, right. I was going to say, thanks for the breakfast. That was a bit, er, embarrassing. I hope you didn't jump to conclusions.'

She shook her head and turned to the two young people in front of her as they walked from table to table: one girl very much in control; one boy like a lovestruck puppy.

'Yo, bro,' said the ebullient Ross, who appeared behind them, giving Ruaridh a heavy brotherly thump on the shoulder. He then proceeded to wrap his arm around Marcie's shoulder as he leaned into her. 'Can I introduce you to my new sous chef?'

'Are *you* cooking?' queried Ruaridh, a horrified look spreading across his face.

'Don't look so afraid! I'm only on desserts because it's an assembly job, but feel free to send no orders into the kitchen and ask only for ice cream. I *can* work a scoop. I'll do you a very generous portion,' she replied, 'and squeezy chocolate sauce.'

'There's an invitation!' said Ross and gave her a little pull, which she noticed Ruaridh watched closely. 'Right, Mossie, kitchen. You two' – Ross whistled to Hannah and Dax – 'final instructions, step to it!'

'Has he always been so bossy?' Marcie asked Ruaridh, finally looking up at him.

Ruaridh simply sighed. 'Is Ally on the bar?'

'Yeah, she'll be out in a minute,' she replied and watched as he ambled slowly over to the counter and leant his foot on the brass bar below. She walked over, placed her hand in the small of his back.

'You okay? You'll have a good night tonight with the team,' she said with a genuine concern.

He looked wounded. 'Tippety-top,' he lied. 'Good luck in there.'

He checked himself in the mirror, and thought his brother's comments earlier in the week were true; he still looked a shadow of his former self.

Marcie had begun to make her way back to the kitchen when she caught sight of Dieter.

'I've been trying to search you down all day!' He rested his hands on her shoulders as he greeted Marcie with two kisses on the cheek and then took a glass of Prosecco from the perfectly still tray of Hannah.

Marcie automatically went to take a glass from the tray before Hannah gave her a wide-eyed look, and Marcie apologised with a heartfelt *sorry*.

'But I see that you have been busy.' He smiled.

'Oh, this?' said Marcie, holding out her newly bought and slightly too-big shirt. 'We're all just helping out Heather while she gets a night off!'

'I was hoping to invite you to this special dinner. I had invited my wife, but she was too ill to come to Scotland, as you know. It is a get-together of the most generous type. The people of Strathkin have been most kind to us – a friendly German invasion, if I can say such a thing.'

'You can and very nicely put,' said Marcie and took hold of the hand he held out to her.

'I made a mistake in a message I sent to my wife, and I called it S*tathkind* because truly that is what it means to us, and it is now what we all call it.'

'Oh, Dieter, that is so nice,' agreed Marcie and put her hand on her heart.

He took her by the arm and steered her away from the other chatting figures around them.

'And with regard to that other thing we have in common,' he began.

'Ah,' she managed, 'about that. I've been thinking, and I'm not...'

'I have some news for you from my man.' They were standing in the vestibule, and he was about to tell her the latest from his private investigator when a familiar scent appeared all around them like an aromatic haze.

'Well, well, well, lovelies. I thought you of all people might 'ave made an effort!' said Maureen as she sidled up to Marcie, her eyes casting a glance at the monochrome uniform, and she curled her lips.

'I'm working here this evening, Maureen.' Marcie gestured around to the busy room next door.

'Oh? Really? That fancy big job in London and whatnot not working out? Never looked like a lawyer to me, to be fair. Find out you couldn't cut it?' asked Maureen, unable to give even a backhanded compliment.

Marcie raised her eyes to the ceiling. 'This was a private conversation,' she began.

'Well, this lovely young man invited me along to this special supper so *I'm* a guest. I'll have a G&T if you're actin' as the waitress, dear. Large one. As quick as you like, if you don't mind. Now, Mr From, where exactly *are* you from?'

'Frum,' he corrected.

'Oh, really, is that in Austria then?'

After raising her eyes to the ceiling again in despair, Marcie left with a motion to Dieter that they needed to meet later. She made her way back into the kitchen as Bella was rushing out.

'Where have you been?' she asked quickly in passing.

'Just catching up with people.'

'You're not a guest!' warned Bella as she headed out into the fray.

Marice turned and walked straight into Ross, arms folded in front of him. She gazed at his strong ink-free forearms, and her mind began wandering to the story behind the tattoo and where else they would be on his body.

'Socialising?' he asked.

'Um...' She turned away, avoiding his gaze as Dax came into the kitchen.

'Dax, my man, once the first orders are out, I need you on dishwasher duty. I've seen you at home so no worries – stacking, twenty-minute fast wash, then plates out and away. We need a clean kitchen to work in. Got it?'

'Yup,' agreed Dax.

Marcie observed the exchange and was surprised at how Ross was in control of what could easily be chaos. Just the *right* kind of bossy, she thought.

'Mossie, front and centre,' he ordered her, and she made her way quickly to where he was in front of the stainless-steel counter. He dished out orders, pointed at bubbling pans, told her what she needed to do and deftly started plating up while she stood in awe at his skill and confidence in the kitchen. It ran like clockwork under his clear direction and cool demeanour, and she stepped to one side of the kitchen so as not to stop the flow of culinary artistry that was going on in the middle of the space on the long steel counter. She found herself slotting into the group and agreeing to his every challenge as he made demands and then, suddenly, he was thanking them for the efforts and their help.

Marcie glanced up at the large kitchen clock and wondered where the time had gone. Everything had happened so fast when she knew that as a diner, everything was at a slower pace on the other side of the pass. Hannah was instructing Dax where the washed plates had to be stacked and started refilling the dishwasher like a pro as Bella piled up plates beside her, emptying anything uneaten into a bin at the end of the kitchen. Marcie was genuinely surprised as to how all these people worked together in tandem, each slotting into each other's space effortlessly. She was delighted and knew that Heather would be ecstatic to find out that everything had gone so smoothly. And then, the kitchen was empty, the last dessert plates coming back with not even the garnish still on them, dishwasher filled and cleaned plates stacked away. Everything was pristine once more.

She opened the door slightly to listen to the chatter outside, which was loud and full of laughter. A buzz was spiriting around the room, and she watched people's faces as they threw their heads back, enjoying each other's company. She felt Ross at her shoulder.

'Well, everyone looks happy, and no one has keeled over yet,' he said as he joined her gaze out into the dining room.

'Early days,' she joked and felt him nudge her.

'If the same amount of people leave that came in, then that's a good service,' he said and went back into the kitchen.

Her eyes flitted around the room, and she saw Ruaridh leaning back in his seat, nodding intently, arms folded, sleeves of his plaid shirt rolled up, as he exchanged stories with Lachie Bateman. She noticed Ruthie talking to Maureen near the door as people started to drift away.

'Thoughts?' Ross was asking her, behind her once more.

'Hmmm?' She turned around, not listening to what he had been saying.

'I said, if you want to stay for a drink, I'm happy to drive you back up the road?'

Marcie bit her lip at this scenario, which she admitted to herself was fraught with danger – her emotions in turmoil and her fertile imagination in a state of flux.

'I've decided to stay at Sweet Briar tonight with Callum due home. I wanted to start to get the place freshened up.'

'Closer. That's handy,' he said into her ear and then wandered back into the kitchen.

Her body gave a little shiver then watched as Ruaridh left the table and made his way to the bar. People continued to drift away from tables to the bar and the room emptied. She went out and started clearing away plates that had been left on the tables while observing the movements at the bar. After Maureen passed Marcie on her way to the toilets with a pat on the arm and a 'good job dear – lovely tea,' she made her way over to where Dieter sat at the table alone. He was pleased to see her.

'I bet your ears are crying out in mercy.' She smiled to him.

'I don't quite understand?'

'Maureen can be quite a challenge.'

'She is such a delightful woman. I am quite overwhelmed at her kindness.'

'Really?' Marcie shook her head. 'Oh well. Each to their own.'

'Listen, I really do need to speak with you about that person we have in common. My man says he is on the move although we do not know where. He seems to have disappeared. Are you still willing to help me? To put a stop to him?'

'Well, I've been thinking, Dieter, you see, and I'm not sure if...'

'Please do not let me down. We have both suffered immeasurably.'

Marcie knew he was right, but she was trying to put events behind her. She had started her own journey of revenge with so much hate in her heart. But with Callum settled and her own life moving in a different direction, she had decided, like Ruaridh, that she wanted to close the door on her old life to enable her to open one to a new life. And that was a life that did not have something inside that was eating away at her daily, tearing her emotions to shreds, not allowing love to be the driver to her future. She had had therapy, counselling and even a meditation retreat but even so, sometimes she struggled to put her feelings and emotions into words. She did not want to go back to events of the past that had Poytr Medvedev at the centre. That was another time. It was in the past and that's where she wanted it to remain. She shook her head and tucked her hair behind her ear, then ran her fingers over her lips.

'Listen, Dieter, my uncle is back soon. Could I talk with him first? It doesn't just affect me...'

'I understand. I just don't want him to turn up unexpectedly. My man is paid a lot to keep his eye on him, but I can't let him get away. He's currently gone to ground.'

'Why doesn't your guy know where he is?' asked Marcie, and at the same time a chill ran through her.

She had a feeling of uneasiness. Her eyes drifted out to the loch in front of the Inn and Swanfield directly across the water. With no moonlight and no lights from the building opposite, the area where her childhood home used to illuminate the water was now entirely dark.

'I've decided to throw out some crumbs.'

'What? What do you mean?'

'Oh no, no, once I have a plan fixed in my head, I will follow it through. I have every confidence he will take the bait.'

'I don't know what you're planning, Dieter, but this guy is so, so clever. If you have tempted him with bait, I hope you can pull back at any time?'

'I have placed an advert, looking for a companion, and we believe he has responded in a positive way. Wherever he is, he will be tempted out with money from a supposed wealthy woman.'

'Positive? Meaning?'

'We will be making arrangements to meet. I will agree, but not to somewhere remote. I am aware of what you said about him. I have seen some areas around here, places where it would be problematic for him to do anything, wide-open spaces, overlooking the sea.'

'To meet?' A horrified look spread across her face. Her life in the past few years had seen its difficulties and disappointments like most people. But now, she seemed to lurch from crisis to crisis, and the last thing she wanted was to have the threat of Brodie Nairn or Poytr Medvedev or whatever he was calling himself now, back in it. She knew that placing adverts and following through whether online or in traditional print media, was best left to late-night television with a glass of wine

and a laugh with girlfriends. She rested her elbow on the table and her hand took the weight of her head which, suddenly, was heavy and confused. She saw Maureen head their way and she stood up.

'Who else knows about this?'

'Just me, my man and you. There is no one else who needs to know. If you choose to tell your uncle, I can understand that.'

He smiled as if he had the best plan in the world laid out, but the clever and elusive Poytr Medvedev knew that was exactly what he wanted you to think. Just when you thought you were one step ahead of him, Marcie knew, he appeared out of the woodwork with another plan up his sleeve. And with Callum coming back for a joyous return when they would *chase the sun* together, Marcie realised the last thing he needed in his new life was to come face to face with the man who almost took his life – not once, but twice.

'Are you okay?' Dieter queried as she stood and appeared a little unsteady on her feet.

She felt his hand on her elbow.

'I'm fine. I'm fine.'

She smiled at him weakly and was glad that she had made the last-minute decision earlier that morning to stay at Sweet Briar. But wasn't that also fraught with danger if her nemesis was anywhere in the area? Although Dieter appeared quite confident that he had everything under control, *isn't that when things usually go wrong?*

'Please keep this as quiet as possible. Please, for everyone's sake. I understand if you don't want to get involved but I am quite capable of handling this man by myself.'

Marcie nodded and, looking around, noticed most of the bar had cleared. Ruaridh had left, Lachie Bateman from the MRT was still talking to Ruthie, and only a few scattered people now remained in the vestibule.

Marcie walked over to the window and gazed across the

water. A cloud briefly moved away from the moon and for just a moment Swanfield was visible. She headed out and made her way into the cool, still air, walking to the edge of the small wall that separated the car park from the shore of Loch Strathkin. A couple nearby were chatting animatedly, toxic smoke from cigarettes drifting upwards and disappearing into the clean and clear night. She thought about The Retreat and its premise. *Dignity in dying* was certainly available there – if you had the money and the means, open to the wealthy few, not people with limited funds where it could actually have helped. And what of Swanfield now? If Angelina's plans came to fruition, her former home could be turned into something that would save so many lives from being wasted. It could allow people to heal and to recover from love that went wrong, abusive relationships. Strathkin cared for people. Like Dieter Frum had mistakenly called it – *Strathkind*. Was this where her future lay? Not in a big city fighting against the system but back in her small village where she could make a difference? She and Heather and Bella doing what Dina would have wanted – showering strangers with love and kindness? Maybe this was her purpose, her new focus. Sharing Strathkin with people who needed to escape to a better future, in a way, like her. *Was she really seeking out something that would bring clarity back to her complicated life?* Making her money work for the better – her experience in legal matters being put to good use rather than lining somebody else's pockets. She missed Callum's wise counsel – *could this be something that might tempt him, too, back to the land of his birth?* There was so much to consider and so much to walk away from. But there was also so much ahead that was making her heart thrill with expectation. She heard a crunch of gravel behind her and turned around to see Ross Balfour stepping out of the wide porch and into the car park. He was standing like a warrior before battle, arms folded, watching. Waiting. She caught his eyes before looking away. *Was she ready for this next step?* Her body was telling her yes. Her mind was telling her to wait. Everyone seemed to be giving her warnings about this man who had turned up unexpectedly and seemingly on a one-man mission. Her eyes again rested on Swanfield. The couple who had been laughing and talking slid into their car and drove away and another parked car in the corner switched its lights off. Ross wandered down to where Marcie was standing at the end of the car park at the small wall, and he rested his boot on it. A gentle ripple made barely a sound as it lapped the shore in front of them. His eyes settled on the building opposite.

'It's a pity, isn't it?' he said.

'Hmmm.'

'It must be saved. Something as magnificent as Swanfield can't be left like that.'

Marcie turned to look up at him but was unsure if he was talking to her or just saying words to himself. She looked back to the house where her memories were born. *What a mistake, turning my back on such a place*, she thought to herself. He stood next to her, his bare arms brushing against hers, and she felt it again. Like a spark. *It's energy*, she said to herself, *it's just energy*.

'We're having a drink inside, if you're up for it?'

'Sure, why not?' she agreed.

He turned to go back into the hotel, but she stayed for a moment looking over to what had been her childhood home then gave a little shiver. 'Oof. Somebody's just walked over my grave,' she muttered to herself as she shook her shoulders and walked up to the main door, completely unaware of the man in the dark Lexus far away from the one single light in the car park who was watching her every move.

By the time Marcie made it back into the dining room, Hannah and Dax were sitting cosied up at the end of the banquette.

Ross had sat next to them, and Bella was relaxing next to *him* with her arms spread out on each side of the plush seat and a contented smile on her face. Marcie pulled up a dining chair and sat down heavily, resting her arms on the side of it. Ally walked over from the bar with a tray of drinks, and she deftly put them down in front of everyone – a zero-alcohol shandy for Dax made up from the top of the bottle of Ross's zero per cent lager, a Diet Coke for Hannah and red wine for everyone else. Marcie pulled over another chair next to her and indicated to Ally to take a seat.

'I've got to hand it to you, Ross, you played a blinder,' said Bella and raised her glass, everyone clinking their glass against hers. Hannah turned around and gave Dax a cheeky grin and he smiled back, looking as if he'd realised that suddenly, he was at the grown-ups' table because that's exactly what he was.

'You all did, it was teamwork,' Ross agreed. 'That's what we do, isn't it, Daxy? Team Balfour all the way.' He reached over and hit his glass against his nephew's, who beamed in agreement.

'Team Balfour,' he repeated and under the table placed his hand on Hannah's knee, and she covered her hand over his.

'Now, you can't leave,' continued Bella, shuffling in her seat to edge herself a little closer to Ross, 'you're woven into the Strathkin folklore, and you'll never be allowed to go back to New Zealand!'

'Is that right, now?' he asked and took a sip from his bottle of beer. He watched as Marcie took a large gulp of her wine then turned to compliment Ally on the choice.

'Don't tell H – it's out of the *special* wine crate,' replied Ally, making a face.

'Oh, I don't think she'll mind,' reassured Marcie. 'She will be absolutely delighted at the success of the night. Everyone was full of praise for the chef and the waiting staff.'

Marcie turned from Ally to see Ross watching her. She saw

that Bella had followed Hannah's lead and placed her palm flat on Ross's knee, but he paid no attention to it; rather, he followed Marcie's gaze as she turned to look across the loch. She felt a strange unease. Was it the thought of Angelina San returning or was it something else? Or maybe Dieter Frum and his plans which she had grave concerns about. Marcie ran her finger round the rim of the glass. She shook her head and brought herself back to reality.

'Dax, how was your first big night of working?' Ally asked the boy at the end of the table.

'Oh, I work all the time with Dad,' he answered, trying to sound as if this was a normal everyday occurrence now that he was a grown-up.

'But this was your first time in service?'

'Er...' he stumbled, unsure of what Ally meant.

'Well, you know what happens after service?' she said, with a smile and wide eyes.

Dax eyed her suspiciously, and Hannah nudged him.

'Tips!' said Ally enthusiastically. 'And I'm pleased to say that here at the world famous Strathkin Inn, all tips are generously shared out amongst all the waiting staff! *Immediately!*' She put a pile of bank notes on the table, and Dax stared at them in wonder. He'd never worked with, or for, 'real' money before now, his parents providing him with a bank card from an online bank on his twelfth birthday. In reward for chores, they would put a little on it each week so that he could access his own money and become accustomed to budgeting from an early age, so this look and feel of real money was a strange concept to him. And there was a pile of it sitting directly in front of him on the table.

'Everyone kinda left a fiver but some put in a tenner, so it works out at thirty-four pounds each.'

'*Each?*' asked Dax in astonishment. 'For, like, working here? Tonight?'

'Hey, don't think this is a regular occurrence, sometimes you won't make that in a good week. It's a planned function tonight so it's always a little bit more and these guys are super generous. Plus, they heard about Adam, so they're just delighted it wasn't cancelled!' qualified Ally as she divided notes and coins down in front of everyone.

Ross rubbed his hands in apparent glee, picked up the three ten pound notes and four one pound coins and made a big gesture of putting it into his pocket. However, under the table, Marcie saw him nudge Hannah and pass his portion of the tip to her. She turned to say something about being reluctant to take it, but he shook his head at her, and she took the money secretly. Dax glanced at Marcie, noticing that she had seen what had occurred and she, too, motioned under the table and slipped her own money into his hand. He looked at the cash, then back to her but did not know what to say. He began to count it, not believing his luck. He leaned over to Hannah and said something unheard but included the word 'Inverness' and they both smiled shyly at each other.

'Excuse me, ladies,' said Ross suddenly, 'I'm going to nip up and see the *real* chef. Check in on him. Back in a tick.' He squeezed out past Bella, who leaned back ever so slightly to allow him to squeeze by, and she watched him leave, eyeing him up and down.

'Who's up for a coin toss? Anyone after a fine piece of Scottish beef?' she said jokingly before covering her mouth when she remembered the two young people at the end of the banquette. Hannah and Dax, however, were too engrossed in giggling with each other to hear anything anyone else was saying. Ally spat out her wine at Bella's comment.

'You're unbelievable.' She laughed at Bella's embarrassed face.

'I'm heading off, too, I think,' said Marcie. 'I'm not used to all this hard physical labour.'

'You sliced a courgette!' said Bella, eyeing Marcie over her large gulp of wine.

'Three courgettes!' Marcie held up three fingers. 'And they were *ribboned*, not *sliced*.'

'He's some worker, though,' said Ally, nursing her glass and licking her lips. 'Adam can stay sick as far as I'm concerned!' Bella laughed at the comment and held her glass out to Ally, who tipped hers until they rang out with a loud *ting*.

'Dax, will I walk you back up the road?' suggested Marcie, only to be met with a look of horror from the young boy.

'Er, no, thanks!' was the response, and Marcie shrugged her shoulders and stood up, momentarily forgetting what it was like to be in the first flushes of young love.

'I can see him back if he ever wants to leave,' said Bella, whose house at the Trekking Centre was only steps away from Lochside Croft, which in turn was only moments away from the Inn.

'Well, I'll see you ladies tomorrow just in case you have a late one,' said Marcie, as she leaned her hand down on Ally's shoulder then took her hand and squeezed it, 'but seriously, girls, you played a blinder. Heather will be over the moon. You were amazing – just pulled it all together.'

'And thanks to you, too,' said Bella, holding her glass up and seemingly settling in for a long session.

At the back door, Marcie glanced at the clock as it neared midnight but stopped as she heard someone on the stairs on their way down. Ross stopped as he neared the bottom of the wide staircase and leaned on the wall.

'I hope you're only going to the little girls' room. I've just found a great playlist for late-night classics on Spotify, smooth jazz, good for a wee slow dance.'

'I'm heading off.'

'Oh,' he sighed, disappointed.

She walked over to look up at him on the stairs as he folded his arms.

'How long are you going to be here? I think the girls are waiting for you to go back in to join them. I'm sure they'll be up for a move on the dancefloor.'

'Depends if I get a better offer.' He waited.

She pondered.

'How about if I cook you breakfast?' she suggested.

'I'm outta here!' he said, launching himself down the last two stairs and heading to the still-open door. 'C'mon, it's only early!' he said eagerly with a glance to the clock.

'I'm not offering anything other than breakfast,' she confirmed and remained where she was in the vestibule. He had a quizzical look on his face. She threw him her car keys. 'I'll tell you en-route,' she said and caught up with him as they headed to her car. 'Aren't you going to say goodbye to the girls?'

'Och, they'll think I'm still tending to a sick Adam, and my street cred will go up.'

'They'll see us on the CCTV, Sherlock.'

'Well, it's your street cred you've got to worry about then, isn't it, Mossie?'

TWENTY-SIX

Ross was open-mouthed when they reached Sweet Briar, a cottage he had not been in since his young teenage years. Like Tigh-na-Lochan, it had been decorated in muted tartans and selected highland-ware which gave it a feel of contemporary elegance. Its look was classic but modern; stags and thistles without being twee. A copy charcoal drawing of Landseer's *Monarch of the Glen* hung above the fireplace in a huge silver frame and was a perfect fit in this Scottish retreat.

'It's got her written all over it.' He took a cup of herbal tea from Marcie and sat down on a well-worn leather sofa, refusing her offer of a fine wine. Dina, without doubt, had beautiful taste and a perfect eye for detail. Her interior decorating skills were well known amongst her group of friends, and if her life had not been cut so tragically short, she would no doubt have gone on to bigger and better commissions once her family had grown.

'I miss her every day. I can only imagine what Ruaridh and the boys feel and of course little Mari who simply won't remember her at all,' sighed Marcie as she sat down on a chair opposite, preferring to keep away from the large sofa for want of *inviting trouble*, as Lisanne would have said. She took her wine with her and a large glass of water to accompany it.

'He certainly does struggle. He's definitely a changed man,' said Ross and gazed into the empty grate. 'You and him not, eh...' he began, 'like before?'

'I've told you. No.'

'And you and your husband? No chance of...' His eyes were scanning her, not letting up.

'We've had that discussion. I'm not going there again.'

'And, so, I'm here tonight as a bodyguard? Just getting the ground rules squared away.'

'I'm just feeling a bit uneasy, as I said in the car. Callum's back soon and I wanted to start getting the place ready for him, and with Tigh-na-Lochan being so far away...'

'That's fine. Just as long as I know I'm here as Tom Cruise, not Kevin Costner then?'

'What are you taking about? You're twice the size of Tom Cruise.'

'What I'm saying is, I'm here as the tough guy, not the romantic hero?'

'Hmmm. Yes, I suppose so.'

'The frog rather than Prince Charming?'

'Hmmm.'

'The bad cop rather than the good cop?'

'Exactly.'

'Tom rather than Jerry?'

'Good gawd! I'm beginning to regret this already. I said to you in the car, sometimes I just worry about that guy coming back. It doesn't always happen but sometimes I get a little uncomfortable. Sometimes when I'm on my own. Just tonight, I feel a little bit, not scared, just anxious.'

'I'm getting the lay of the land, Mossie, no need to get your knickers in a twist. Oops, sorry! Mentioned knickers in your presence!' He covered his mouth in fake disgust, and she threw a velvet cushion at him which he caught with one hand and rested on his lap, giving her a wide-eyed look. She giggled, shook her head.

It was obvious he was a Balfour – the cheeky demeanour and incessant flirting a dead giveaway – and she knew what was happening to her despite her efforts to dampen her feelings. She also wondered if the time was now. The time to bring things out into the open. He was sipping on his camomile tea, and she followed his gaze to the fireplace. He started to say something, his facial expressions showing that he was working something out in his mind. She knew this because she was doing the same. Was it time to stop playing games? She put down her wine on the small table and took a breath.

'Just to clarify...' she began.

'Uh-huh?'

'You're here just to make sure nothing happens.'

'You've made it perfectly clear; nothing is going to happen,' he qualified her statement.

'I mean with anyone out there,' she said and gestured to the window with the curtains still open.

'And in here.' He nodded, firmly.

'You're incorrigible,' she said and expected him to give the Ruaridh retort of *once I look that up in the dictionary, I'll come back and agree with you*, but he simply gave an exaggerated nod of the head. 'First up makes breakfast?'

'I thought you invited me? Okay. Yes, ma'am.'

She decided there and then to call it a night and stood up, her wine not touched. 'And there's a lock on my door,' she said as she walked past him, heading to the door to her bedroom.

He grabbed her hand.

'And you'll be using it?'

'Indeed,' she responded. 'Nightie night.'

She wriggled free and switched the light off as she left, leaving him in the soft glow from the large outside lantern.

With teeth brushed and pyjamas on, she was lying with the curtains open and under a light duvet when she heard her door handle being turned from the outside. She took a sharp intake of breath.

'Just checking, scaredy cat!' he shouted as he passed. 'I'm heading for a shower. Just letting you know in case you hear any strange noises. It's only me making them. Sleep tight, Mossie.'

She laughed into her pillow, her insides churning and her heart beating out of her chest.

'*Self-control,*' she said quietly to herself, '*self-control, self-control.*'

Marcie slept more soundly than she thought she would under the circumstances. She awoke with a stretch and to the smell of coffee drifting though the cottage. 'Mmm,' she said as she pulled the duvet around her. It was only when she opened her eyes, she realised that the smell was so strong because a mug of coffee was beside her bed. 'What the…?' she thought and pulled the quilt from her, feeling at her hair to see if it was as bad morning hair as she usually had, mussed up and sticking out.

She leapt out of bed to check herself in the mirror. She did look as if she had had a late night. She heard footsteps outside and raced back to her bed as the door knocked.

'Yes?' she squeaked.

'Are you decent, Mossie?'

'COME IN!' she yelled, trying to flatten her hair, pinch her cheeks to pinkness.

Ross came in with a bed tray on which was a freshly warmed croissant and a small dish with her own homemade blackcurrant jam. It sat next to a side plate with some scrambled eggs and a slice of buttered toast. There was a shot glass of orange juice on top of a napkin.

'First rule to the scared out of wits. When locking one's

door, make sure you don't leave the spare key hanging up. Enjoy.'

He had left before she had time to speak and started laughing. *So, turns out he is a gentleman*, she thought to herself and decided to take ten minutes out to enjoy the fruits of his labour before heading for her own shower and getting dressed to face him in a more respectable manner.

When she did meander through to the kitchen, there was a pink sticky note on the empty table that simply said:

IN THE INN

'Fair enough,' she said and rinsed her dishes, setting them to dry on a kitchen towel on the worktop. Glancing around, she realised she was missing her furry friend and wondered if Atlas was thinking the same – *missing her* – then realised it would be Ross that the cat was pining for. She enjoyed their one-sided chats, and now that Atlas was becoming more adventurous in the great outdoors, she only saw him rarely and normally when he was spread out, belly up, on her bed before she climbed in at night. She drained the last of the coffee from the French press and went outside to look across to Lochside Croft. How things had moved on in just a few years. A glance to the side showed her the scaffolding firmly affixed to Swanfield, and she bit her lip, wrapping her fingers around the mug. Would Ruaridh and Arshia make a go of it? Would Dax and Hannah become a well-recognised couple in and around the village? Would Maureen outlive all of them?

She was laughing as she made her way back inside then thought she really needed to discuss the Poytr issue with Callum, and suddenly she remembered she hadn't confirmed the hotel she had booked for their yearly getaway. Two rooms at a small hotel at Dunnet Head, facing the beach. She cursed herself. Without a deposit paid, the rooms had probably been taken. She tried to rebook quickly on her phone, but they had disappeared from the booking site. She sat at the table for a moment, chin in her palms, as she tried to think of a place that did not involve camping or *roughing it* when her phone buzzed. It was Heather with a message.

> I'll be back at the Inn in half an hour – need to speak urgently!!! Hx

It was the exclamation marks that made Marcie think – Heather was not one for dramatic punctuation. A glance at her watch told her it was too late to go back to Tigh-na-Lochan if Heather wanted to see her right away. Her mind was working overtime. There was a decision to be made. If Angelina's plans were to be approved and Swanfield turned into a women's refuge, surely this should be where her focus was. Ruaridh was also on her mind. He felt it was time to move forward with his life, and she was clearly now only best friend material. She appreciated his honesty, his upfront discussion and plans for his own future. If he – the man who avoided decision-making at all costs – could plan a way forward, then she, *too*, would have to do the same thing. Now it was Simon's turn to occupy her thoughts in what was increasingly a butterfly mind. She dialled Simon's number and got what she expected – the message saying the phone was switched off. She dialled the home number that no longer went to voicemail. It simply rang out. And that made her decision for her right there and then. She wanted to expedite everything.

Calling Richard MacInnes, she left a message with Margaret Tulloch who was unusually chatty about the weather, the forthcoming summer solstice, and her recent visit to Strathkin, which Marcie found rather odd. It was as if she was trying to tell her something without trying to tell her something.

She grabbed her jacket and began to walk to the Inn, completely oblivious to the figure of Poytr Medvedev in a hard hat and reflective jacket with a clipboard at the house next door, not studying building plans, but studying the woman he had come back to finally erase from his life.

She zipped up her red fleece as she walked, her mind running over phrases like *irreconcilable differences*. Is that what the expression was? How long would it take? Six months for a dissolution or divorce. There were no children to consider. The property in London's Southfields was bought with her money, just as the flat in Southampton Row on the other side of the city was bought as a joint venture. So, no significant issues there. Money was not an issue for either of them, but she felt an overwhelming sadness that it had come to this. She was sure that, if allowed, he would be open to a conversation; there was still a kind of love there. She could see his mother in her mind's eye, more than likely opening the letter from Richard before it landed in his hands and giving her version of events to the man who once shared her life.

Marcie thought of the charcoal drawing of her beautiful wedding dress that hung in the alcove in Tigh-na-Lochan. She was reminded of the lovely weekend away in Edinburgh with Heather and Dina, and their giggling afternoons in the wedding boutiques and high-end stores of the capital. They were having such fun until they stumbled into one expensive wedding shop in George Street. She recalled how they all stopped dead, mouths open as they gazed in awe at the ivory silk gown that was on a mannequin and about to be placed in the window display. She slipped into it effortlessly only moments later, and the assistant made various adjustments with bulldog clips and pins and suddenly she was looking at her two teary friends as they stood in front of her with glasses of Prosecco. It was a lifetime ago. Dina glowing and Heather smiling dreamily. Bella still in what she referred to as her secret *getaway*.

How things change and move on in little over two years. Dina now gone and Heather with the man she should have been with all along, and Bella, well, Bella sharing her days with Maureen Berman, which bore little resemblance to a normal life. But Bella had told Marcie they had 'an arrangement'. It had been agreed between them that Maureen would 'see her all right' if she was well looked after and was despatched quickly when the time came, desperate as she was to meet her Brian in the afterlife or wherever he had taken up residence. 'Each to their own,' Marcie had said to Bella when she offered an explanation about the woman who came to recuperate after the devastating fire at Swanfield and who never left.

As she reached the head of Loch Strathkin, Marcie took in the length of the water before her as it flowed finally out into the Minch and then the Atlantic Ocean and the open sea. How lucky she was to have been born here, to be able to return here and in the not-too-distant future, maybe settle back here permanently. She thought of Ross and what he had said about the pulling thread that tugged at her to guide her back home. Was this what she was feeling? Was this what this pang was that had started to beat inside her? The invisible thread to home. This deep, deep longing. Everything that had gone before, had it simply happened for the sole purpose of eventually bringing her back here? Was her previous life with Simon a road she had to travel on before setting her on the right path, a journey she had to take to finally lead her to where she now found herself? And was there someone else out there with a Marcie Mosse stamp already branded onto their heart? Was he already in her life? Is that what Ruaridh had noticed and, as he asked her to release him, was he also releasing *her*? Had he seen into her future the way she was looking into his? Had she simply chosen the wrong Balfour?

Marcie stood and let these thoughts linger for just a second more. She started to meander on the road to the junction where she once again stopped. Left to Strathkin, the village hall, the Inn, Lochside Croft, her posse of childhood friends, a melange of scattered little cottages along the water's edge as they led up to the next junction that took visitors to Strath Aullt and Strathdon. And then the single-track road that took visitors to the burial ground and up again to the left to Tigh-na-Lochan and her own new little life. She looked to the right, the road that would lead her back to the city and the airport and, she now wanted to admit, her old life. Behind her, a past life at Swanfield and Sweet Briar next door. She was at her own crossroads. Take this way and continue in the past; take that way and change her future. For better or for worse? Maybe it was all for the better. Maybe her future had more than a change of job in it. Maybe Angelina's plans for the new Swanfield were exactly what she needed. And maybe it *was* Dina who was answering her prayers. She was a new Marcie Mosse. She felt Simon invade her thoughts and she knew there and then it was for the last time. She had done all the chasing and had been met with a wall of silence. She had stood at the door, she reminded herself, hundreds of miles from here in the pouring rain, begging for forgiveness that was not hers to give. *Enough. I'm not spending any more time on this.* She turned left and walked into the village of Strathkin.

The Inn was quiet, and Marcie saw Heather in their usual seat at the window of the restaurant on her phone, texting. She stood up as Marcie came in. Marcie noticed her friend's worried look and sat opposite her.

'That's a face I haven't seen in a while...' she began.

'You want a coffee? Tea?' suggested Heather.

'No. Stuffed. Had a huge breakfast made for me.' She didn't say by whom.

'Listen, thanks for stepping up to the plate. You lot played a blinder. There were so many grateful emails on my phone this morning. Seriously, I'm so thankful and so is everyone.'

'Anytime!' Marcie smiled. 'It was an eye-opener for me in a lot of ways, I can tell you!'

'Jamie's been suspended,' Heather blurted out before Marcie had finished her sentence.

'What?'

'Well, we went down to Inverness thinking this was the moment he was going to be promoted. I mean, he was a bit surprised when he realised he was the only one there, but I guess he just thought he was special. Instead of promoting him, they suspended him.'

'Why?'

'I don't know!' said Heather, with a pleading look on her face.

'Well, they can't just suspend you and say nothing. They must have told him.'

'He is being quite evasive, but I'm just not sure.'

Marcie reached out and took her friend's hand across the table.

'It'll be something and nothing. I wouldn't worry about it. Not at this point anyway. What happens next?'

'No idea. He said something about an investigation, and he's suspended until that's concluded, I think.'

'Odd. Is it serious?'

Heather shrugged. Marcie was perplexed.

'Apart from that – everything going well?' A broad smile across the table from Heather revealed that this new relationship was going more than well, and they hugged.

'As I said, I'm sure it'll be something and nothing,' reassured Marcie. 'Try not to worry about it. These things happen all the time and they're usually over quite quickly. They'll keep everything under wraps until they're ready to reveal their findings but, really, it's just an oversight or something, I imagine. He'll have forgotten to file something or run out of time on submitting paperwork.'

'What if he gets a punishment post?'

'A punishment post?' queried Marcie.

'Yes, where they post you somewhere remote as a form of punishment if they think you need sorting out?'

'Come on, Heather, surely that's a thing from the past. I wouldn't think they'd do that nowadays, plus, as I said, it'll be something and nothing. Really, just wait and it will sort itself out, these things usually do. I'll speak with him. Don't worry! It'll sort itself out!'

In the kitchen at the back of the Inn, Ross was chatting to Ally about the success of the previous evening's dinner, with her heaping praise on him for his valiant efforts in the kitchen and, being a Balfour, it was no more than he expected. He leaned to one side as he saw Jamie MacKay appear at the back door, excused himself away from watching Ally wrap cutlery in napkins for the bar meal service, and wandered out to greet his friend.

'Hey,' he greeted Jamie but noticed he appeared a little unkempt, hair not its usual neat crop and unshaven. 'Heavy night? Lucky you.'

Jamie motioned for Ross to walk with him, and they strolled out and started along the road that took them moments later to the village hall, where Jamie wandered along the side of the building that took him down to the shore.

'You're making me a wee bit uneasy, pal,' said Ross finally and Jamie checked around several times as if he was under surveillance.

'Got a problem,' he announced and walked to the low wall that separated the car park from the shore and the gentle lapping waters of the loch beyond.

Ross watched his friend stare out into the middle distance, his eyes settling on Swanfield opposite.

'I've been suspended,' he said suddenly, catching Ross unawares.

'Oh?' replied Ross.

'Was hauled in yesterday to Professional Standards.'

'What's that?'

'Used to be Complaints and Discipline. Now it's the department that holds up the professional standards of the organisation and looks down on the rest of us lowly coppers trying to do the right thing.'

'And what were you doing?' quizzed Ross.

'You *know* what I was doing,' responded Jamie, turning around to face him. 'I was looking up an old file to finally find out if the car we tampered with was Marcie's mum and dad's.'

'Ah,' Ross sighed, placing his hands in his pockets, rooting his feet to the spot. 'Sorry about that.'

They both stood, looking at the small cottage of Sweet Briar that sat in the shadow of what had been the grandest house in the area.

'I'm not sure I should've agreed to do it.'

'Well, you wanted to find out as much as I did,' said Ross, not wanting to take full blame for what had happened.

Silence descended.

'And?' asked Ross, reluctant to know what the answer would be, but determined to tick this box off in his mind and to close this part of his childhood for good.

'Nothing,' began Jamie. 'The file was closed. It was an accident, according to the Collision Investigation Team that was on duty at the time. There was a full and thorough investigation, and nothing unusual was found on their car.'

'Nothing?'

'Nothing.'

'So, it was *definitely* old *two suits'* car that we tampered with, not the Mosse's Volvo?'

'Definitely not theirs. The accident would always have

happened. The other guy was a tourist, a French driver in a Citroën, who came out of the junction at Carrbridge and on to the wrong side of the road. They didn't stand a chance. Everyone was killed. Him, his passenger. Marcie's mum and dad.'

Hearing it said aloud like that sent a shiver through Ross. He and Jamie in their youth. Known to be naughty but not bad. Young and stupid as opposed to cold and calculating. Rumours about their teacher's proclivities with students swirled around, and when the man known as 'two suits', because that was his entire working wardrobe, brought his car into Jamie's father's garage, they thought they would tamper with the brakes. *Give the old guy a scare,* they agreed. It was a bit of fun for them at their young age, knowing deep down that the teacher drove everywhere at no more than twenty miles an hour, thinking any higher speed would wear out his tyres quicker and cause thrown up stones to ruin his paintwork. Never known to leave the village apart from his daily trips to school, they would be happy if he drifted quietly into a hedge or into a gully where Jamie's pa would then retrieve him later with his tow truck and a chain. But there were two dark Volvo estates in the garage at the same time, and they simply did not think. It did not turn out quite as they imagined, and they both had lived with the guilt for nearly twenty years.

Ross knew that it was this possible wrongdoing that had made Jamie turn his back on his father's offer of partnering him in the family garage business and instead join the police. He had felt the need to atone for something he may – *or may not* – have done but which had eaten away at him for all this time. It was without a doubt a relief for Ross to know neither of them had been responsible for the deaths of Marcie's parents, but he had carried that guilt with him, too, from the moment he stepped on a plane at Inverness Airport to get as far away from it as possible. That, and the other reason – the reason that had made him come home.

And how was that going? Not as well as he had planned. He had not imagined the tug of home to be so strong from the moment he pulled his car into the car park of The Strathkin Inn and certainly hadn't imagined the strength of attraction to the woman he had come to... *was avenge too strong a word?* His inner voice had told him many times that once he had found out the truth about their deaths, he would make his mind up about his next steps but that was just not going as well as expected. Marcie had captured his brother's heart all those years before. She had been the feisty no-nonsense girl in their tight group of schoolfriends but what was happening now? What was unfolding between *them*? He realised he should have listened to the sensible side of his brain and not done anything like contact the solicitors in Inverness before he had figured out what exactly he wanted to do. And here he was now, responsible for the professional suspension of his greatest friend for some misdemeanour that was clearly his doing, and there was no doubt in his mind that he was falling for the woman he thought he would be battling with in the coming weeks. He was too late to stop this train that was coming down the tracks a lot quicker than he had thought, and he was going to have to fess up or he would be, once again, forced to do what he didn't want to do – travel to the other side of the world to escape his past.

TWENTY-SEVEN

Maureen sat at her favourite place – the banquette of the lounge at The Strathkin Inn. There was no local café in the village unless you could persuade someone to drive you to The Aizle or the bigger and newly opened, but equally as busy, Stag and Thistle restaurant and gift shop, both situated on the road that led back to Inverness. So, the Inn had become her local coffee morning drop-in if Bella was out, and she was in danger of regaling lengthy stories of the past only to herself. Everyone paid their own way at their impromptu coffee mornings and only occasionally was a free coffee on offer. Heather sought out the best local produce to promote to her guests, often selling it onsite for a small profit, which was then churned back into the business. Maureen loved these tastings. And she particularly loved the chat with the driver from Only Coffee Roasters in Beauly, the little village just outside Inverness. He would flirt and wink at her and occasionally give her samples that she would take back and share with Bella. Maureen revelled in her popularity. Sometimes she found a willing victim in a visiting guest, and sometimes she could capture Ally until the woman's eyes glazed over when the one-sided conversation simply became too much. This morning it was unusually quiet. Guests had been up and away early on their tours, and the ticking clock in the vestibule was Maureen's worst nightmare, sounding as it did every second left of her life. She had been mulling something over and over in her head and knew it was now time to confront it.

Dieter Frum bounded down the stairs and made his way over to her with a broad smile and outstretched arms.

'Mrs Berman!'

'Hello, luv,' was Maureen's warm greeting in return.

'I just want to thank you for being my guest at the dinner – you are such charming company.'

'Oh, lovely, dear.' She smiled in acknowledgement and in the realisation that he was completely right.

Maureen was distracted as Hannah came out of the kitchen with a tray of wrapped cutlery to lay it down on a small table in the dining room. Hannah glanced up at the chatting older couple, smiled and moved back to the kitchen. Maureen saw Heather talking to Marcie in the lounge bar and gestured to her if she wanted coffee or tea, and Heather replied with a shake of the head. Hannah disappeared into the kitchen to bring out another tray to collect salt and pepper pots and take them to the kitchen to be refilled.

Hannah was lost in her own thoughts as she went about her tasks. She had grown to love this remote and out of the way place and, in her head, she thanked the person who had suggested it. She was wearing a long-sleeved white T-shirt today and dark blue jeans and sandals, far removed from the completely black outfits that she had been prone to wearing – as if they were a mirror image of the black moods that would come down on her like a cloak and which now seemed to be lifting. Here she felt lighter and her mood sunnier. She only had to be told to do a task once and she absorbed it into her daily routine. Plus, she knew for a fact that her boss was delighted with her work.

Hannah and Dax had planned a special picnic lunch at the place where her new boyfriend had said was one of the best places in the world to watch the ocean, at the other side of the Drovers' Road at somewhere called Atlantic Point. She wanted to stay here so much despite the fact she had a small tingle of an inkling to go back to Kent to see the only family she had left behind. Instead, she had asked her boss for a pen and a piece of paper and had a half-written letter in her room to her grandmother and money on top of it to buy a stamp.

The German guest was leaving when she went back out into the lounge area, and Maureen gave her the international signal for ordering tea – holding both an imaginary cup and saucer and raising them high for her to see. Hannah acknowledged it, went into the kitchen, and started making the woman a pot of tea for one just the way she liked it – with Ceylon tea bags. In a generous mood, she plucked two pieces of shortbread out of the big plastic box of homemade treats and laid them on a side plate on the tray. Maureen stared into space as Hannah poured the tea and asked if she needed anything else.

'Oh, I don't think so, love,' said the older woman, eyeing the perfect circles of shortbread with relish, and Hannah turned, taking her tray with her. It was only when she was two steps away from Maureen that the woman said, 'Thanks, Suranya, appreciate it.' And the self-styled Hannah Hurley stopped in her tracks.

When Heather left Marcie at the table to continue with some tasks held over from the few days she had taken off to go to Inverness, Marcie remained in her seat. She sat at the table and set about answering Callum's emails and owning up to the fact that she had been so distracted, she had forgotten to confirm their solstice booking but was devising another plan in her mind. It was a workaround of something they had never done and that was to stay in Strathkin at summer solstice. She had asked him several times about his arrival date, how long he was planning to stay, and his responses were vague and changeable. She knew he wanted to come back for their yearly tradition, but he had made it plainly clear this was a visit like last year – a catch-up, an exchange of plans and promises and a departure at the airport filled with tears and emotion. But maybe, just maybe, this time she could persuade him to stay.

Ross wandered into the dining room and glanced in the kitchen. He was about to leave when he saw Marcie sitting alone at the table, her fingers working overtime on her phone. He walked over, his mind full of what he and Jamie had discussed, and when he neared her, he felt an overarching desire to say, *it wasn't me, I know this now*, and *I know I wasn't responsible for your pain*, but this was a secret he and Jamie would continue to keep. Instead, he paused for a moment to take her all in.

'Working?' he asked. 'I won't disturb you if you are in the throes.'

'Just catching up with Callum. Trying to organise something. Two continents and a phone – you of all people must know what it is like?' she said, not looking up but continuing to tap.

When she sat back, Marcie gave a sigh and it was only when she looked up at him, she realised he had been gazing at her for some time. She turned away and tried to ignore what her body was telling her.

'In my new job of bodyguard,' he began, 'does it come with perks?'

She turned to him. 'Such as?'

'Taking my boss to dinner? I suggested it before, but we never got round to fixing a date.'

'Depends,' she said, and while her brain was telling her one thing, her heart was telling her another.

'Well, I was going to suggest somewhere away from here... somewhere *far* away,' he began, his feet taking root in front of her and his hands finding his pockets.

They were interrupted by Dieter Frum who had been out to his car and had rushed back, phone in hand.

'Ah, Marcie!' he greeted, and she smiled at him, not exactly glad of the interruption but ever wary of what his plans entailed.

His eyes fell on Ross.

'He's fully up to speed,' she said to Dieter with a nod to the handsome man in front of her.

'We don't want too many people to know of our plans,' he replied with a glance to Ross.

But Ross had too much on his mind to be fully aware of anyone's plans bar his own. He remembered Strathkin as a sleepy backwater, the Toy Town to the bustling metropolis of Ullapool (population fifteen hundred) but it was so full of secrets and hidden stories, and every corner revealed another paradox. Had it always been that way? He had found the answer to one – needed to find the answer to another – and here was something else raising its head again just when he was dealing with enough complex problems of his own.

'We have him in our sights,' said a clearly enthusiastic Dieter Frum.

Marcie's heart sank a little. 'Dieter,' she began, 'I'm not sure you understand what you're dealing with. This guy is—'

Dieter held his finger up to his lips in a *Shhh* gesture. 'I think we need to keep this as quiet as possible,' he suggested.

She glanced at Ross and bit her own lip slightly. What Poytr Medvedev, in the guise of Brodie Nairn, had subjected them to was bad enough, but she could not keep playing scenes and scenarios over and over in her head. She had started with hate in her heart for this man, but after the death of Dina she had come to realise that life was too short to continue to bear grudges. She was beginning to regret her discussion with Dieter about bringing the man down.

Marcie had made her mind up. She was going to forge a new life with only positive people in it. Cancel out negativity and try to meditate more. She wanted to share this new chapter with people who shared her values and principles and goals for the future, and already she was laser focused on forging a new life which had Strathkin at the heart of it and her friends at the centre. No matter her issues in the past with Angelina San; on hearing her backstory, she realised, along with Hannah and Maureen, that there was a need for women to support women in whatever way possible. What had happened to Swanfield may have been the catalyst that was needed at this moment in time.

The two men in front of her awaited an answer to a question she hadn't heard, lost as she was in her thoughts.

'I really do need to think about this, Dieter. He's devious and cunning and I'm worried that whatever your plan is, he is one step ahead of you.'

'I know my plan is tempting him.'

Marcie turned to Ross who was shaking his head very slightly.

'No, no, no. I'm sure of it. I have planned well. I think he has already taken the bait, like I said.'

He was convinced he was fully on top of whatever he was organising, and that alone gave Marcie a shiver down her spine.

Dieter's phone rang and he made an apologetic sign to take the call and turned away.

'Not convinced?' asked Ross.

'Not in the slightest,' replied Marcie and put her own phone on the table. 'People just don't know what this person is really like.'

Ross shrugged with a 'meh,' his shoulders moving up and down.

'Seriously, people have no idea. He's a sleekit bas—' She was about to launch into a diatribe when Hannah popped her head round the corner.

'Have you seen the boss?' asked the young woman. 'If you do, can you say I'm just taking a little time out to speak to Maureen?' She pointed to where the woman, dressed head to toe in leopard print, was nursing a pot of tea and wiping biscuit crumbs from her pale Coral Reef lipstick.

'Sure,' agreed Marcie, just as Ross slipped into the other side of the banquette and opposite the woman he could not take his eyes from. He watched her as her finger drew an outline on her lips.

'You have a tell.'

'Hmm?' She looked up as his eyes bore into her.

'When you're deep in thought or plotting.'

'I know, I do it unconsciously. Well, sometimes unconsciously...'

'It's very... distracting.' He said it so low it almost sounded like a whisper.

'Sorry.'

'Oh, not in a bad way.'

'I'm just...'

'You're worried about something, I can tell.'

'I don't think Dieter knows what he's doing.'

'You need to stop worrying about other people. He's a big boy. I'm sure he can handle it.'

'This guy is ruthless. I've looked at him in his black eyes. He's terrifying. He has complete disregard for human life, and Dieter's a surgeon whose only concern is to save people's lives.'

'What can you do about it?'

'I don't know.'

'If you can't do anything about it, you need to let it go.'

'It's not in my nature.' She sat back. 'You know I'm a meddler.'

'It has been mentioned.'

'Who mentioned it?'

'Oh, just everybody.' He laughed, and she turned away, stifling the overwhelming desire to reach over and kiss him. 'Let it go, Mossie. Everything is probably going to be okay.' He rested his hand on hers.

'It's the word *probably* that scares me the most.'

Hannah strolled over to where Maureen was sitting drumming her fingers on the table, and she, too, slipped into the banquette, a mirror image of the window seat in the other room. She did so reluctantly, knowing she would not have to keep her secret any longer. They eyed each other for a moment.

'It's a nice name, Hannah Hurley. It's got a ring to it. Where did you come up with that one?' asked Maureen.

Hannah remained mute.

'We've all got our secrets, H. I'm sure Rita will have told you some of hers. Your granny, that is. 'ow's the old gal doin'?'

'She's in a home now but she's doing good.'

'Was it 'er what told you to come up 'ere?'

Hannah nodded.

'We 'ad some laughs, your Rita and me. People see an old woman or an old man and think they've always looked like that. They can't see into the soul of the person and see they're still twenty-two in their heads, you know, inside, inside 'ere?'

Maureen placed her hand on her chest and gazed longingly into the distant past. She started to describe her friendship with Hannah's grandmother as the young woman sat forward.

Suddenly Maureen had painted a picture in Hannah's head of a vibrant young woman on the verge of the rest of her life. *Like her*. Maureen had a wistful look come over her as she described a sixties London, and she raised her hand to her face.

'So, did she tell you to come up here then, away from your *business*?' she said, while air quoting her statement. 'What's going on then?' she added bluntly.

'I met this guy, and everything was fine until...'

'It wasn't. Same old, same old.' She shuffled in her seat, settled down and Hannah prepared herself for a lecture. 'Problem with men, luv, is they're simple creatures, know what I mean? They want to eat and sleep and have a bit of 'ow's yer father every so often. But, really, some of them? They're just animals, they hunt in packs, one wants to be the alpha male, then they get challenged. But here's the thing. You ever watch any David Attenborough? It's the survival of the fittest. Animals take out the idiots and they're left with the top of the cream, know what I mean, luv? But in our life, it doesn't happen often enough, and the idiots think they can take out the alpha males. Well, at the end of the day they're just weak so they prey on the next best thing. Us women. Us *strong* women. Women like you – me – Rita. Us alpha females. Problem is, we ladies are told to behave like ladies and act like ladies and please these no-hopers just so we don't get left on the shelf and become wizened old spinsters. So, we pander to their every need and what do we get in return? A slap every now and then if they think they can get away with it. Your granny, Rita, she was the best of the best, she was. A total joy to be around. Her mum and dad, you'd never have known them – Elizabeth and Winston. The best this country ever had to offer.' Maureen's hand was on her chest again and she took a moment. 'What was your one called then?'

'Chester.'

'Asshole, was he?'

The blunt language took Hannah aback for a moment, but she agreed.

'You're beautiful, Suranya. I know his kind. The *If I can't have you then nobody will* type. The weak little man who's been a mummy's boy all his life. Oh yes, I had one of those. 'orrible to me, 'e was, 'orrible. And I could only confess to your Rita because she was going through the same thing. You think women of today stand for that kinda nonsense? Some do but most of them will stand up and fight back, and they don't like that. Oh no, they don't.'

Hannah glanced around and could see Marcie through the mirror talking to her boyfriend's uncle.

'My Ange has got the right idea about that place across the loch, and that's where you need to be workin'.' Maureen had glanced to Marcie, threw a quick look to Swanfield and shuffled in her chair again with an indignant look on her face. 'So, what brought you up 'ere?'

'Granny always told me to have...'

'Running away money,' they both said together. 'She was spot on. She was spot on, my Rita.'

Hannah felt she had to fill in the blanks now she knew she was on safe ground.

'Granny saw the accident you were in, the fire, in the paper. She cut it out. She said she hadn't seen you in years but you and her, you had a pact. And if I ever got into a sticky situation then you'd help me out.'

'We did that, yes, indeed we did,' confirmed Maureen. 'We would always look out for each other, me and your gran. We had a safe word, a phrase, at one point, I remember.'

'*Meet me at the corner shop,*' they both said together, and then they unexpectedly laughed, Maureen placing her hand on Hannah's resting on the table. She looked closely at this young woman, barely seventeen and on the cusp of the rest of her life.

'Granny give you a drawing I did for your mum? Little bird?'

Hannah nodded.

Maureen did, too, remembering the charcoal on paper she had drawn for Rita's only child, Suranya's mother, all those years ago.

'What happened to him, this Chester bloke? Does he know where you are?'

'He... died.'

'Died? Accident or was it someone else who took him out?'

'I think he fell down the stairs.'

'I know that scenario.' Maureen sighed and sat back. 'You sure he fell down the stairs?'

'Well, I found him at the bottom.'

Maureen raised her brows and gave a throaty cough.

'Who knows you're 'ere?'

'Just Granny.' Hannah, like Maureen, sat back.

'Keep it that way. You can reinvent yourself – well, it looks like you 'ave.'

Hannah agreed.

'It's so perfect up here,' she began, 'it's another world. Everyone helps everyone else. Everyone looks after everyone else. Granny said it's what it was like in the old days. I think I was just existing in my past life. Here I'm really living. You meet so many nice people, genuine people, and everyone seems so glad to see you. And it's not like it's a pay-off. You've not got to do something first to earn a friendship.' Hannah glanced around the empty room they were in, but even though there was no one in at this time of the day, the Inn still had a warmth about it, a welcoming ambiance.

'It's the summer though, innit? Everyone is on their 'olidays so they're all upbeat and happy. Wait till you've been here in the winter – it's freezing and it's dead. Nothing to do except contemplate how much snow is going to keep you in and not get down 'ere for a wee G&T.'

Hannah laughed slightly at Maureen's south London accent trying to master the use of the word *wee*.

'It's no laughing matter, I tell you. I wrapped myself in a duvet and 'ibernated for six months.'

'Six months?' asked Hannah, horrified.

'Well, two, three at the most.' They both shared a little laugh. 'You going to make it back down to see Rita? She'll be getting on now, like me. You don't want to leave it too late, gal.'

'Oh. I'm definitely going to go and see her. I have some money. Probably have to plan it sooner rather than later.'

'You wouldn't mind taking an old bird with you? For old time's sake and all?' suggested Maureen, and Hannah looked enthusiastically at her.

'Of course!' she said with a genuine wide smile.

Although she wanted to tell Maureen about everything she had been through, true to form Maureen ended up talking about herself and her life with Brian. Her hand was on her heart again and she was in a wistful dream for a moment until she looked squarely at Hannah.

'But it's not gone by me or anyone else, for that matter, you're hanging around with a Balfour boy, the eldest, Drax.'

'Dax.'

'That's what I said, love. Drax. He's a lovely young man. Handsome like his father, gentle like his mother.'

'Did you know his mother?'

'She was a beauty, I can tell you. Gorgeous. I don't think that family will get over her death. So quick, so sudden. Like my Brian – 'ow is it the good ones always go first?'

Hannah gave a little shrug.

'He's tall, too, still growing, I imagine. Lovely nature. You could settle here, you know...' Maureen went on.

'Well, I'm not sure now. You said it was *really* cold!' Hannah laughed, her face glowing.

'Oh, it's not bad really, luv. Not if you have 'im, that Drax one to keep you warm, know what I'm saying?'

Hannah gave a little snigger, and Maureen gave her a theatrical wink under her large sunglasses.

'You'll be fine here, darlin'. I'll look after you. Problem with places like this, though, is sometimes you never want to leave.'

'Oh, I don't ever want to leave. I'd fight to stay, Maureen, I would. I'd do anything… anything.'

'We all would, love. They'll have to carry me out of 'ere in a box. An 'orse box if that Bella's got anything to do with it.'

Hannah gave another little chuckle, suddenly glad of the release of telling someone why she found herself in Strathkin and that it was no accident.

Maureen laid her hand on the young girl's arm. 'You'll be fine here. He's a lovely young man you've hooked up with, he'll look after you. Just you two be careful, and you'll soon forget about the past. The future's going to be good to you pair, I can feel it in me old bones.'

TWENTY-EIGHT

Ruaridh was leaning on his kitchen worktop, watching his eldest son make sandwiches – a rare occurrence, Dax being the one to usually stand at an open fridge staring at the full shelves and complaining that there was never anything to eat. Home-cooked ham delivered by his maternal grandmother the previous day, had been carefully sliced and he had managed to keep his father's hungry hands away from it. He had wrapped the sandwiches carefully in greaseproof paper and, with his mother on his shoulder, had tied hessian ribbon on each one to seal it, which she always believed made it both appealing to look at and inviting to eat.

'Looking good, Dax,' his father said as the boy began filling a picnic basket with a delightful outside lunch. A hot plate was bursting with warmth, and the young man turned four peach halves until they were charred and then sat them face up on some kitchen paper to steam until cold and suddenly there was dessert. He then filled a small plastic lidded tub with Greek yoghurt and placed it carefully in the basket.

Ruaridh watched all of this with an enthralled fascination.

This boy he had held in his arms as his firstborn – and not too long ago, in Ruaridh's mind – was taking a girl out and in a way he and his mother had done for years. Pre-children, post children, on anniversaries and birthdays, an outdoors picnic (and sometimes an indoor floor picnic when the weather or the midges changed plans at the last minute) was something to be treasured, and he had the feeling that Hannah Hurley had never picnicked in her life. Ruaridh was an open father with his children and spoke to them from when they were young about what he still referred to as *the birds and the bees* and was confident Dax would not let him down in his desire to be a perfect gentleman.

'Have you made sure you've packed everything you might need?'

'I've just to grab the tartan rug out the back of the car, the one with the waterproof...'

'I was meaning something else...'

'DAD!' the young man complained, red in the face at his father's lurid suggestion.

'I'm just suggesting, you're sixteen and I'm too young to be a grandfather, Daxy,' he said and gave his son a nudge.

Dax took his red face out to the side of the house to collect the thick blanket from the car. His twin brothers were on the shore playing with a drone, flying it low and slow over the water, low enough to have the loch ripple in its wake and then high enough for them to see the abandoned jetty from a grand height. Ruaridh, sceptical at first about the gift from Ross, had agreed it was a fabulous addition to their world of board games and outside Jenga. Their screams and yelps of delight warmed his heart, and he had a moment when he had stopped for a second inside Lochside Croft as he thought about Dina. An unexpected day off from school due to a staffing issue. These were the days she loved. Listening to screams and shouts of delight and happiness. He took a deep breath and blew it out in a steady stream.

'Get a grip,' he said to himself and went outside to sit on the bench and watch the two boys playing and staring into the sky. They were at the water's edge, and he had taken the laptop from their 'office' which was, in effect, an old, reclaimed school desk with a wicker chair in front of it in the corner of the room that held the laptop and an ancient printer. It felt like a perfect day as the boys whooped over the machine that had been gifted by their Uncle Ross on the understanding that they kept their abandonment at Achmelvich a secret. They agreed, but after just one question from their father, they all squealed in unison.

Later that morning, at Atlantic Point, Hannah was lying on a rug, eyes closed, while Dax set out the picnic from an old dry and cracking wicker basket. Now, he was sitting up against a large boulder that shielded them from the blazing sun, a baseball hat pulled down tight, his sandy blond hair escaping the white cotton. She was the most content she had ever been and felt the warm sun soak into her skin, deep into her bones. She had never seen the water so close-up – a lake in a park or the water of Loch Strathkin – but here she had seen the ocean stretching as far as the eye could see. She was mesmerised. They initially sat on a bench with a clear view of the Atlantic Ocean, then moved behind a huge boulder for shade. The cliff face was directly in front of them, dropping straight down to the rocks. Waves loudly crashed against the short rocky shore below. Nothing, as Hannah had said to Maureen, was going to stop her from starting her new life here. Content and with an overwhelming feeling of security, she drifted off, the smell and taste of delicious food lingering in the air. Dax lay down next to her, her bare arm casually thrown across his chest.

Like his new girlfriend, Dax was feeling loved and warm

and only wished his mother was at home so he could excitedly tell her about his day and how kind he had been – just like she had told him to be with everyone, not just girls. 'People won't remember if you got the qualifications you wanted, the job you wanted, the car you wanted. What people will remember is that you were kind to them. That is the young man we brought you up to be.' He could see her in his mind's eye. She was half sitting up on pillows, he remembered. She sounded weak. She had disappeared from his life completely just a few days later. He felt his lip tremble and wanted Hannah to hold him, but he also did not want her to see him that way. To her he was strong – not emotionally complicated. 'It's all right to cry. It's just your inner self rebalancing itself, releasing too much water that's gathered inside,' his father told him, but it had taken *him* a long time to cry and then, one weekend, he recalled his father was nothing but a ball of tears for what felt like days on end. They had all gone to stay with their grandmother and when they came back, he looked different – hair cut short, beard almost gone. He was like another person, and something had changed, like they had turned a corner. And then they fell back into their normal routine as if a wife and mother had simply slipped into the room next door for a fleeting moment and would return at a time of her own choosing.

Dax rolled onto his side, reached out and ran his hand through her thick, dark, soft hair and then down her forehead and along her small perfect nose. He continued to her lips, and she opened them to playfully bite his finger. They both laughed and he leaned over to kiss her softly then they began to drift off into sleepy silence, two hearts, two different souls and just one thought in their minds – each other.

Nobody heard the commotion that took place as the two men struggled, one overpowering another to wrap gaffer tape round his wrists, ankles and across his mouth. The heavily bound man was dumped unceremoniously onto the long bench seat that faced out to sea. He was barely conscious, having been pistol-whipped as soon as he had stepped out of the car on the small road that led halfway up to Atlantic Point. He had managed to send a text, *The meeting is on*, before he was dazed.

Dieter had dropped a pin of his location which had pinged on Marcie's phone just as she was leaving the Inn to go to The Aizle, a twenty-minute drive away. She was still pondering what to do when the ambling figure of Jamie MacKay meandered up to her. Tired and unshaven, he had red eyes behind his black square-framed glasses.

'Someone stolen your bed?' she asked, trying to lighten the mood, seeing just how tired Jamie was, the closer he walked to her.

'Ha, bloody ha,' he sighed. 'Not seen Ross around, have you?'

'He's just dropped in to see Ruaridh,' she replied, pointing to the short walk to Lochside Croft. She expected him to leave immediately but he hovered around, stepping from foot to foot as if he wanted to say something.

'Everything okay?' she ventured. 'Heather told me. Is there anything I can help you with?'

He opened his mouth as if to say something but then backed away, biting the inside of his cheek as if this would prompt him into speech. Instead, he remained pained.

Marcie looked at him oddly, her head to one side – this man always in control and who suddenly appeared lost.

'Jamie, you sure everything's okay?' She placed her hand on his forearm, and he shook his head.

'Heather told you what happened?'

'Uh-hu...'

'Well, nothing fresh to say.' He concluded it with the finality of someone who had accepted his circumstances.

'Okay. Is there *anything* I can do?'

He shook his head, and his eyes settled on Lochside Croft.

'I'll see you later, Mars. Need a quick word with Ross.'

He left her standing, puzzled at this strange set of circumstances. She wandered over to her car and thought for a moment about how she could help Jamie out of the predicament he was in, and what got him into it in the first place.

When Jamie reached Lochside Croft, both Ruaridh and Ross were outside laughing and joking with the boys as they played with the machine that flew over their heads, swooping above them and then gathering speed as it headed out over the loch. Ruaridh was looking at the images on the laptop while Ross sat next to him on the bench, and they shouted directions to the youngsters about how and where to guide the drone next.

'So, this is where it's all happening?' asked Jamie as he joined the two seated brothers, the other two younger brothers whooping and giggling on the shore.

'I have to say, I'm pretty impressed, and that's from a guy who thought Pacman was the height of sophistication.' Ruaridh laughed.

He passed the laptop to Ross, who was intently focused on the screen and the drone's incoming images. 'Hey, boys, take it over to Swanfield. Let's see what's going on in the big house!' He pointed and they both followed his instructions. Immediately the drone changed course and began its journey to the charred house across the water, scaffolding surrounding its walls.

'Hey, wee man!' he shouted to Ruaridh, now talking to Jamie, and pointed to the screen. 'What a mess!'

Both Ruaridh and Jamie took a few steps back and looked at

the images on the laptop, both realising the building wasn't in such a bad state when viewed from above.

'You know what they want to do with it?' asked Ruaridh.

'No?' both men responded.

'Like a women's refuge or something,' said Ruaridh, Maureen finally giving up to him what Angelina San was really coming back for.

Ross moved his head from side to side and gave a noise of approval.

'Why?' queried Jamie. 'It's in the middle of nowhere?'

'Exactly,' said Ross, and it was Jamie's turn for the penny to drop.

'Of course. A pretty good idea. Another big refurbishment, eh? Will cost a fortune.'

Ruaridh's phone buzzed a message at the same time as Ross's. Ruaridh's was from Callum. Ross's was from Marcie.

'Feck, Callum is arriving in a couple of hours! I've missed his messages and I've not to tell Mars!'

'I've got Mars here. I've no idea what she's on about.'

Jamie stood in front of them, hands in pockets and quietly seething that no one had asked him how he was handling this bizarre situation he found himself in.

'You couldn't look after the boys for a wee while, mate?' asked Ruaridh urgently.

Jamie shrugged. 'S'pose.'

'Great! Off the hook!' said Ross as he jumped up and handed Jamie the laptop before walking quickly down the side of Lochside Croft and back to the Inn.

Jamie sat down on the bench, laptop on his knee, and sighed more in annoyance than acceptance.

Outside The Strathkin Inn, Ross opened the door to Marcie's car and peered in.

'Can you explain in English?' he asked of her bizarre, forwarded text to him.

'Well, it's a message from Dieter to meet him at Atlantic Point, but I'm not exactly sure what he's asking? He's sent a pin. I was going to find Ruaridh and suggest he comes up with me, but I know he's got the boys.'

Ross took the phone and the message that started with regular text then changed into nonsense as if someone were typing with their eyes closed. He was as puzzled as Marcie was looking at the pin.

'So, you want me to come with you?'

'Well, you're always hanging about with nothing to do apart from telling *me* what to do on the estate, and I figured Ruaridh would be tied up.'

'Just the twins. Douglas and Mari are with Granny. Dax is out with Hannah apparently.'

'I need to go to The Aizle first if you're in the mood for a coffee?'

'Nah, let's head up to the Point and see what's doing now you've got my attention. Anyhoo, the wee man needs to do an airport run, new guests or something. Jamie's on babysitting duty.'

'Listen, I'm worried about Jamie. You think he's okay?' said Marcie with a voice of concern.

'He'll be fine,' reassured Ross.

'I'm not sure what happened – one minute he's going for promotion, the next he's on forced leave.'

She pulled the car out and on to the road and turned it towards the sea.

'He'll be fine,' Ross said again, aware he was largely responsible for his best friend's suspension.

'I mean, it must be pretty serious,' Marcie continued.

'There's a shortcut if you go past the big house,' explained Ross, changing the subject, and then he stopped as they neared

Swanfield.

'I didn't think anyone knew that shortcut?'

'I was brought up here, Mossie. Everyone knows the back road.'

'Oh. Okay.'

It was a steep, narrow road up to the cliffs and was mostly overgrown. It was known locally as the *secret passage* and most newcomers to the village were unaware of the back road which led to a small area called the *flat top* that would take two small cars or a large Land Rover with an amorous courting couple.

Marcie pulled the car into the vacant space, and they waited for a moment in silence as she switched off the engine.

'Is there anyone in Strathkin who *hasn't* been here!' She giggled and glanced across to Ross who seemed in a little dream of his own. She leaned over and nudged him. 'Cat got your tongue?' she joked, and he turned to her.

'You mean it wasn't with you?' He gave her a wink, and she gave him an incredulous look.

'Cheek!' she said and pulled herself out of the car. He was about to say he had a racy story about a couple at the *flat top* that Ruaridh had spoken to him about years before but decided to keep it for some other time.

Although the walk up to Atlantic Point wasn't far, it was a slight scramble as they had come the circuitous route. From a distance they saw Dieter Frum sitting, relaxed, on the bench with a view out to the wide-open sea beyond, and Marcie stood for a moment taking in the incredible view. The Atlantic Ocean stretched out in front of them, and she knew from Callum's outdoor geography lessons, the next stop would be Canada.

'Quite something, eh, Mossie?' Ross stood behind her, his eyes gazing at the stunning vista before them.

'Don't do it,' she began just as his arms reached out, gripped her forearms, and pointed both straight ahead.

'Newfoundland,' he began.

'I know, I'm not an amateur!' she protested, but only slightly.

He took her right arm and pointed it upwards.

'Not clearly seen, but the moon is almost two hundred and forty thousand miles away,' he said as he took her left arm. 'Most of the Outer Hebrides out there.'

'We went to the same school,' she protested to no avail until he spun her around quickly. 'We had the same geography teacher. You just have a better memory,' she joked and felt her heart beginning to beat a little faster. 'I'm awfully close,' she said, almost in a whisper.

'Not nearly close enough,' he began as he pulled her towards him, her pupils dilating, a protest of gentle denial making them both smile, until she heard her name being called.

She turned to where Dieter was still sitting, some distance away on the bench.

'Does he look okay to you?' she asked Ross as she saw Dieter gently slide to one side and his head thud onto the bench. A sudden chill ran through her, her eyes widened, and she began to try to wrestle herself free from Ross. 'I don't like this,' she said suddenly, panic in her voice.

'Believe me, you won't be disappointed...' he began then realised Marcie was looking around in what could only be described as distress. He released her immediately from his bear hug but kept a tight grip of her hand. 'What is it, Mossie?' he asked and immediately he felt a rush of protection for her. He wanted to pull her close, tightly, and fight off single-handedly what was causing her to have a look of fear creep across her face.

'I don't like this,' she repeated and immediately felt her stomach churn. She turned to see a large boulder, then the wide-open sea in front and the man on the bench who she suddenly thought may or may not be alive. She released herself from Ross who let her go with some reluctance.

'Mossie...' he enquired of her as he followed her to the bench. He reached out and grabbed her hand again so that it was she who was leading him towards the man in the pink shirt who seemed barely alive. Marcie let out a gasp as she was first to see him and immediately noticed the tape across his mouth, bindings on wrists and ankles. Then she simply said, 'Trap!'

'We really should stop meeting like this... *Mossie*,' said Poytr Medvedev, hovering no more than a few hundred yards from where she and Ross were standing.

Marcie gulped, turned around, taking Ross with her, and faced the man who had caused her to question her own sanity in the months and years since he had appeared in her life.

'You utter shit,' she said viciously, so he could hear the venom in her voice.

'Once again I come across an Anglo-Saxon who thinks they can outsmart me.'

'Hey, pal,' shouted Ross, 'I've got the Viking blood in me so leave all your so-called Anglo-Saxon nonsense for further down south, eh?'

'Ah, the distant brother with the dodgy past. I know who you are.'

Ross had pulled Marcie towards him and she was standing next to him. He was gradually and very, very slowly moving her around so that she was now half behind him.

Marcie realised what he was doing and was quite happy to go with this plan, as her heart was beating so fast, she thought it was in danger of pounding out of her chest. She ended up behind Ross, facing back to her car, as they very slowly and steadily shuffled away from the cliff edge, Poytr Medvedev mimicking their every move in front of them as he edged closer.

'What is it you want?' asked Ross.

'She knows what I want but she's too scared to face me.'

Marcie was standing with her back pressed against Ross as he leaned round, his hands gripping her arms and pushing them downwards to his side. She was held in this protective grip, knowing he would do all he could not to have her face this wicked adversary.

'See that big stone over there?' Ross glanced to the large boulder where, unbeknownst to him, Hannah and Dax were lying and just slowly awakening in the warm sunshine. 'How about you crawl back under it?'

Don't goad him, Marcie's inner voice was saying.

'She's not going to face you. You want her, you go through me.'

Poytr lifted the gun he was holding and pointed it straight at Ross, who drew in a deep and sharp breath. Marcie felt this movement against her own body, and she closed her eyes as his grip on her arms felt so tight she was sure he was going to cut off her circulation.

'Too easy,' laughed the man who held their lives in his hands. 'This man' – he turned to where Dieter was propped up on the bench, restrained and semi-conscious – 'another one who thought he could outsmart me. Look where all this pretence and *catfishing* has got him. One gentle little push and off he goes into the sea.'

Ross took a step back, slowly inching his way backwards to where he knew Marcie could escape; if he released her at the right point and she could scramble down to the car, she could at least go for help.

'Look, mate,' he began.

'Oh, not another one who thinks calling me *mate* and *pal* will endear them to me,' sighed Poytr. 'Give her to me.' His voice had changed from flippant to demanding.

Ross remained stock still. Marcie was breathing hard while telling herself to slow down and calm down, to think her way out of the situation. A noise above them made them all look up as a buzzing machine flew low overhead so quickly it was gone before they realised what it was. Poytr appeared perplexed for a moment then snapped back to reality.

'Do you want me to count to three and then you can hand her over? She knows – I don't really do games.'

'What do you want her for? She's of no use to you. I know what you like and it's not strong women like Marcie Mosse. Am I not more your type?'

The two men stood looking at each other, Ross thinking of a plan to release Marcie where she wasn't in danger of becoming another victim, and Poytr thinking of how to finally get rid of his nemesis without having to take two people's lives in the process. In the end, however, what was two against one, when one had a gun?

'She's spent all her money, you know. She's opening a women's refuge to provide a safe space for women to escape thugs like you.'

'Oh gawd,' thought Marcie and closed her eyes, waiting for the loud bang that would first hit her protector and continue to then take her life.

'I've come to realise, Mr Balfour, money means nothing when you can have revenge. She robbed me of my future so, really, I no longer need the money. I just want to close this part of my life down then I can continue with the rest of it. A new future, if you will, so one last chance to save your own life and write your own new chapter.'

He held the gun up and took a few steps away from the side of the bench, walking slowly backwards and then to the side. Ross stood firm and if he could have gripped Marcie's arms even closer and harder, he would.

When the shot rang out, loud and reverberating, Ross had closed his eyes and tensed his body. Marcie felt her knees give way. Then they heard a noise like a thud and Ross saw it was the body of Dieter as it hit the concrete plinth. But the bullet had not been for either of them as they found out. The second shot happened so fast after the first, it had made them both think he had missed with the first shot, but it was the noise of the drone above them that made Marcie open her eyes and look up. He had fired at the drone, not Dieter, and had missed both times, such was the speed of the small mechanical device. It hovered for a second then darted away to the side again. Her heart was beating so fast she could see the beats through the cotton of her shirt. She realised she was shaking, shaking but very much still alive.

Ross had not looked up at the drone, as his eyes had remained tightly shut from when he realised the gun from Poytr Medvedev was pointed straight at him, directly at his head.

'You want her, you go through me first... try me,' he demanded as he faced down the man in front of him.

Poytr laughed a high-pitched comical sneer at Ross's statement. The Russian continued to snigger as he approached the large boulder then the smile began to disappear from his face as his foot stuck in what looked like a divot near to it. As he attempted to pull it out, cursing at himself, he tried to straighten himself up before he realised that instead of pushing him forwards, gravity was in fact pulling him back.

Ross watched in horror as Poytr's arms began first to steady himself then to flail as he realised he was falling backwards – the consequences of this loss of balance so very clear. Ross suddenly let go of Marcie and ran towards the man who moments earlier was about to take his life. A look of terror spread across the man's face as Ross automatically reached out to save him, fear and panic screaming from his eyes. But it was too late. Ross scrunched his own eyes shut tightly and raised his shoulders, waiting for any noise to come out of the man who seconds later had simply disappeared from sight. There was no quiet thud. There was simply silence and the sound from the crashing waves below. Ross looked up to where the whirring noise of the drone that had been hovering above them whizzed out of view. He turned sharply to where Marcie was still facing in the opposite direction and when he raced towards her, he spun her round and she clung to him, tears rolling down her cheeks, shaking.

'What happened?' she gasped as she looked up.

He took in the whole of her and pulled her close to him, shaking his head.

'Uncle Ross?' asked a quiet voice behind him, and he turned to see his nephew and Hannah standing by the large boulder, looking quizzically at both Marcie and the man still dazed on the bench.

'Over here, kids! Now!' demanded Ross and they quickly made their way to him where he scooped them up into his quartet of protection, and they stood wrapped in his arms for some moments. When he let them go, Marcie turned to where Poytr had previously made his threats and where there was now no sign of him.

'Guys, do me a favour and make your way to the car, eh? I'll take you back over the road in a minute...'

'But... was there another man here?' Dax began to wonder, looking to the large stone where Ross could now see the remains of a picnic spread out on a familiar family blanket.

He looked at Marcie and she knew what he silently asked. She turned to lead the two young people towards the small incline down to the car while Ross quickly made his way to the picnic spot and gathered up the remains of half-eaten food and bottles of water and juice. He took a sharp intake of breath and stepped carefully to the edge of the cliff. He leaned down and saw nothing but crushing waves. Sideways on, he moved forward slightly and looked at a crop of rocks, but the body of the man who had terrorised his home village had quietly but violently been surrendered to the wild Atlantic Ocean.

He ran over to where Dieter was slowly wakening from unconsciousness. After a brief acknowledgement of what had happened, he helped the man to his feet, released the tape and they walked slowly but carefully back to where the car was parked.

At Lochside Croft, the twins had been whooping and laughing as they teased the drone in and out of the trees and up over the hills behind Swanfield, along the Drovers' Road and up to Atlantic Point. Jamie watched it on the laptop in the kitchen, where he had retreated out of the warm sun. He watched the scene the machine had captured with interest before it morphed into horror. The identity of the man with the gun had not escaped him. There was no doubt what was going on. A man on a bench, a man with a weapon, a couple in close contact then a couple behind a large rock. As it played out in real time, Jamie felt he was watching a horror movie. The man raised the gun to the couple he could now identify as Marcie and Ross, then looked down sharply as if his foot was caught in a trap. Jamie watched in despair as Ross, like a greyhound out of the traps, ran to the struggling man in an effort to save him from certain death. For a moment Jamie's heart was in his mouth. *What if he grabbed him and they fell together?* Jamie looked away, out the window to the shore to where the two boys were laughing and giggling. When he looked back at the screen, Ross had the people gathered around him like a protective parent. The body of the assailant was nowhere to be seen, taken by the waves.

As an upholder of law and order, he realised what he had just witnessed, clearly an accident. He reached for the SD card that held the images and pulled it out, shoving it in his pocket. Jamie was a good man, an honest man, a decent human being. But deep down he knew the dead man had brought so much pain and hurt to his people, and he had absolutely no remorse over the death of this monster.

Jamie strolled out to the shore where the boys had the drone now swooping low over the water, still whooping with delight, and he tapped his pocket. He would take a drive up to Atlantic Point later to make sure the rough waters of the wild and stormy ocean really had taken the body out to sea. Then he would destroy the SD card that had captured the death of Poytr Medvedev. And he would try over time to forget the horrible scene he had witnessed.

Just a half hour later, when Marcie unexpectedly flagged down Doctor Arshia Brahmins outside The Strathkin Inn, her mind was racing about the lies she was going to tell to have her examine Dieter Frum.

'Lucky I was passing.' The doctor smiled as she headed up the stairs to his room. Dieter was sitting on top of the bed, clearly out of his state of shock and more compos mentis about what was going on. Marcie had explained what had happened and a look of what could only be relief settled on his face.

'We just found him like he'd taken a little turn or something outside. He didn't want to say anything, but we thought it best to have him checked out just in case,' Marcie explained.

When she entered the bedroom, Ross was sitting on the armchair next to his bed. Marcie caught Dieter's attention and gave him a wide-eyed look of *say only what you need to,* and Ross stood up and suggested he leave her to it and joined Marcie in the corridor.

'What do we do now?' Marcie asked the man standing in front of her who was staring into the middle distance. He remained silent as he bit the inside of his lip.

'I dunno,' he replied. 'I can't believe he just... he just fell...'

'Do we go back and look?' she suggested, hoping his answer would be exactly what she was thinking.

'Not a chance,' he said, and she sighed in agreement.

He glanced up and down the corridor then took her hand, leading her to where he knew there was a linen cupboard. He pulled her in. It was half in darkness and for the second time that day, she felt her heart begin to beat just a little bit faster as he stood close to her.

'Nobody knows about this. Nobody *needs* to know about this,' he began. 'You saw nothing. I saw nothing. The kids are too wrapped up in each other to have seen anything.'

Marcie gazed up at him and thought of this secret which now bound them together. He was holding up his hands, gesturing as he spoke.

'We just continue, carry on like before. Dieter isn't likely to say. He wasn't conscious of anything.' He leaned his hand on the wall behind her. She could feel the rise and fall of his chest. She shook her head. 'He was out of it anyway. When I told him, he was just relieved that he didn't have to do anything and to all intents and purposes, he did it to himself, didn't he?'

She nodded.

'What about the drone? You heard it? Do you think it was there at the exact time that...?'

'Leave the drone to me.' Ross was breathing hard as if his brain was working overtime.

'We should work on a plan. Do you want to come up to Tigh-na-Lochan later?' she suggested, but working on a plan was the last thing on her mind.

'It's another secret of Strathkin and it's likely to stay a secret. Got it?' he said, leaning down close to her ear.

As he leaned in, she closed her eyes and opened her lips slightly before she realised he was bending to reopen the door, which he left slightly ajar as he exited. She puffed her cheeks out and let air escape.

When she made it back downstairs, Hannah and Dax were sitting in the nook at the window. She stopped at the bar, made an order then joined the couple.

'Dax, could you get the stuff from the bar, save Ally coming over?'

'Sure.'

He left them and Marcie slotted into the seat he had vacated. She took Hannah's hand. 'Sorry to have interrupted your picnic today.'

'It's okay, it's summer, there's going to be others.' The young woman was clearly unaware of what had happened at Atlantic Point, just feet away from where she and Dax had been enjoying the sunshine and each other.

'Can I tell you something?' she began, and Marcie gave her an encouraging nod. 'I don't want to leave here. It's magical and everything I never thought I would like. I think I now know running away from my other life was the best thing I ever did.'

Marcie wrapped her arm around her, and Hannah's head rested on her shoulder.

Dax brought back two Cokes and two packets of crisps, also completely unaware of what had gone on at Atlantic Point, and thought it odd Marcie was being so affectionate to his girlfriend for no apparent reason.

Marcie reached down and whispered something in her ear then they locked eyes for a minute before Dax watched Marcie slip out of the banquette, patting him on the shoulder as she walked away.

Hannah smiled at him and his beautiful innocent face and patted the seat vacated by Marcie. He sat down and she took his face in her hands and kissed him long and slow. She was at the beginning of her new life, and with Marcie and Maureen in her corner, she knew she could close the door on her past and finally let the healing begin.

Ruaridh looked at his watch, then up at the airport information board, and down to his watch again. All passengers had disembarked, and he began to think he had either taken note of the wrong flight number or that his passenger had missed the connection, when the smiling figure of Callum MacKenzie came strolling through the arrivals hall chatting animatedly to a tall blonde member of the Dutch cabin crew. When he caught sight of an agitated Ruaridh, he thought it wasn't possible for his smile to be wider and more genuine. They hugged before exchanging any words, a gesture of reconnection between two friends.

'Thought I'd missed you!' said Ruaridh, releasing the man from his tight grip.

'Och, you know what it's like, son, once you get talking. That was Ardi, what a belter...'

Ruaridh laughed and took the wheelie case from his passenger, and they wandered out to the car that was full of snacks, water, chocolate, and cans of cold coffee.

'So, son, what have I missed?' joked the older man, and it made Ruaridh laugh knowing that Marcie's weekly FaceTime calls to Callum meant that he was more up to speed than most of the patrons of The Strathkin Inn, who treated the bar area like the front office of a gossipy newsroom.

'Same old, same old,' replied Ruaridh and switched on his 'Driving to Strathkin' playlist which would immediately make his passenger feel at home, the music taken directly from Heather's jukebox.

'I'm in danger of dozing off so can I ask you to do one thing for me?'

'Sure,' agreed Ruaridh.

'Wake me up when we get to the high ridge.'

'Not a problem, boss,' he agreed and before he turned to tell him about Ross's return, he noticed that Callum was fast asleep, head resting on the window, and he smiled.

. . .

Well over an hour later, and as if on autopilot, Ruaridh pulled the car slowly up to the viewpoint.

Callum awoke, stretched and announced, 'I'm home.'

Ruaridh waited in the car while his passenger made his way up the ridge to the highest point reachable by foot.

Callum surveyed the village that stretched out before him, the silence of the air all around and the peace that he knew he would feel deep inside once he breathed in the clear, clean air that drifted down from the mountains, and which shielded the village like a comforting hug. He closed his eyes. He had dreamed of this moment; it was everything he had imagined, and his heart was at last filled with joy.

It was like role reversal from only a few years before as Ruaridh pulled the car into the driveway of Sweet Briar and Marcie ran towards her beloved uncle, embracing him in a torrent of tears. She knew she would be excited to see him, but the emotions suddenly overwhelmed her. When she last saw him almost two years ago at Inverness Airport, they would not have expected to have seen so many changes in their small village. People departing, people arriving, babies being born, residents traversing the mountains and the road south to seek a better life only to return to raise children and hopes. They linked arms, chatting animatedly into the kitchen, and Ruaridh stood looking lost on the path with a case at his feet until Marcie ran out, took his hand and dragged him into the warmth of Sweet Briar.

Like Swanfield of old next door, the cottage was enveloped in a haze of inviting aromas from the oven, and Callum breathed in the scent of home like he was a child again. Conversation was sharp and pacy, funny and tragic all at once, and tears as well as howls of laughter were all around.

Ruaridh watched the pair, sitting back, arms folded, and smiled at their exchange as if no time had passed between them. Images of Dina around this very table flashed through his mind, and he took in a large gulp of air. *When will this stop?* he thought to himself as the other part of him wished it would never stop – that one day he would stop remembering her. He was trying to build a new life, a new relationship for him as well as his children, but deep down he was not ready to relinquish the old one. He had enjoyed Arshia's company, he didn't feel any chemistry yet, but it was early days, he told himself. He watched as Marcie threw her head back, laughing as Callum comically recounted a story of his first try of jerk chicken that had made him cough so hard that his nose began to run, and she laughed until she snorted herself into covering her mouth in embarrassment. Ruaridh watched the scene, moving his head to one side to take it all in. He still loved her in his own way, but he had to move on. Deep down, though, was he ready, *really* ready? Only time would tell.

He left them, disappeared without them even knowing, and returned to Lochside Croft. He could see the light of Sweet Briar from his seat on the blue bench, drinking a fruit tea and hoping it would lull him into sleep. Ross had told him he was going to Tigh-na-Lochan to feed Marcie's cat and not to wait up as he was heading to Inverness tomorrow and would leave early.

The lights stayed on until the early hours at Sweet Briar, with discussions and catch-ups late into the night, continuous long hugs of welcome and copious amounts of tea from the silver Carlton teapot.

In the morning, Callum was having a jetlagged long lie which enabled Marcie to make excuses for her trip to Inverness. And here she now stood outside the main door to Richard MacInnes' office, the fast-flowing water of the River Ness behind her. Yet another day of secrets and revelations. The meeting hadn't taken long, and she spent most of it staring into the middle distance.

Is everyone's life like this? she thought to herself. Her phone pinged in her handbag, and she ignored it for a moment. She was in the city, a long way from Strathkin. If someone wanted to speak to her today, they could wait until she returned. She was everyone's go-to person when things inevitably went wrong, or they just needed to speak to a voice of (mostly) reason. She thought of Heather, on the verge of a wonderful new part of her life, then it all falling apart. Ruaridh was about to embark on a new relationship which he so desperately needed even though he couldn't see it himself yet. And Bella – they fought like sisters sometimes do, but she so wanted her to be happy it pained her. She had told Marcie that Maureen had written a new will and that she was one of two beneficiaries. Marcie had finally relented, after a long conversation with Callum, where he had told her she should do the right thing and gift the stable back after being its custodian for so long. She had huffed and puffed but – as usual – Callum was right, and she had a plan in her head to do just that.

Marcie's phone pinged again. *I come to Inverness to escape, and it turns out there is* no *escape*, she complained to herself and fished in her bag for her phone: both messages were from Ross. She put her phone back in her bag without opening them and began to walk along the riverside. She stopped and leaned over the railing that separated the water from the grass and the path. Some ducks floated up to her on the off chance she was going to feed them, but she left them disappointed, watching as they squawked away to someone further down the path who was obviously a regular visitor, their paddling becoming faster as they approached the woman. Marcie realised it was Margaret Tulloch, and she watched as the older woman threw in feed to the waiting fowl.

'Oh, what secrets we keep,' said Marcie to herself as she continued to walk along until she reached the crossroads that would take her directly into the city centre. It was only now she delved into her bag and took out her phone. She shook her head. *Not a chance* said her internal voice of reason, but her heart and her body were telling her something different as blood coursed through her.

> I'm at Rocpool Reserve

The first message included a room number,

> if you want to talk

'Ha!' she said aloud as she walked. 'Not after all I've heard from Richard MacInnes. As if.' But despite her mind playing out this scenario in her mind, she found herself walking purposefully across Ness Bridge and then turning right and suddenly she was on Culduthel Road. And then she was outside the hotel. She had walked as if on automatic pilot. Knowing and yet not knowing what she was doing.

The room door was unlocked, and she pushed it open. He had his back to her, standing at the window in that familiar Balfour stance – legs apart, hands in pockets surveying the scene outside his window. She kicked the door closed with her left foot and it made a heavy sound. He waited a moment before he turned around, and this infuriated her. She felt like she had been summoned and, like a lamb to the slaughter, she had walked into his den, but she had no patience for standing around and he knew it. It was like he was waiting for her anger to build up. Which, of course, he was.

When he did turn, she felt her heart give a little flip as if it had stopped for a moment before readjusting its rhythm. They stood like gladiators awaiting the signal to go into battle. He sat down on the deep windowsill, crossed his legs casually like it was just a normal day for him.

'I don't know how much Richard told you.' He looked like

he was at the start of the opening of negotiations. She remained silent. 'You would have done the same,' he continued as if to justify his actions.

'You could have told me,' she said quietly.

'Like you didn't know already. Like you weren't hiding it yourself.'

'Is that when you were flitting from croft to croft? Looking for the birth certificate to try and prove a lie as well as find your mother's letters?'

'Bit of both.'

Marcie dropped her shoulder bag to the floor and folded her arms in defiance. 'How dare you entice me up here to justify your actions.'

'Entice? You came here of your own accord. Your own curiosity got the better of you.'

He was right, of course, but she wasn't about to give in easily.

'I admit I made a mistake. I made the mistake of thinking I was coming back to the same old Mossie. Forgot, of course, that you'd grown up into the Lady Laird.'

She stood, arms folded, waiting for the explanation she was sure would come, blood still coursing through her.

'You'll know why I left,' he began and stood up again, turning to face the window, 'being told I was the rightful heir to Swanfield and that I'd always be denied. I tried to put it out of my mind, but then after all that business with Callum, I began to think maybe that's why he didn't inherit, nothing to do with him batting for the other side – that was just a smokescreen for the village. Maybe she thought it was still about Callum being Cameron's boy and not her husband's.'

It still made Marcie gasp. When she had found the birth certificate with her grandfather's name wiped out in white correction fluid and Cameron Balfour's name inserted as the true father of her uncle, it had made Marcie stare at her grandmother's writing in astonishment. But it couldn't be proven, could it?

Until this morning.

Until this morning when Richard told Marcie that the challenger to the Estate had withdrawn all his demands and wanted to dismiss everything he had pushed for at their last meeting. No explanation given. But Richard was open with Marcie about the real story. Margaret Tulloch said that she was there the night they met, Lisanne MacKenzie and Cameron Balfour, and there was no doubt there were fireworks. Then there was a wedding which led to the birth of a bouncing baby boy in the marital bed at Swanfield. But in her meticulously kept diaries, the dates were wrong. Alastair MacKenzie was there when people were gossiping, as they do, that it was Cameron Balfour. And whatever Lisanne had thought about her brief liaison with Cameron Balfour, Margaret had to admit to both Gus McSporran and Richard MacInnes that it was an improbability, and that simply gossip and rumours had fuelled these tales. Tight-knit religious families had listened to the hearsay until they had to hide what they believed was a family scandal. The secret had been kept hidden until Ross overheard his father and grandfather talking one night, confronted them and was warned never to speak of it again. He had watched his own parents struggling with four strapping boys to feed while they worked on the Estate and the family across the water in the big house wanting for nothing. He threatened to expose them, the secrets and deceptions which he was told was the gospel truth and his own grandmother none the wiser. And then he was told this was neither the time nor the place, it was best if he left, took his grievances elsewhere – and he did. And despite his travels, his jobs, his children, and his new life, this had eaten away at him as time passed, and the death of Lisanne and then Dina and thoughts of his rightful inheritance had been the catalyst for his return.

'You know, I saw the way the wee man was struggling after Dina, and I thought, why should Mossie have everything and it's not even rightly hers?'

'Of course, it's rightly mine. Stop using your brother as an excuse!'

'I'm not using anything as an excuse. I can fight my own battles; God knows I've had to when I left here as a youngster. When I look back, I wasn't even twenty. I wasn't much older than Dax.'

'So, what was your plan? Lure me into your lair and then pounce and take everything away from me? Like you deserved it more? Lead me along then empty my bank account?'

'You make me sound like an animal but, well, yeah, it was kind of my plan to start with.' He slipped off the window seat and came towards her. 'If I'm being honest, it was what I wanted to do, sitting on that long flight planning how I was going to do it – get back my rightful inheritance.'

He stood in front of her. 'But what I hadn't planned on was seeing everyone again, seeing everything in black and white and how much older everyone was getting and people saying let bygones be bygones.'

'So, all the stuff about the crofts and getting the cat and helping me out – it was all just a game.'

'Well, I won't lie, it started out like that. I wouldn't call it a game but, yeah, I suppose it was.'

She opened her mouth to blast him with expletives until he held up his hand. He could tell she was furious. 'But I hadn't taken into account the Marcie Mosse effect.'

She bent down and picked up her bag, slinging it over her shoulder, preparing to leave.

'Thing is, I had no plans to fall for the woman I thought had stolen my life.' He said it so matter of fact, so casual, it was almost lost on her. He stretched over and opened the door, placing his hand on the top of it, his body against it. 'As I said, you're free to go any time you like.' They both waited. The only sound was a distant car and their hard, loud breathing.

'Everyone told me to be wary of you, I should have listened. *Ross Balfour always has an agenda*, they said. *Why do you think he left in the dead of night?* they said.'

He signalled the door, the space out into the corridor. She glanced at it. He nodded out to the empty hallway.

'And what's your plan now? Richard said you had withdrawn everything. How magnanimous of you,' she hissed at him.

He smiled and gave a little laugh.

'You do *not* give up, do you? Can't you just accept the fact it's all over? All over now that I'm thinking of coming back for good. *Now* that I think my life lies in Strathkin and not the other side of the world. *Now* that I see *this* part of the world has a lot more to offer me. Truth be told, I've fallen for you, Mossie.' He sighed, his eyes not leaving hers. 'And you know it. Why do I know that? Because you feel *exactly* the same, and there're no bloodlines to get in the way.'

'I don't believe you,' she stated, feet firmly rooted to the spot.

'Try me.'

'It's just another smoke screen.'

He took a step forward. 'Try me.'

'You're not to be trusted.'

He took another step forward. She could feel his breath on her.

'Try me.'

Ross leaned forward, cupped her face in his hands and kissed her. And with that, Marcie took a step to the side, dropped her bag to the floor and let her left foot kick the door closed for the second time that day.

. . .

Five weeks was all it took. Five weeks for Marcie's life to be turned around and flipped over. And here she was, on a hilly path that meandered from Tigh-na-Lochan to the bottom of the mountains that surrounded the little valley at the far end of the Swanfield Estate. Bent over, palms on her knees, panting hard and feeling the warm sweat run down her back to be absorbed in the wick-away fabric that covered her from head to toe. She stood up and stretched, looking around at the hills, and smiled at the colours that shone back at her, foliage dazzling in front of her as she absorbed its beauty. It was a glorious day in this part of the western Highlands, and she closed her eyes, imprinting the image in her memory bank. Mountains and lochs bedazzled her in this bright sunshine. Although Marcie had always made excuses to avoid running before, Ross had dragged her out to stretch her legs in the warmth and the rain and had gently persuaded her when she complained. He had encouraged her into mindfulness. She had even managed not to giggle when he told her to chant her fears away. She had taken indefinite leave from her high-powered (but somehow suddenly uninspiring) job in the city. She had complained to her friends that her lack of success in her legal life had prompted all these sudden changes, when in fact it was the man she was still trying to figure out who had inspired her. Ross Balfour had unexpectedly returned to Strathkin, waltzed into her life and it had exploded in more ways than one. Marcie hadn't expected to fall in love so quickly, hadn't expected her life to take such a dramatic turn and certainly hadn't expected to be living with the older Balfour who now shared her bed and her world. He was as spiritual as she had been consumed with material wealth. He was grey where she had been strictly black and white. But somehow it worked. He had a calmness about him that all the Balfour boys and their children displayed, but somehow, he was different, unique.

She had taken this time out from work at his insistence,

brought herself back to her childhood home of Strathkin with a new outlook after years of what seemed like trauma bestowed upon her – and she felt at peace. It was a strange feeling. A feeling she never thought she would ever experience. She knew she had been what her friends had called a *marmite* figure. You either liked or disliked Marcie Mosse. She could be charming, she could be imperious, she could be generous, she could be greedy. But what she realised now was that she had been mostly lost. Growing up without parents, with a strict grandmother, and a gentler carefree uncle, though she had a tight group of girlfriends from her childhood who could guide her when she needed it, mostly, she made her own way in life. She had separated from, and was in the process of divorcing, the man she thought she would spend the rest of her life with. She realised, in moments of reflection which she was now prone to do, that her marriage to Simon was never going to last the distance. She knew deep down she could never give him the security he craved from the only woman in his life who was prepared to shield him in his vulnerability. She had been cut off and cut out of his life. And where once she would have never given up the fight for what she believed was hers and hers alone, this time she had simply walked away, only glancing back once. Then in a plot twist nobody saw coming, and still in her own raw emotional trauma, Marcie had fallen for the man she now shared a horrible secret with – a secret that needed to remain locked away in a vault deep inside their souls. A secret they never talked about, but which occasionally made her shiver as she thought about the day at Atlantic Point. She had never been back. And knew now she would never go back to watch the wild Atlantic Ocean. And she and Ross never discussed it; it was like it never happened. Now when she stood at the window of the beautiful cottage that looked out onto a still green lochan that lay like glass in front of the small white croft, she had a deep feeling inside that the past was the past and the only thing that mattered was the future.

She was still panting as her running partner meandered his way down the small hill and back to her, where she now stood, hands on hips. He made a gesture that he was trying to get around her but instead picked her up and threw her in a full circle before planting her firmly back on the path.

'What happened to you, lazy bones McMossie?' he complained as he stood back, hands on hips.

'I just couldn't go any further, my legs are like jelly.'

His arm fell around her shoulder, and he turned her to face the way they had run so that they could walk back to the croft they now shared on the vast Swanfield Estate. She raised her hand to entwine her fingers in his then leaned up so that he could give her a lingering kiss that still gave her a tingle.

'You could be getting more of the good stuff if you'd finished that run, slacker,' he suggested and then tightened his grip on her for a second as she laughed, trying to match his wide stride.

'I just need a bath. I'm not training for a marathon. This is supposed to be fun.'

'It *is* fun! You could be running for a big red Routemaster bus in London to get to a meeting with boring clients but instead – look at this!'

He stopped and gestured to the scenery all around them, a gentle breeze with a slight chill blowing in her hair, and she appreciated the country in all its beauty. She agreed. She had a lot to be grateful for, and as they walked at a brisk pace – despite her complaints – back to Tigh-na-Lochan, she knew he would draw her a bath, make her a late breakfast and more than likely suggest an afternoon of playtime to which she would hastily agree. Marcie Mosse had a new look about her and was grinning like the cat who got the cream.

Her friends knew she was in love. Bella had said the month that she came back from Inverness she had love hearts in her eyes. Heather said she looked as if she was walking on air. Maureen simply said Marcie's new relationship was the *world's worst kept secret, innit*.

The solstice was so close to the anniversary of Dina's death that Callum was in full agreement that he and Marcie should stay in Strathkin this year to enjoy the longest day. Ross suggested a huge paella cook-out and some Spanish music on the beach. When he suggested adding a firework or two, a new plan began to take shape.

And this summer solstice wasn't an invite for two – the entire community of Strathkin had been invited to share the moment as one. Villagers now gathered on the beach in chairs and on rugs and with tables scattered along the shore. The little hamlet had been through so much that it was Marcie's idea to round up as many people as possible together to share food and stories, plan their futures and say goodbye to the past. It was a time to allow everyone to come together, out of the confines of the village hall on this cool clear night. The jetty had been stocked and stacked with pyrotechnics for a midnight display that everyone eagerly supported and had contributed to. Ruaridh stood with his feet in the water not far in front of Marcie, Arshia Brahmins, hands clasped behind her back standing next to him. To her right, Heather was looking up, eyes wide and bright as the starburst of shimmering pyrotechnics began to light up the sky. Jamie leaned down and said something in her ear and as she turned to him, her hand rested on his cheek and she reached up to kiss him, then wiped the lipstick from his mouth.

Marcie felt a nudge and Ross appeared next to her, handed her a plastic tumbler full of wine and rested his arm over her shoulder.

'How about it, Mossie?' he enquired.

'And they say romance is dead,' she sighed and took a sip of the cold red wine.

'Romance, schmomance. Look what you've managed to do?' he said as he gestured to the couples around him.

Further down the shore, Dax was standing behind Hannah, wrapping her up underneath his red hoody as he leaned close to her. Marcie thought, *he's probably telling her about his amazing mum.*

The young woman was smiling as she gazed up in wonder to the most spectacular sight she had ever seen as the bright colours of the dazzling display reflected in the still loch. The only ripple in the water came from Callum's boat as it swayed slightly off anchor, the two Balfour twins sitting far back in the vessel, well out of the way of the fireworks' path.

'Look, even those two are in a stable relationship,' joked Ross as he turned to see Strathkin's famed equestrian, Isabella Forrester, sitting in a festival chair next to Maureen Berman, who was complaining about the noise. At their feet, Douglas Balfour was lining up that day's collection of shells into a very straight line.

'So, we're making a go of this? I mean, I know it's hard for you to resist the Balfour charm.' He stood back, gestured to his strong fit body from head to toe and cocked his head to one side, waiting. She made a face and took another sip of wine. 'You're one tough cookie, Mossie,' he complained.

'For a start, you can stop calling me Mossie,' she retorted and nudged him fiercely. 'You Balfours are so cocky, as if you rule the place.'

'Hmmm, up for debate,' he said and shoved his hands into his pockets. 'Hit me with another one.'

She thought for a moment.

'Oh! I know how to persuade you!' he said and moved in front of her, taking her face in both hands and gently kissing her.

It was longer than she expected, softer than she expected, and surprisingly delightful now that his beard was shaved and his skin fresh from an avocado facial. When he moved away, she was still poised, with her head up, eyes closed.

'Do you know,' he whispered in her ear, 'you should always kiss for more than six seconds as it releases oxytocin into your bloodstream and makes it more pleasurable – for both parties involved.' Their eyes locked for a moment as he winked at her, then she looked up when a huge firework exploded above them, spreading out and falling in a feather display.

'Is this a scientific test then?' she asked, her tongue running over her lips.

'I've been carrying out these tests for years. Had to travel the globe for research.' He moved round to stand behind her and lifted both her arms. She was immediately taken back to him doing the same thing the first time at the Inn when she stood in front of a slot machine, which now felt like a lifetime ago. 'I had to travel way over there,' he said, taking her limp left arm and pointing it west, 'then I had to travel over there,' he went on, forcing her arm to the east, slowly this time, making sure the wine she was still holding remained in the glass. Marcie giggled, finding his antics genuinely funny. Still holding her arms, he folded them over on each other as he wrapped her up.

'But I think I need to take stock,' he said close to her cheek, and she felt the smoothness of his skin, 'and really put it all into practice, preferably in a darkened room.'

She leaned back into him. She let out a sigh of utter joy.

'What about...?' Marcie began. She wanted to talk about the past that they shared, the secret of Atlantic Point, the fact that if his stories had been right, she would have had a battle on her hands for the place that meant so much to her. Could she truly be in love with the man who could have taken it all away?

As if sensing the question, his finger rested on her lips.

Ruaridh turned around. He smiled at her like it was the

most natural thing in the world, as if he were giving his approval.

Marcie smiled back. She recalled something she had read in a letter, a letter she had found at one of the crofts. Discarded notes, unread messages of comfort from a sorrowful mother to a boy she desperately missed. *Memories fade. New ones are made.* The author was right. Marcie was in charge of making *her* new memories and she intended to make magical ones.

A LETTER FROM THE AUTHOR

Once again, a huge thanks to everyone who took the time to read *Return to Loch Strathkin*. I think this book brings together a lot of loose ends (and maybe lays out some more – who knows!). I know from engaging with a lot of my readers on various social media platforms that some of my characters are challenging and sometimes frustrating, but I know from others that it's what makes them feel real and authentic. They, like us all, have flaws, and I think when you want a character to feel genuine, you need to see them in the raw. I actually love Marcie's bossiness and haughty air; I adore Heather's laid-back attitude to life and I'm sure Bella will find her elusive potential someday soon! And of course there's adorable Ruaridh. People have told me they would love to go for a pint with him (men and women) and wish he was real. I'm sure once readers get to know his big brother, Ross, there will be a disorderly queue forming in a fictional village pub in a virtual world. I know because I'll be at the front of it.

If you want to join other readers in hearing all about my new releases and bonus content, you can sign up for my newsletter.

www.stormpublishing.co/elayne-grimes

If you enjoyed this book and could spare a few moments to leave a review that would be hugely appreciated. Even a short review can make all the difference in encouraging a reader to discover my books for the first time. Thank you so much.

I've said before that I started writing this series at a writing retreat. I knew where I wanted the book to be set – in the mysterious and stunning setting of Wester Ross. I am incredibly lucky that I used to live and work in the Scottish Highlands so to write about the wild and unforgiving scenery is a joy. If you follow me on Instagram, you will know that I recently took a trip back to Torridon to revel in its glorious landscape, the natural features of the surroundings such an inspiration to an author, and I wrote and wrote and wrote. If you get a chance to go, please visit. You will see Strathkin come alive in front of you as you pass real places and see vistas described in my pages. Its beauty will make you gasp and if you're really lucky, there might be a Balfour around for a virtual chat and a dram.

Thanks again for being part of this amazing journey with me and I hope you'll stay in touch – I have so many more stories and ideas to entertain you with!

Elayne Grimes

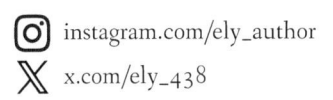

instagram.com/ely_author
x.com/ely_438

ACKNOWLEDGEMENTS

While it may be one person who writes a book, the author is supported by many people who give time, encouragement and assistance throughout its journey, from an idea, to the page, and finally a reader's hand.

Those who have helped me by allowing me time to create and take time out, I thank you. Every writer knows what a lonely time it can be crafting, drafting and rewriting so a huge thanks to the fabulous friends I call Team Tuscany. I had a deadline falling on a fabulous holiday and you let me disappear into the quiet solitude to allow me to finish without interruption. Kathleen Hogan Ehrlich, Steven Ehrlich, Belinda Barron, Ted Kirchner, Jessica Benoit – I cannot tell you how grateful I am for your support and thoughtfulness. See you at the pool soon. Thanks also to Scottie (Lachie) Bateman for all his help on drones. Whilst a lot of it didn't make the final cut, I'm sure I could hold a decent conversation now that I know the ins and outs of drone piloting!

As ever, the wonderful team behind Edinburgh Writers' Forum who are there to encourage and support those taking their first steps to those who have several books in their writing arsenal. They are welcoming and encouraging so if you have a kernel of an idea, want to share with fellow writers, come along to the party.

Again, thanks for the continuing support of fellow writers, Claire MacLeary and Kirsty Mooney, and my early reader, Helen Sturrock.

Once again, a huge thanks to Oliver Rhodes at Storm for allowing me the opportunity to share my stories with grateful readers and my fantastic fellow gelato aficionado, my editor, Kate Smith. Additionally, I have to mention Rosie Cooper, who designs the most stunning front covers, and Janette Currie, copywriter who whips me into shape to make the book sound better, sharper, pacier and more engaging.

Finally, my sister Juliet, holiday companion second to none. And Skips x

Printed in Dunstable, United Kingdom